TH

"[Castle] gives her multitude of fans another wonderfully witty, futuristic-set romantic suspense with the incredibly exciting *The Hot Zone* . . . A superb addition to the brilliant Rainshadow/ Harmony/Arcane series . . . This highly talented author never disappoints readers. I am always looking forward to her next novel."   —Fresh Fiction

"Castle weaves a suspenseful tale complete with murder, mayhem, and escalating danger that kept me on edge . . . Best dust bunny EVER."   —Caffeinated Book Reviewer

"Inventive and brimming with whimsy, this pleasing escapade gives sexy new meaning to the term 'fire and ice' and carves another brilliant facet in Castle's mesmerizing futuristic world. Great fun!"   —*Library Journal*

"In her own mad-genius fashion, Castle combines a perfectly matched pair of protagonists with a riveting plot filled with plenty of sexy twists and dangerous turns, and adds just the right dash of dry wit to cook up another riveting addition to her futuristic Harmony series."   —*Booklist*

"Definitely hot in more ways than one. The world and characterization continue to expand and evolve in the most delicious of ways. I recommend to all readers who enjoy a more suspenseful PNR."   —Smexy Books

"Erotic thrills ensue . . . Breathless narrow escapes and familial conflicts . . . made intriguing by the otherworldly and esoteric setting."   —*Publishers Weekly*

"The intensity a Castle hero projects toward [his] woman is what makes these books for me. It is why I keep coming back for more."   —Fiction Vixen

continued . . .

"Castle's newest heroine . . . is utterly compelling from the first page . . . An out-of-this-world must-read . . . No shortage of heart-stopping action and thrilling romance." —*RT Book Reviews*

Praise for

DECEPTION COVE

"Another wonderful addition to this entertaining series. Jayne Castle again proves her writing prowess with *Deception Cove*."
—Fresh Fiction

"In her usual spot-on fashion, Jayne Ann Krentz, writing as Castle, serves up another riveting installment in her futuristic Harmony series, and the resulting fast-paced, witty, sexy romance is guaranteed to keep readers enthralled with its danger-spiked plot and compelling characters." —*Booklist*

"Castle continues to expand her world and draws on an engaging cast of characters to make it come further alive for her readers. *Deception Cove* certainly lived up to its name, and I look forward to my next visit to Harmony." —Smexy Books

"Full of suspense, passion, and discoveries that both answer and leave more questions . . . I can't wait for the next venture into this world. To say that I Joyfully Recommend this book as a must-read is putting it almost too simply, but I do whole-heartedly." —Joyfully Reviewed

"Three-word review: suspenseful, romantic, and entertaining . . . Fans of romantic suspense in a futuristic setting will enjoy *Deception Cove* and the Rainshadow series. You just have to meet a dust bunny! Four cups of coffee out of five."
—Caffeinated Book Reviewer

Other titles by Jayne Ann Krentz

TRUST NO ONE	DAWN IN ECLIPSE BAY
RIVER ROAD	SOFT FOCUS
DREAM EYES	ECLIPSE BAY
COPPER BEACH	EYE OF THE BEHOLDER
IN TOO DEEP	FLASH
FIRED UP	SHARP EDGES
RUNNING HOT	DEEP WATERS
SIZZLE AND BURN	ABSOLUTELY, POSITIVELY
WHITE LIES	TRUST ME
ALL NIGHT LONG	GRAND PASSION
FALLING AWAKE	HIDDEN TALENTS
TRUTH OR DARE	WILDEST HEARTS
LIGHT IN SHADOW	FAMILY MAN
SUMMER IN ECLIPSE BAY	PERFECT PARTNERS
TOGETHER IN ECLIPSE BAY	SWEET FORTUNE
SMOKE IN MIRRORS	SILVER LININGS
LOST & FOUND	THE GOLDEN CHANCE

Specials

THE SCARGILL COVE CASE FILES
BRIDAL JITTERS
(writing as Jayne Castle)

Anthologies

CHARMED
(with Julie Beard, Lori Foster, and Eileen Wilks)

Titles written by Jayne Ann Krentz and Jayne Castle

NO GOING BACK

SIREN'S
CALL

A RAINSHADOW NOVEL

JAYNE CASTLE

JOVE BOOKS, NEW YORK

JOVE

An imprint of Penguin Random House LLC
375 Hudson Street, New York, New York 10014

SIREN'S CALL

A Jove Book / published by arrangement with the author

JOVE® is a registered trademark of Penguin Random House LLC.
The "J" design is a trademark of Penguin Random House LLC.
For more information, visit penguin.com.

ISBN: 978-0-515-15574-7

PUBLISHING HISTORY
Jove mass-market edition / August 2015

PRINTED IN THE UNITED STATES OF AMERICA

10 9 8 7 6 5 4 3 2 1

Cover art by Craig White.
Cover design by George Long.

Penguin
Random
House

*For Lorelei—you'll look fabulous
on the cover of* Harmonic Bride *magazine*

A Note from Jayne

Welcome back to my other world—Harmony—and another adventure on Rainshadow Island, where everyone has a past. The local inhabitants are good at keeping secrets—their own and those of their neighbors. On Rainshadow you don't ask too many personal questions. The island has long been a refuge for people who don't fit in anywhere else.

Those who make their home on the island are also accustomed to dealing with the dangerous mysteries concealed in the ancient underground catacombs and inside the forbidden territory known as the Preserve. Rainshadow, it turns out, was once the site of ancient Alien bioengineering labs. (What could possibly go wrong, hmm?)

The tight-knit community on Rainshadow figures it can handle the monsters, the reverse-engineered dinosaurs, and the deadly legends that seethe just beneath the surface.

The real problems, as usual, are caused by humans.

Chapter 1

IT WAS THE WEDDING OF THE SEASON AND IT WENT OFF flawlessly—right up until the moment when the bridesmaid announced to the bride, the pastor, and the crowd in the pews that the groom had murdered his first two wives. . . .

"If anyone knows why this man and this woman should not be married, let him speak now or forever hold his peace," the pastor intoned.

Ella's cell phone rang. Everyone grumbled at the breach of good manners, although several people surreptitiously checked their own cell phones to make certain they were switched off.

But Ella dug hers out of the middle of the bouquet where she had concealed it and read the text, her pulse racing.

"Stop the wedding," she shouted.

All three hundred guests, the bridal attendants, the best

man, and the wedding singer stared at her. She focused on the message she had just received and then looked at the bride.

"Karen, you can't marry him. His real name is Leo Bellamy and he's wanted for the murder of his first two wives. He's also wanted for questioning in the murder of another woman, a fiancée."

Karen Leggett, a delicate blonde draped in yards of white tulle and silver satin, was nearly speechless with shock.

"Ella," she finally managed. "What is wrong with you? Have you gone crazy?"

Ella moved to stand between Karen and the too-handsome, too-perfect groom. Her senses were heightened and she could see the cold, dark shadows in the dreamlight fields of Bellamy's aura. She knew a monster when she saw one, and she had known Bellamy for what he was ever since Karen had introduced them a few weeks earlier.

"I sensed that there was something off about you the first time I met you," she said. "I had a private-investigation agency take a closer look into your background."

Violent energy spiked in the groom's aura but his expression was one of calm, compassionate concern. He was a chameleon-talent, Ella reminded herself. He had a talent for deception.

"Karen, your friend is having some sort of nervous breakdown," he said gently. "Someone should escort her to the emergency room at the nearest para-psych hospital. Perhaps one of our guests will volunteer to assist her."

"I'm not going anywhere." Ella held up the phone displaying the text message she had just received. "This is from Jones and Jones, Karen. It says that the man you know as Charles Forbes is a chameleon-talent whose real name is Leo Bellamy. He lied to you from the start. Lied to the matchmaking agency, too."

It was the *Jones & Jones* name that finally penetrated Karen's state of stunned shock and sparked a wave of low-voiced concern among the wedding guests. Like Ella, Karen and many of those present were members of the Arcane Society. Within Arcane, everyone was aware of the organization's storied investigation firm.

Unfortunately, Leo Bellamy recognized the agency's name, too.

"Shit," he growled.

Before anyone realized that he was not going for the ring, he pulled a small mag-rez pistol out of the pocket of his tuxedo and grabbed Ella. He put the barrel of the gun to her temple.

"If anyone moves half an inch, the bridesmaid dies," he shouted to the crowd. "She and I are leaving now. If I see a cop in the rearview mirror, Miss Morgan is dead."

He edged toward a side door, dragging Ella with him. The pistol never wavered from her head.

The crowd watched in horror.

Bellamy's arm was around Ella's throat. She put her fingertips on his bare hand. He ignored the light touch, intent on hauling her through the doorway and out into the parking lot.

Ella pulled hard on her talent. She had physical contact.

That was all she needed. The delicate crystal chimes on her bracelet shivered. They weren't absolutely necessary but they helped her focus.

She began to sing.

It was a silent, psychic song, audible only to Bellamy because he was the focus of her paranormal music. The crashing, soaring chords drew power from the far end of the spectrum. She wove ominous, compelling harmonies that ensnared Bellamy's dreamlight and pulled him down into the depths.

No man could withstand such violent notes. All of Bellamy's senses—normal and paranormal—foundered on the rocks of oblivion.

The pistol fell from his limp hand and clattered on the floor. He made a weak attempt to tighten his grip on Ella's throat but she slipped effortlessly out of his grasp.

He stared at her with eyes that were glazed with the unnatural sleep that was swiftly dragging him under.

She thought she read belated comprehension and horror in his gaze. His mouth opened on a single word spoken so softly that only she could hear.

"Siren."

In the next instant he crumpled to the floor in a deep coma.

She decided to play it safe and give him a small encore just to make sure that when he woke up—if he woke up—he would not have any clear memories of the bridesmaid he had attempted to use as a hostage.

She crouched beside him and touched his throat as

though checking his pulse. The little bells on her brace-let shivered again.

She sang a few more bars, aiming the crushing waves of music at his aura.

Bellamy twitched a couple of times and then lay very still.

THE DRAMATIC ENDING TO THE WEDDING OF THE SEASON got full media coverage and made the front pages of every newspaper in Crystal City. The police and the medical professionals concluded that Bellamy had suffered from a previously undiagnosed aneurism that had burst under the stress of the moment. The mainstream press focused on the story of the wealthy bride who had almost married a two-time wife-killer.

For the most part everyone forgot about the brides-maid who had been held hostage for a short time at the altar. That turn of events was fine with the bridesmaid.

Bellamy eventually surfaced from the coma but his senses were severely scrambled. He was deemed incom-petent to stand trial and was sent to an asylum for the criminally insane. The para-psych doctors noted in their reports that the patient was obsessed with painting. He worked on his pictures as though consumed by a fever.

All of the images featured the same subject—a woman sitting on rocks that jutted out of a wildly churning sea. In the paintings, the lady on the rocks played an ancient stringed instrument and sang to the drowning sailors who had been summoned to their deaths by her music.

Ella did not breathe a sigh of relief until the media frenzy died down. In the end only the *Curtain*—a notorious tabloid that catered to fans of conspiracy theories, scandals, and assorted exposés about women who claimed to be pregnant with Alien babies—came anywhere close to getting the story right.

WEDDING OF THE SEASON ENDS
WITH ARREST OF GROOM

DID A SIREN SING KILLER INTO COMA?

Ella tossed the paper into the recycle bin. Fortunately, very few people took the *Curtain* seriously, and even fewer believed in the Sirens of myth and legend—women who could sing men to their deaths.

A MONTH AFTER THE NEAR-DISASTER, KAREN TOOK ELLA out for drinks.

"I don't know how to repay you, Ella." Karen picked up her glass of white wine. "The matchmaking agency I used said he was a perfect match. If it hadn't been for you I probably would have become Dead Wife Number Three. How did you figure out that Bellamy was a chameleon?"

"Jones and Jones came up with that information," Ella said. "I just knew there was something off so I hired J and J to look into Bellamy's past."

"'Something off' is putting it mildly." Karen shuddered. "Bellamy is one of the monsters—the kind of evil talent they write fairy tales about. And to think I nearly married him."

"You didn't marry Bellamy, that's the important thing."

Karen raised her glass. "Here's to the next Mr. Right."

"To Mr. Right."

"It's your turn, pal. When are you going to register with a matchmaking agency?"

"Someday."

"I'm surprised your family isn't pushing you hard to register."

"They understand that I'm trying to get a career going first," Ella said.

"Let's face it, you'll never get anywhere if you stay with the Wilson Parsons Talent Agency. Parsons won't let you establish a name for yourself. No matter how good you are at dream counseling or how many clients you attract to his firm, he'll always take all the credit."

"Between you and me, I've been thinking about going out on my own. The problem is that the dream counseling business is very competitive, especially at the low end of the market. A lot of people, including a lot of frauds and con artists, think they can analyze dreams. The secret to success is to project an upmarket image and that's expensive, what with rent and advertising costs."

"You can do it," Karen said. "You're good. And as soon as you get established you'll register with a matchmaking agency, right?"

"I'll think about it," Ella said.

And she would think about it—she would think about it a lot. But she would never register.

Registering with a matchmaking agency would mean having to lie on the questionnaires. It would mean lying to the marriage counselors. It would mean lying to a prospective husband. And if she ever did marry, it would mean that she would have to live a lie for the rest of her life.

The last thing she wanted was a marriage based on a lie. She wanted a real marriage, one founded on love and intimacy and passion and all the other things that she would probably never experience up close and personal.

"Thank goodness your intuition was better than mine," Karen said. "More acute than the matchmaking agency's programs, for that matter."

"Just a lucky hunch on my part," Ella said.

She could not tell Karen or anyone else outside her own family the truth—she had recognized the monster for what he was because he had touched her on a few occasions in an effort to charm her. The contact had been fleeting and casual—the light brush of his fingers when he handed her a glass of champagne; his hand under her arm when he assisted her out of a car. But that was all she needed.

No, she would not be registering with a matchmaking agency. There were no fairy-tale endings for women like her. When it came to identifying the monsters, the old saying held true. *It takes one to know one.*

Chapter 2

THE ALIEN MUSIC LOCKED IN THE GREEN QUARTZ WALLS sang to her senses. Gorgeous notes floated in the paranormal currents. Haunting bells chimed their ethereal harmonies at both ends of the spectrum. The dark thunder and lightning of crashing chords reverberated in the atmosphere.

Ella did her best to ignore the thrilling music in the tunnel walls so that she could concentrate on her driving.

"You know," she said to the dust bunny clinging to the utility sled dashboard, "I'd assumed my first client would be human."

The dust bunny responded with a low, rumbling growl. Not so much a warning or a threat, Ella concluded; more like an urgent plea for speed. Then again, what did she know about dust bunnies? The one perched on the sled's dashboard like a hood ornament was the first one she had ever encountered outside of picture books and cartoons. Every kid on Harmony had read the tales of *Little Amberina and the Dust Bunny*.

Dust bunnies had a cute mode—hence their popularity in children's literature. When fully fluffed they looked like oversized wads of dryer lint with six little paws and two big, innocent blue eyes. The one on the dashboard of the sled, however, was not even trying to look adorable. She was fully sleeked out and her second set of eyes—the fierce amber ones that were designed for night hunting— were open.

"I'm sorry," Ella said. "I've got the sled rezzed to the max. I can't drive any faster."

They were whipping through the maze of ancient Alien tunnels at a speed that was only a little faster than the average person could run. The sled looked a lot like a golf cart and it moved like one, too. It was powered by a sturdy, but simple, old-fashioned amber-based engine. Low-tech was the only option in the heavy psi-environment that permeated the catacombs and the great subterranean Rainforest. The Underworld had been engineered by the long-vanished Aliens, who had relied on as-yet little understood forms of paranormal energy. Sophisticated human technology such as high-powered engines, computers, and guns either exploded in your hands or simply flatlined in the eerie realms the vanished civilization had created below the surface.

"I really hope you know what we're doing," Ella said. "Because I'm going to owe Pete a big favor once he finds out that I borrowed his sled."

Pete Grimshaw was the proprietor of Pete's Underworld Artifacts, the shop next to her new office in the Old Quarter. A retired ghost hunter, he had closed early that afternoon in order to have a few beers with some old hunter pals.

Ella had opened her little one-person consulting firm—Morgan Dream Counseling—less than a week earlier, but she had already discovered that short workdays and long nights in the local bars was business as usual for Pete. There had been no time to find him and ask permission to take his prospecting sled. The dust bunny that had scampered through her doorway a short time ago had been frantic. You didn't have to be psychic to know when an animal was anxious and desperate.

Ella drove the sled into a large circular chamber and stopped. There were more than half a dozen intersecting tunnels, each glowing with the acid-green energy infused in the quartz that the Aliens had used to construct their underground world. She looked at the dust bunny.

"Which way?" she asked.

She knew the small creature could not comprehend what she was saying, but under the circumstances, she figured her meaning was clear.

The dust bunny faced toward one of the vaulted entrances and bounced up and down, making urgent little noises.

"Got it."

Ella rezzed the sled and drove into the indicated tunnel. The dust bunny did not protest, so she concluded she'd made the right choice.

It had been like this from the moment they had descended into the Underworld and commandeered the sled. Every time they reached an intersection in the maze, the dust bunny chose the tunnel.

Ella glanced at the handful of simple instruments on the dashboard. The signal from the tuned-amber locator was still strong. Her route was clearly charted so she could find her way back. The tunnels were impossible to navigate without good amber, and Pete, being an old Guild man, was obsessive about keeping the sled's amber tuned. In addition, she had plenty of personal tuned amber on her. There were nuggets in her stud earrings and a nicely carved piece on the pendant that she wore around her neck. She also had another chunk stashed in the heel of her shoe.

Unlike Pete, who often searched for relics in the maze of the Underworld, her day job rarely took her into the catacombs. But the Alien music that sang in green quartz often proved irresistible.

She had learned that she could find a kind of peace in the strange harmonies. On the nights when she knew that she was dwelling too much on the lonely future that awaited her—a future in which she was fated to be always a bridesmaid and never a bride—she sometimes descended into the Underworld and gave herself over to the ethereal music until dawn.

Bright yellow warning lights flickered on one of the locator screens. The sled was nearing an uncharted sector. She wasn't lost yet but she was in danger of driving out of the mapped zone. Even with good amber, that was a dangerous place to be. There were a lot of hazards in the uncleared regions of the underground, most of them fairly lethal.

Now that the initial rush of adrenaline had started to wear off, common sense was flooding back. What was she doing, allowing a dust bunny to lead her deeper and deeper into the tunnels?

Her first thought—the one she had leaned on to rationalize the daring escapade—was that someone was in trouble down below. Children's books were replete with stories of heroic dust bunnies that saved little kids who had been foolish enough to go into the Underworld alone.

Right, she thought. *That would be children's books, as in pure fantasy. Get real.*

But the dust bunny on the dashboard was real.

The yellow lights on the locator screen turned red. That was not good. Ella was on the brink of making the decision to turn around and go back when the hood ornament froze and uttered a forbidding growl.

Ella brought the sled to a halt and looked down a seemingly endless hallway. Vaulted entrances to rooms and chambers loomed on either side of the corridor.

"Okay," she said. "Now what, pal?"

The dust bunny leaped from the dashboard to her shoulder, startling her. The creatures were predators, she reminded herself. There was a saying about dust bunnies: *By the time you see the teeth, it's too late.* Panic flickered through her. If the thing went for her throat she was doomed. . . .

But the dust bunny didn't attack. It made more anxious

noises, bounded down off her shoulder, and dashed through the entrance of the nearest chamber.

Ella double-checked her personal amber. Satisfied that she could retreat if necessary, she followed the dust bunny. At the doorway she paused to glance back over her shoulder, making certain that she could still see the sled. The invisible rivers of paranormal energy that flowed through the Underworld played tricks on human senses. Losing visual contact with your transport was not smart.

She went through the opening and stopped short. She was not certain what she had expected to find at the end of the frantic race through the tunnels—an injured prospector or a lost child, perhaps.

The reality was a long workbench, two strange crystal devices that did not look as though they had been designed for human hands, and a row of small steel-and-glass cages. The locks on the cages were old-fashioned padlocks that required keys. High-tech security devices would not function in the paranormal environment.

Each cage contained a sleeked-out, mad-as-green-hell dust bunny. There were six in all. Rage and fear radiated from the trapped creatures. They watched her with suspicious eyes, not certain if she was friend or tormentor.

She took in the situation at once. Outrage flashed through her. The crystal relics on the workbench were the telling clues. Someone had discovered a couple of Alien weapons and was planning to run a few field tests using the dust bunnies as targets.

"Bastard," she whispered.

The dust bunny that had come to her for help dashed

frantically back and forth across the room, chattering anxiously.

"I'll do my best," Ella said. "There's probably a hammer in the sled's tool kit but I don't think it will work. That glass looks like the kind they use in banks and shark tanks. But lucky for your buddies, it's still just glass. People like me are good with glass."

The dust bunny chittered and dashed around her ankles.

"Okay, okay, give me a minute."

She went to the first cage in the row and flattened one hand on the front panel. Gently she rezzed her talent, searching for the right frequency. The tiny bells on her bracelet shivered.

"Got it," she said to the dust bunny.

She focused on the cage.

You had to be careful working with glass. It was a unique substance in terms of para-physics because it possessed the properties of both a solid and a liquid.

"Don't worry," she said. "I know what I'm doing. I broke a lot of Mom's best crystal stemware when I first came into my talent."

The dust bunny stood on its hind paws and quivered. All four eyes were open very wide.

"And just how did you know that I could help?" Ella asked softly. "What are you? Psychic?"

The faint tinkling of the bracelet's bells grew louder and more resonant.

For a moment there was no visual evidence of the effects of the destabilizing energy, but Ella sensed that the internal structure of the glass panel was weakening.

A couple of seconds later the entire front of the cage dissolved into a pool of liquid crystals.

"Just like melting a Popsicle," Ella said. "Easy-peasy. But I'm a professional. Don't try this at home."

Great. Now she was talking to animals.

The freed dust bunny chittered madly and bounded down to the floor. Ella moved on to the next cage. Now that she had the frequency it was easy to melt the glass. The process went smoothly and swiftly.

A couple of minutes later the last of the dust bunnies was free. They chortled at each other and at Ella. She got the impression they were grateful, but they did not show any inclination to hang around. All but one dashed to the doorway and promptly vanished out into the tunnels.

Ella recognized the one remaining dust bunny as her client.

"Don't worry about my fee," she said. "It's probably good karma to open a new business with a little pro-bono work. Now, you'll have to excuse me. I need to get back to the surface to make a phone call. The Guild and the FBPI will be interested in whatever is going on here. Looks like you and your pals got caught up in some black market Alien-tech dealing. The authorities frown on that sort of thing."

The dust bunny chortled cheerfully and dashed away through the door. Ella crossed to the workbench and considered her next move. The question that confronted her was whether she should collect the two crystal weapons and take them back to the surface or leave them where they were.

The relics constituted evidence, but if she left them at the scene there was a real risk that the arms dealer would return before either the Guild or the Federal Bureau of Psi Investigation arrived. As soon as the dealer spotted the melted cages he would know his lair had been discovered. He would grab the artifacts and run.

On the other hand, if she showed up on the surface with two Alien weapons worth a fortune in the illicit underground market, there would be a lot of questions to answer. Somehow, she did not think either the Guild or the FBPI would buy a story involving a bunch of imprisoned dust bunnies. She could easily come off looking delusional at best. If things really went down the dust bunny hole, she might get arrested for possession of illegal Alien tech.

As the proprietor of a new dream counseling business, the last thing she needed was a lot of unpleasant publicity. Bad press would lead potential clients to conclude that they should take their business elsewhere—say, the Wilson Parsons Talent Agency, for example.

Discretion was a prime virtue in her profession. Dreams were intensely personal matters and those who sought her services would want to keep them that way—personal. No one wanted an analyst who was known to report stuff to law enforcement.

Just having her name linked to the FBPI could prove disastrous. She had caught a break at Karen's wedding when the authorities concluded that Leo Bellamy had suffered a burst aneurism. She might not be so lucky in a second encounter with the forces of law and order.

She studied the devices. Each was gracefully curved

and about the size of a man's hand. Like a lot of Alien relics, they looked like works of abstract art. The crystal was faintly green in color and utterly transparent. There was no chamber for bullets or any other sort of projectile, but she was certain that the artifacts were weapons. She could hear the music locked inside. Amid the harmonies that emanated from the green quartz chamber she could discern the darker notes that spoke of power and destruction.

Dread mingled with fascination. She had been able to detect Alien music since she had first come into her talent in her early teens, but she had never heard songs like these—songs of senses-dazzling chaos.

The thing about Alien machines was that very few people, including her, could activate them. She could *hear* the music in artifacts and she could generate counterpoint melodies, but she could not focus the power in the relics.

As Pete often said, it was a damn good thing that only a small number of highly specialized talents could channel Alien tech. There was no telling what sort of destructive forces might be unleashed accidentally or intentionally if an Alien weapon fell into the hands of someone who could unlock and focus the energy inside.

That fact, however, did not lessen the value of the relics on the black market. According to Pete, it actually made the artifacts all the more attractive to a certain category of obsessive collectors that included dangerous eccentrics, cult leaders, and mob bosses—not to mention the government.

Mere rumors of the discovery of an artifact that might be an example of Alien technology intrigued conspiracy theorists and others who lived paranoid lives on the fringe.

Many were convinced that the government and its corporate contractors had already discovered some truly bizarre Alien machines and were busily conducting experiments on them in secret labs. The *Curtain* was filled with such stories every week.

Not that she read the *Curtain*—at least not in public.

She decided to leave the weapons where they were. Better that they disappear than that she be caught with them. She would go back to the surface and make a couple of discreet, anonymous phone calls to the FBPI.

"Well, isn't this interesting. Who are you and how the hell did you find my little workshop?"

Chapter 3

THE SHARP MASCULINE VOICE CAME FROM THE ENTRANCE
of the chamber. Panic flashed through her. She whirled
around so quickly that she nearly lost her balance. Reflexively, she grabbed the edge of the workbench to steady
herself.

A tall, distinguished man walked a few steps into the
chamber and stopped. He assessed her with cold gray eyes.
Everything about him, from his elegantly cut hair to his designer trousers, was smooth, polished, and sophisticated—
everything except the flamer in his hand.

Her first irrational thought was that he didn't look like
a man who dealt illegal Alien tech. But with her talent
flaring she could see the dreamlight energy in his aura
and it told her the truth. The man was prepared to com-
mit cold-blooded murder if necessary. Selling hot tech
on the side would not be a problem for him.

"Who are you?" she asked, trying to establish some control.

"Allow me to introduce myself. Thomas Vickary." He gave a short, mocking inclination of his head. "Maybe you've heard of me?"

"No. Why would I . . ." A belated jolt of disbelief shot through her. "Wait. You're not going to tell me you're Vickary of the Vickary Gallery."

"I'm afraid so."

"Good grief. You're one of the most respected antiquities dealers in the city-state."

He raised his brows. "And you are?"

"Why should I give you my name?"

"One reason that comes to mind is that I'll send you on a walkabout of the catacombs minus your amber if you don't answer my questions."

He had as much as told her that he would kill her if she did not give him answers. But she was very certain that he had no intention of allowing her to return to the surface alive under any circumstances. A man who was dealing dangerous relics like those on the workbench could not afford to let her live. She knew who he was and she knew his secrets. Those secrets could get him locked up for years in a federal prison.

She folded her arms and tried to appear calm and in command. "You were planning to test these devices on a bunch of innocent little dust bunnies. How many did you kill before I got here?"

"None, actually." Vickary grimaced. "The little rats are damned hard to catch and even harder to keep inside a cage. The first batch escaped. I finally had to go with the glass reptile cages and some serious, old-fashioned padlocks, the kind that require a key." He studied the cages. "What did you use on the glass, by the way? It was supposed to be shatterproof."

She ignored the question. "How did you catch the dust bunnies?"

"That part wasn't so hard. I put out some pizza laced with a heavy-duty sleeping drug in the tunnels beneath my shop."

"Why did you choose dust bunnies for your horrible experiments?"

"Isn't it obvious? They can survive in the catacombs. The animals from the Rainforest don't last long outside that ecosphere, and the energy down here makes surface animals act in highly unpredictable ways. Even rats don't venture down into the Underworld." Vickary smiled a thin, humorless smile. "But I'm sure you know that. Common knowledge."

"I'll bet the FBPI is closing in on you as we speak. I made a phone call before I came here. You'd better run while you can."

It sounded weak, even to her.

"No." Vickary shook his head with grave certainty. "You didn't call anyone. If you had, the FBPI or the Guild would have arrived by now. They sure as hell wouldn't have allowed you to come here on your own. Which brings me back to my questions. How did you find this chamber and what the hell did you do to my glass cages?"

"You're going to kill me regardless. I can see it in

your—" She stopped herself before she blurted out the word *aura*. "In your eyes."

"Don't be so melodramatic. I just want answers."

"Liar," Ella said. But she said it very quietly because she was focusing her talent, getting ready to sing, and that required concentration.

Normally, she needed physical contact to manipulate the dream currents in a person's aura with psychic music, but down in the psi-hot tunnels almost anything could serve as a conductor of paranormal energy, including the glowing quartz walls and the floor on which she and Vickary stood.

"You want to know how I melted the glass cages?" she asked softly. "I'll show you."

A sudden chittering sounded from the doorway, breaking her concentration. Her dust bunny client had returned. It sleeked out, showing all four eyes, six paws, and a lot of teeth, and leaped at Vickary's trouser leg, scampering up toward his throat.

"*Shit,*" Vickary yelled. Caught off guard, he instinctively jumped back, swiping wildly at the dust bunny with the flamer.

The dust bunny narrowly avoided the weapon and vaulted nimbly to the floor. Vickary aimed the flamer at it and rezzed the trigger.

"No," Ella shouted, horrified.

The dust bunny made it safely out through the doorway just before a volt of fire seared the atmosphere over its head.

Ella pulled hard on her talent and focused again on Vickary's aura. The bells on her bracelet shivered with the dark music of endless sleep. Energy burned between her and her target, traveling through the psi-infused quartz floor like electricity through water or a wire.

Vickary jerked violently when the full force of her song slashed through his aura, overwhelming the dream-light currents in powerful waves of darkness.

His mouth opened. He stared at her with shocked eyes. "What the hell are you doing?"

He could barely get the words out. His eyes started to roll back in his head.

He tried to retreat, staggering backward, but as long as his feet were in contact with the floor there was no escape. The thin leather soles of his designer shoes blunted some of the hot energy she was directing into his aura but they were not a significant barrier.

Infuriated by the attack on the dust bunny, Ella hurled wave after wave of fierce energy at her target, drowning Vickary's dreamlight in irresistible songs of oblivion.

The results were devastating. Dreamlight was, after all, the conduit between the normal and the paranormal. Any assault on those currents had serious repercussions on all of the senses.

Vickary tried to rez the flamer but he could not summon the energy. The weapon fell from his nerveless hand. He crumpled to his knees.

"No," he whispered. "What are you doing?"

"Giving you a private concert," Ella said.

He managed to lift his head one last time. He stared at her, horror and comprehension sparking briefly in his dazed eyes.

"Siren," he whispered.

"Oh, yeah."

"Impossible." Vickary folded up and collapsed on the floor. His eyes closed. "You don't exist."

He sprawled on the green stone, unconscious.

Ella abruptly cut her talent. She stared at the stricken figure on the floor.

"I get that a lot," she said.

That was not, strictly speaking, true. The exact nature of her talent was a deep, dark family secret, the kind of secret that could destroy her career as a dream consultant and put her on an FBPI watch list.

But she had just sung a very powerful song and she was buzzed. Her voice was shivering and so was she. It wasn't panic or fear that was causing the reaction now— her inner Siren was flying. Using her talent at full power had that effect. It unleashed a volatile cocktail of bio-psi chemicals. Later she would pay a price for such a heavy expenditure of psychic energy, but for now she was definitely in high-rez mode.

The dust bunny reappeared in the doorway, still sleeked out. Ella laughed. "Are we a great team or what?"

The dust bunny fluffed up and chortled.

"Right." Ella took a deep breath and pulled her dazzled senses together. "Okay, I need to act like a responsible citizen now."

She crouched beside Vickary to check for a pulse, more than a little afraid of what she would discover. She was not certain of her control when she was pulling the darker harmonies. The problem was that it was impossible to practice

without putting someone at risk. She had nearly killed Leo
Bellamy, and a few weeks ago she'd put a Wilson Parsons
client into a deep sleep that had lasted nearly two days. The
client had survived and recovered with no clear memory of
the events leading up to his unexpectedly long nap, but if
she accidentally murdered a leading antiquities dealer, her
life might get very complicated, very fast.

It occurred to her that this was the third time she had
used her talent to such devastating effect in the past few
months.

"Getting to be a bad habit," she said to the dust bunny.

She breathed a small sigh of relief when she discovered Vickary's pulse. It was slow, indicating a state of
deep unconsciousness, but it was detectable. The depth
of his dreamstate was a good thing, she told herself. The
odds were excellent that he would not remember her, at
least not with any clarity. She would become a fragment
of a dream to him.

She rose, stepped back quickly, and looked at the dust
bunny.

"I don't know about you, but I'm getting out of here,"
she said. "The last thing I need is to get caught in a room
full of Alien tech with this guy."

"Too late." The voice from the doorway was male and
freighted with the kind of power and authority that usually was accompanied by a badge and a mag-rez gun. "It
looks like you do have a room full of Alien tech and a
body to explain."

Chapter 4

SHE STARED AT THE MAN IN THE DOORWAY, STUNNED. HIS
collar-length, night-dark hair was brushed straight back
from a sharp widow's peak on his high forehead. He had
a hard profile, a lean, tough, broad-shouldered build, and
a raptor's eyes. But it was the invisible shock wave of
dark energy that infused the atmosphere around him that
riveted her senses. It was as if he had brought an invisible
thunderstorm into the chamber.

The sound of bells clashing discordantly made her realize that her talent was still sparking and flaring, no doubt
intensifying the impact the newcomer was making on her
overheated senses.

Deliberately, she reined in her talent. Not much changed.
The man in the doorway remained a force of nature with
the power to dazzle her senses.

Get a grip. You're still riding the rush. You need to settle down and think clearly. He might be working for the good guys, but that did not make him any less dangerous.

Ella heard a small chortle. She glanced down just in time to see the dust bunny vanish out into the hall. She was on her own.

She looked at the man in the doorway.

He held a flamer somewhat too casually in his right hand. It was the easy, sure grip of someone who'd had a lot of experience with the weapon.

She finally managed to breathe. "Let me guess— you're Vickary's client?"

"Not exactly." He flashed a badge with his free hand. "Rafe Coppersmith, consultant for the FBPI and Guild task force that has been planning to take down Vickary's operation for the past five months."

So much for making a couple of discreet, anonymous phone calls to the authorities.

She cleared her throat. "I can explain this situation."

"That will be interesting. Who are you?"

"Ella Morgan. I'm just a dream counselor. I'm not running Alien tech. I'm not involved in this operation, I swear it."

"You can explain the rest later. One thing I do know, you're not the client Vickary was expecting today, so we need to get you out of here before he arrives. Go. Now."

He glided into the room and moved the flamer in a small arc, urging her toward the corridor.

As a rule she was not big on taking orders, but in this instance there did not seem to be any reason to refuse. She started toward the door.

But it was too late. Three men barred her path. One was dressed in an expensively tailored business suit. He would have looked like any other high-powered executive if it were not for the two men at his side. They were built like bulldozers and their eyes were pitiless.

Enforcers, Ella thought. The one in the business suit was no doubt the boss.

"Trent," Rafe said. "Fancy meeting you here. I'm afraid there's been a change of plans."

Trent glanced down at Vickary and then looked at Rafe. "Who the hell are you?"

"Let's just say that I'm taking Vickary's place. Are you still in the market for Alien tech?"

Ella realized that Rafe was improvising. He was literally making up the script on the fly.

"Depends." Trent looked at Ella. "Who is she?"

"My assistant," Rafe said without missing a beat.

"Yeah?" Trent looked amused. "What kind of assistant would she be?"

"She does odd jobs for me," Rafe said. He smiled a knife-sharp smile. "Like taking care of Vickary, for example."

Ella froze. Rafe had just told a mob boss that she was his personal hit woman. Visions of her future as a top-flight dream counselor were going to go up in smoke if the situation did not improve.

Trent raised his brows and gave Ella an appraising look, one that held a measure of curiosity as well as a hint of respect. "You're that good at assisting?"

Ella shot Rafe a veiled glance. She had no idea where

the script was going, but it was clear he had just given her a part to play.

"I'm very, very good," she said with what she hoped was the right degree of professional-hit-woman cool. After all, she reminded herself, it wasn't as if she didn't have a talent that would have taken her far in that particular field—assuming she had been a total sociopath.

In spite of her best efforts, she knew she hadn't done a terrific acting job because one of the enforcers snorted in disbelief. But the other one contemplated Vickary's prone body with a thoughtful expression. When he turned back she thought she saw a little wariness in his eyes.

"You want to go through with the buy or not, Trent?" Rafe asked. "Because if you're no longer interested, I've got a long list of clients who will be happy to take your place."

"I definitely want the artifacts," Trent said. He gave Rafe a considering look. "I was hoping to establish a long-term business arrangement with Vickary but it looks like he's out of the picture. And as it happens, I'm not in the mood to negotiate." He spoke to the enforcers without looking at either of them. "Burn 'em and dump 'em in the tunnels."

The thugs responded immediately. Two violent balls of green energy coalesced in the chamber, charging the atmosphere. Ella's hair was suddenly standing on end.

Ghost fire. The small storms of lethal energy that drifted randomly through the catacombs were one of the many hazards underground. There was nothing supernatural about them. They weren't real ghosts. But the early settlers had bestowed the nickname on them two hundred years before and it had stuck.

The technical name was UDEM: Unstable Dissonance Energy Manifestation. Only those with a unique talent could summon a ghost or control it. Flamers were useless against a UDEM.

Ella watched Rafe, hoping for direction. He looked bored.

"You're an idiot, Trent," he said. "We both know you can't work those relics."

Something akin to lust flashed in Trent's eyes. "Maybe not, but I've got the kind of money and connections that will allow me to buy the talent I need." He moved one hand in a slicing motion. "Burn 'em. Now."

The ghosts moved toward their targets. Ella rezzed her talent and prepared to sing. She had used a lot of energy on Vickary but she had not exhausted her psychic senses. Her target would not be the ghosts but rather one of the men who had generated the fireballs.

"You dumbasses." Rafe shook his head. "You really think we're that easy to kill?"

"Don't see what's stopping us," the first enforcer said. He was flushed with a disturbing excitement. Clearly he liked his work.

"Try this," Rafe said.

Very casually he put a hand on Ella's shoulder. She flinched at the heat and power of his grip—not because it was painful but because the physical contact sent a shock wave through her senses. The blue quartz ring on his finger sparked with a dark energy. She knew then that he was rezzing his own talent. Whatever the nature of his ability, the power in his aura was breathtaking.

A rush of excitement swept through her. It was not unlike the thrill she got when she jacked up her own senses, but it wasn't quite the same, either. This exhilarating tide of heat was accompanied by a powerful wave of intense, erotic intimacy. She had never experienced anything like it. Vaguely she realized that her own talent was flaring in response to Rafe's hot aura—not just flaring, but starting to *resonate* with it.

A storm broke in the green quartz chamber. Dark energy swirled in the atmosphere. Her bells shivered on invisible currents of fire and ice.

Out of the corner of her eye she saw that Rafe had picked up one of the crystal weapons. Another shock flashed through her when she realized that he had activated it. The artifact glowed with violent paranormal energy.

Before she could grasp the implications of what was happening, jagged bolts of psi lightning danced in the chamber. A great darkness filled the space. In the strobe-like effects created by the bolts of energy Ella saw the three mobsters stiffen and jerk about wildly, again and again.

The green balls of ghost fire winked out of existence.

"Well, damn," Rafe said very softly. "It's a little stronger than I expected." He tightened his grip on her shoulder. "Don't worry, I've got you."

Trent and the two enforcers collapsed and did not move. Ella held her breath. She could not tell if the men were unconscious or dead.

The energy storm was still heating, threatening to overwhelm her senses. She wondered if Rafe had lost control of the weapon.

His hand was still on her shoulder, binding her to him. His forehead was damp with sweat, and when he looked at her she saw that his eyes burned with dark fire. She understood on a primal level that it was sexual heat she saw in his gaze.

The storm intensified. Lightning sparked in the walls. Rafe's hand was a mag-steel chain on her shoulder, locking the two of them together. She knew then that their only hope of surviving the howling winds of paranormal fire was to maintain their physical connection. Together they could ride out the blast.

The tension she was feeling from head to toe was unlike anything she had ever experienced. She was a Siren. She was *always* in control. But she was breathing quickly now, as if she were running. There was a great tension deep inside her. She longed for release; ached for it. The most unnerving revelation of all was that her panties were damp.

It dawned on her that she was on the cliff edge of a truly shattering orgasm.

Frantically, she fought to regain control of her senses. What was happening had nothing to do with sex.

No sex involved.

The problem was that she had been flying high when Rafe had arrived and the ensuing excitement had rattled her already over-rezzed senses. That was all.

No sex involved. Just her overheated imagination and

a heavy dose of adrenaline and other bio-psi chemicals coursing through her blood.

She could see that Rafe was fighting to lower his talent. She knew then that he was standing at the edge of the same damn cliff.

And in that moment she wanted nothing more than to take the leap with him. She held her breath.

Gradually, the fire in his ring faded. The Alien weapon abruptly stopped glowing.

Rafe groaned and took his hand off her shoulder. The place where his fingers had warmed her skin suddenly felt chilled. She wanted to reclaim the heat of his body. It was all she could do not to wrestle him to the floor. This is madness, she thought. What had happened to her?

She watched Rafe covertly, trying to ascertain if the side effects of his talent were business as usual as far as he was concerned.

He took a deep breath. "Sorry about that. Never know exactly what's going to happen when you rez Alien tech."

"Rafe . . Mr. Coppersmith—" She broke off because she could not think of anything else to say.

Rafe paid no attention. He was suddenly very busy, moving around the room, collecting flamers, locators, spare amber, and knives from the three mobsters.

"Are you all right?" he asked over his shoulder.

She took another deep breath and let it out with control. She was a Morgan and she was a Siren. She could do control.

"Terrific," she said. "You?"

Her control may have been excellent, but when he

glanced at her, eyes tightening at the corners, she knew he had caught the thin, sharp edge of sarcasm in her voice. And he had the nerve to be amused.

She glanced at the artifact that he had just used. "You can activate Alien tech."

"It's a side effect of my talent. I've got an affinity for hot crystal and quartz. Since the aliens used those materials in their technology I can usually figure out intuitively how to activate their artifacts. But I prefer to do it under controlled conditions."

"Did you know what those relics could do?"

"Not until I picked up one of them. We knew Vickary had come into possession of a couple of lethal artifacts and that he was planning to sell them. The idea was to take him down at the same time we grabbed Trent. You can see why I was a little irritated when you showed up here today."

She raised her chin. "Why are you complaining? You've got Vickary, Trent, and those two goons. You should be thanking me."

"For getting in the way? I don't think so. You could have been killed. I don't even want to think about the paperwork that would have involved."

"That is not funny."

"Sorry." He ceased rummaging through Trent's pockets and got to his feet. "We don't have a lot of time. I left a message for the head of the task force. If I don't check in from the surface and give the all clear soon, he'll know things have gone south. He'll send the team down here to see what went wrong. So unless you want to explain things to the head of the local branch of the FBPI, you'd better explain them to me."

"You're offering to leave me out of this?"

"My gut tells me you aren't into the illegal tech business but my gut has been wrong before. Either way, you are a complication I'd rather do without. This job was about taking down Vickary and Trent. I've got you at the scene but I don't have a real case against you."

She drew a shaky breath. "Good to know."

"But this is a one-time-only offer. Make up your mind and do it fast."

"No problem. Your offer is accepted. Thanks."

She gave him a fast version of events. When she was finished, he shook his head.

"You followed a dust bunny down here to rescue a bunch of other dust bunnies? What was that about? Read too many *Little Amberina and the Dust Bunny* stories when you were a kid?"

"Sure, blame it on my early reading habits." She gestured toward the melted cages.

"That was your work?" he said. "What the hell did you do to the glass?"

The last thing she wanted to do was tell him the exact nature of her talent. No, she thought, that wasn't the last thing she wanted to do. The very last thing she wanted to do was undergo an FBPI interrogation with the head of the task force. Her career was at stake. Better to answer Rafe's questions.

"I'm a singer," she said. "Not a professional musician. It's my talent. Paranormal music, only. Can't carry a tune when it comes to normal music, just ask my family. Glass has some unique properties as I'm sure you know. Hit the right notes out on the spectrum and it's easy to shatter the stuff."

"Your voice," Rafe said. He regarded her with a thoughtful expression.

She frowned. "What about my voice?"

"Nothing. It's just . . . very nice, that's all. Sort of musical or something. You sound like you could be a professional singer."

"Well, I'm not," she said firmly.

He glanced again at what was left of the cages. "That glass wasn't shattered. Looks like it melted."

She cleared her throat. "If I go far enough out on the spectrum I can melt glass."

"And after you melted the glass you used your talent on Vickary." Rafe whistled softly. "You're a Siren, aren't you?"

"Heavens, no," she said briskly. "No such thing. Myth. Legend. Tales from the Old World. I'm just a fairly strong para-music talent. Actually, I'm in the dream counseling business."

Rafe smiled slowly. There was a disturbingly intimate look in his eyes. "You might be in the dream counseling business but you're a genuine Siren."

"No, really—"

"I sensed the heat in your aura when I touched you. You're powerful. Strong enough to melt glass and sing a man into a coma. That makes you a Siren, as far as I'm concerned."

She braced herself, waiting for him to add the damning

words. After all, everyone knew that Sirens fell into a unique category as far as history, legend, and para-shrinks were concerned—the category that contained *psychic vampires*. It was the *Not Supposed to Exist, but If You Find One, Lock Her Up* category.

Rafe moved on without further comment on her powers.

"Okay," he said. "Here's how we're going to do this. You were never down here, understand?"

"But when those men wake up they might remember me."

"It's unlikely they'll remember much, if anything, about what happened just before I took them down. Unconsciousness often wipes out memories of what occurred just before the trauma. Can I assume your talent has a similar effect?"

For some reason the question outraged her, maybe because he asked it in such a matter-of-fact manner. She waved a hand at Vickary's motionless body.

"How should I know?" she said. "It's not like I go around doing things like this every week or so."

"Right." He nodded once, satisfied. "I think we can make this work. Even if one or two of them wake up with a few vague memories I should be able to convince Harding that the perps suffered hallucinations shortly before they passed out. I can tell him that's a common side effect of my talent."

Another jolt of dismay went through her. "Harding?"

"Joe Harding. He's the special agent in charge of the local FBPI office. You've probably seen him in the media."

"Oh, yeah. The hotshot FBPI guy who always cracks

the high-profile cases. Seems like he's on the evening news every couple of weeks."

"That's Hard Joe." Amusement gleamed again in Rafe's bird-of-prey eyes. "Ever since he caught a two-time wife killer at a big Covenant wedding a while back here in Crystal he's been on a roll."

"Uh-huh."

There was a short, brittle pause. For a couple of seconds she dared to hope that Rafe wouldn't make the connection. But when she saw the flicker of recognition in his eyes she knew it was not going to be her lucky day.

"There was a hostage at the wedding, one of the bridesmaids." Rafe looked dangerously intrigued now. "Bellamy put a mag-rez to her head and tried to haul her out a side door. That was when he had his very convenient stroke."

"Mmm."

"Well, well, well." Rafe's smile widened into a wolfish grin. "You were the bridesmaid, weren't you?"

"I don't see how that matters."

"Not likely that there's two full-blown Sirens in this town. I should have put it together sooner. Damn, you're good, woman."

"Look, if it's all the same to you, I'd just as soon you didn't mention your brilliant deduction to Special Agent Harding."

"No problem," Rafe said easily. "My lips are sealed, et cetera, et cetera. Your talent is your business. Don't worry, we're used to keeping secrets in my family. Yours will be just one more."

"Coppersmith."

"What?"

"You said your name was Rafe Coppersmith."

"Raphael Elias Coppersmith. Call me Rafe."

"Would that be Coppersmith as in Coppersmith Mining, Inc.?"

"Yep."

"Wow," Ella said. She was genuinely shocked. "Your family controls most of the quartz and crystal mining industry. Why are you running around in the tunnels doing odd jobs for the Bureau? I should think your family would have other things for you to do."

"Sure. But with my talent, all I'm really good at is finding deposits of hot quartz and crystal. It's boring work for the most part, although it does have occasional moments of stark terror, as the saying goes. You know, much as I'd love to hang around and exchange life histories, I think you'd better get moving. I've got a few things to take care of before the task force arrives."

"Sure, no problem, I'm on my way." She headed for the door of the chamber.

"Remember, you were never here."

"Don't worry, I won't forget."

"One more thing," Rafe added.

She froze in the doorway and looked back at him. "Damn, I knew this was too good to be true. You're doing me a favor and you want something in exchange, don't you?"

"Are you always so cynical?"

"I'm a realist." She gave him a chilly, totally false smile. "Side effect of my talent."

"Yeah? What does that have to do with being realistic? Hell, never mind. We can talk about it later. As it happens, you're right, I am doing you a favor today. Don't make me regret it."

"I won't. So, what do you want in exchange for letting me go?"

"How about a date?"

She went blank. "A date?"

"We could have coffee and swap life histories."

"Are you serious?"

His eyes heated a little. "Definitely."

"I thought you had concluded that I'm a Siren."

"I like music, so sue me." He shrugged. "About that date for coffee?"

A frisson of recklessness sparkled through her. "Why not?"

"It's a deal."

"You don't even know my name."

"It won't be hard to find out. All I have to do is look up the details about the Wife Killer wedding."

"It's Ella. Ella Morgan."

He smiled. "I'll call soon, Ella."

She fled before either of them could change their minds. The utility sled was right where she had left it. She jumped up onto the bench seat and rezzed the little motor.

She fought back the giddy wave of excitement and forced herself to think clearly and logically about what had just happened. Rafe Coppersmith would never call. He had been riding a tide of after-burn energy, just as she was. The side effects that followed a heavy expenditure of talent were well-known. It sometimes heightened sexual desire in both men and women, which, in turn, led to rash decisions and poor judgment. When Rafe sobered up he would realize that the last thing he wanted was a date with her. After all, he knew what she was.

According to Morgan family tradition, men generally had one of two reactions to Sirens. They either developed a sick, dangerous obsession with them or they ran like hell.

Rafe didn't look crazy so she doubted that he went in for freaky obsessions. That meant he would probably turn out to be the other kind.

Just as well, she thought. The fact that he had guessed her secrets had probably doomed the chances of any long-term, meaningful relationship from the outset.

When he came down off the rush generated by adrenaline and paranormal heat, Rafe would think twice about dating a Siren. He would do what any smart man would do—run like hell.

Chapter 5

"MOM, I'VE GOT TO GO. I ORDERED A PIZZA FOR DINNER and it's due to arrive any minute."

"All right," Sophia said. But she sounded deeply reluctant. A coloratura soprano, she was capable of infusing even her speaking voice with over-the-top operatic emotion. Maternal concern shimmered in her words. "You're sure you're going to be all right on your own tonight?"

"I'll be fine, Mom. But I'm exhausted. I need some rest."

"But what about that FBPI agent? You said he suspected that you were a you-know-what. If he tells his superiors, you'll probably end up on some FBPI watch list. Everyone knows law enforcement likes to keep an eye on certain kinds of talents."

Ella reminded herself that her mother was a longtime subscriber to the *Curtain*. Fans of the paper were inclined toward conspiracy theories.

"I don't think he'll tell anyone about me," Ella said. She was not sure why she was certain that Rafe would keep his suspicions about her Siren talent a secret, but her intuition told her she could trust his promise. "For one thing, he's not an actual FBPI agent. He's a private consultant. He doesn't have the same obligations to the Bureau that an agent would have to his superiors. Besides, it's not a crime to be a strong talent. He's pretty damn powerful himself."

"Well, that probably explains why the FBPI recruited him. According to the *Curtain*, the Bureau uses all sorts of dangerous mega-talents to run secret, off-the-books operations in the Underworld."

Ella thought about the task force that Rafe had mentioned and then she thought about his own ability to rez Alien weapons.

"The *Curtain* may be on to something with that particular conspiracy theory," she said. "Look, Mom, I'm really beat. I need to get some sleep. My friend Lydia Chen is getting married next week. I've got a fitting for my bridesmaid dress in the morning."

"Another wedding? Good grief, is that your third or fourth in the past two months?"

"It's the wedding season, remember? I'm very busy."

"All of your friends seem to be getting married this year."

"Tell me about it. I seem to be the bridesmaid of choice. I'm booked out for the next four months."

"Because you're one of the few available for the position. All of the others are busy planning their own weddings."

"Well, there is that, yes."

There was a short, unsettling pause. Ella braced herself for what she knew was coming next.

"Have you thought about your aunt's suggestion?" Sophia asked.

"That I register with a matchmaking agency and lie on the questionnaire? Sure. It sucks."

"Now, dear, she didn't tell you to lie. She simply suggested that you omit certain details about your talent."

"Mom, it would mean I'd be marrying someone who doesn't know the truth about me."

"Everyone has a right to a few secrets, dear."

"I know, but this is one that would be hard to keep from a husband."

"Not necessarily," Sophia said. "Men are remarkably oblivious about a lot of things, provided the sex is good."

And no one could fake it like a Siren, Ella thought.

"I don't want a husband who is oblivious to my true nature," she said.

"Mr. Right will come along someday, dear."

"Sure. Look, don't worry about me, okay? I'll be fine. Love to Dad. Good night."

She ended the connection before her mother could think of another reason to keep the conversation going.

It might not be a crime to be an off-the-charts talent, but it could put a real crimp in a person's social life, not to mention one's matrimonial possibilities. When the talent in question happened to fall into the potentially lethal category, a Covenant Marriage was almost out of the question.

It was true that the matchmaking agencies sometimes found good matches for powerful talents, but the odds were poor. When the prospective bride was a Siren the odds went down to about zero.

She had known since college that the best she could reasonably look forward to was a series of affairs or maybe a few Marriages of Convenience. In such arrangements it was understood that the relationships were not permanent. The individuals involved in an MC had no obligation to divulge their secrets. Both parties knew that the marriage could be ended on the merest whim—no harm, no foul.

That was not true of the far more binding Covenant Marriage. The laws had eased somewhat in recent years but a CM was still expected to last for life. Getting out of one was so difficult and so expensive and so costly in social terms that people had been known to resort to murder rather than divorce court in order to escape.

She had made the mistake of confiding the truth about her psychic nature to a lover on only one occasion. That had been back in her third year of college when she had still been naïve enough to think that love could conquer all. Things had not gone well. She had learned her lesson.

Coffee with Rafe would be a unique experience. It would be a thrill to go out on a normal date with a man who knew her secret up front.

THE PIZZA ARRIVED A SHORT TIME LATER. IT WAS THE large, family size. She had been starving when she ordered it, but now that she'd had a glass of wine it appeared huge. She suspected she would have leftovers for breakfast.

It would have been nice to have someone else to share the meal with, she thought. What she really wanted to do was talk to someone about the events of the day; someone besides her mother.

But confiding in a friend was not an option. The only other person who knew what had actually happened down in the tunnels was one Raphael Elias Coppersmith, and he wasn't around.

Get over it, she thought. *He knows what you are. By now he's thanking his lucky amber that he survived physical contact with you while you were both running hot.*

Time to be realistic.

She carried the big pizza and a second glass of wine out onto the tiny balcony. She was determined to shake off the wistful sensation. She had a new business to launch. She needed to stay focused. Rescuing dust bunnies and meeting high-powered FBPI consultants was exciting but it did not a career path make. She was a dream counselor, one who had not yet managed to snag her first paying client.

From her perch she had a view of the top of the ancient green quartz wall that surrounded the ethereal spires of the Alien ruins. The Dead City had been constructed from the same impervious stone that had been used to build the catacombs. After dark it glowed with an eerie green energy that enveloped the Old Quarter in paranormal light and shadow.

She settled back, swallowed some wine, and contemplated the view. In addition to the Dead City Wall and the ruins, she could see another structure from her balcony. The gleaming edifice of the newly constructed Crystal Center office tower was also visible.

Someday, she thought, after she had attracted enough clients, she would move Morgan Dream Counseling into Crystal Center. Image was everything in her line. As long as she did business out of a small storefront office in the Quarter, potential clients were likely to view her as just another low-rent psychic. But if she moved into the tony office tower, people would see her as an exclusive dream therapist.

She heard the chortle just as she reached for the second slice of pizza. A large ball of fluff vaulted up onto the railing. The dust bunny had a small object gripped in her two front paws.

Ella suddenly felt much better.

"Hey, there," she said softly. "I never thought I'd see you again. I hope you're not expecting me to go back down below tonight. I need rest. Want some pizza? No sleeping drugs involved, I promise."

The dust bunny bounced off the railing and scurried across the balcony. She hopped up onto the table and chortled enthusiastically. Ella pushed a slice of pizza toward her.

"Help yourself. It's the family size and I don't have any family around to share it."

With the glaring exception of herself, the various members of the Morgan clan were almost always on tour.

The dust bunny tossed the object she held at Ella and went to work on the pizza with dainty greed.

Ella held the rock up to the light. "For me? Really, you shouldn't have."

She opened her depleted senses a little and immediately detected a tingle of energy. Curious, she examined it more closely. In the light slanting out of the living room behind her, the stone glowed bloodred.

A shock of excitement whispered through her.

"Ruby amber," she said. "Oh, my goodness. I'll bet it's worth a freakin' fortune."

The amber was uncut and untuned but there was no mistaking its beauty or its power. She looked at the dust bunny.

"Don't misunderstand, I do appreciate a client who pays her bill, but please tell me you didn't steal this," she said.

The dust bunny chortled and started in on another slice of pizza.

THE FOLLOWING MORNING ELLA TOOK THE RUBY AMBER next door to show to Pete. The grizzled ex-Guild man whistled softly when he touched the stone.

"Never seen anything like it in my life," he said. He put it down on the counter and looked at Ella. "There haven't been any rumors of stolen ruby amber, and believe me, I'd have heard if anything this valuable had gone missing on either the legal market or the black market. That means the laws of treasure-hunting and salvage apply. What are you going to do with it?"

"I want you to arrange to sell it for me, Pete," she said. "For a serious commission, of course."

"Sure. Then what? Going to retire to a tropical island?"

"Nope." Ella looked down at the dust bunny riding shotgun in her tote bag. "Lorelei and I are headed for the big leagues. In my business, image is everything. Morgan Dream Counseling will close tomorrow. The Knightsbridge Dream Institute will soon be open for business in the Crystal Center."

Pete lounged against the counter. "I understand the move to fancier digs. You've said all along that you wanted a polished, professional image because people tended to tag storefront dream counselors as fake psychics. But why the name change?"

"Knightsbridge Dream Institute sounds more exclusive, don't you think?" Ella picked up the ruby amber, tossed it into the air, and caught it in her hand. "This rock is my ticket to the high-end dream counseling market."

IT WAS A GOOD THING THAT SHE WAS VERY BUSY IN THE days and weeks that followed because, just as she had warned herself, Rafe Coppersmith never called. On the positive side, neither did the FBPI.

Rafe might have gotten cold feet when it came to a date, but he had kept her secret.

Chapter 6

Three months later . . .

"NICE OFFICE," RAFE COPPERSMITH SAID. "THE DREAM counseling business must be paying well. Congratulations."

He walked toward her across the elegantly appointed counseling room as if nothing had ever happened between them; as if they were old friends. As if he actually had called to ask her out for coffee.

Bastard.

She wanted to yell at him and maybe throw a few things in his direction, but she reminded herself that she was a professional therapist. She had an image to maintain. She also had a lot of control. No one could fake it like a Siren.

She had been waiting for Rafe all morning, ever since she had seen his name on her appointment calendar. She was booked for the day so it had come as a shock to see that

Darren, her receptionist, had rescheduled another client in order to make room for Rafe.

It was no doubt the Coppersmith name that had convinced Darren to fit Rafe into her busy schedule—and possibly a nice little gratuity on the side. Coppersmiths were rich and powerful and no doubt accustomed to getting what they wanted.

When she had recovered from the shock of seeing Rafe's name she had done some fast research on Coppersmith Mining. In addition to controlling a large chunk of the quartz and crystal market, the firm operated some very secretive high-tech research labs. At the company's website she had found a mission statement that claimed that the goal of the research was to discover new ways to use quartz and crystal to improve people's lives. Ella suspected that the real objective was to find new ways to make even more millions selling various quartz- and crystal-powered products. But, then, she tended to be a bit cynical about anything connected to the name *Coppersmith* these days.

After the corporate-speak on the website, there had been very little information about the Coppersmiths and their company. It was clear that, with the exception of a few sensationalized conspiracy pieces in the tabloids, the reclusive family managed to maintain very tight control of its public image.

Even the tabloid hits were tame for the most part. The most interesting articles were the wild theories that cropped up from time to time in papers like the *Curtain*. Perhaps, predictably, they were focused on the company's R and D work. She had automatically discounted ninety-nine percent of the speculation but that still left one percent. She didn't doubt that there were a lot of secrets hidden in the Coppersmith labs.

One small fact had caught her eye—Rafe was not married. She had verified that immediately after their meeting in the Underworld. Not that she cared, she told herself. It didn't matter now. He had never called, so obviously he had reconsidered the suggestion that they have coffee.

So what was he doing here in her office? Luckily, she'd had plenty of time that morning to practice her *you're just another client* smile.

"Mr. Coppersmith," she said. "What a surprise."

His scarred boots made no noise on the expensive gray carpet. He settled into the leather client chair with the ease of a specter-cat relaxing on a sunbaked rock after a successful hunt. The boots offered silent testimony that the man who wore them had spent some hard time in the field, but it was clear that he was equally accustomed to making himself at home in sleek, upscale surroundings.

Lorelei was on the desk playing with her little collection of small quartz rocks housed in an old Green Light cigar box. At the sight of Rafe, the dust bunny went very still. She gazed at him as though transfixed. But not in an alarming way, Ella concluded.

She felt a little transfixed, too, although she sincerely hoped she did not bear a striking resemblance to a wad of dryer lint that had been struck by lightning. The look was adorable on a dust bunny, but her own hair standing on end would not make a good impression on clients.

In spite of the fact that she was prepared for the

encounter, she got the same senses-rezzing sensation she had experienced three months ago at their first meeting. Nothing had changed. The jolt was even stronger this time.

Damn.

Rafe was dressed very much as he had been three months ago. In addition to the boots, he wore a denim shirt, scarred leather jacket, and khaki trousers secured with a leather belt.

But when he moved his right hand she saw that one thing had changed. The blue quartz ring was gone. In its place was a ring set with a dull gray stone.

"I'll come straight to the point," Rafe said. "I need your help and I'm willing to pay for it."

Whatever she had been expecting in the way of opening lines, that was not it. So much for hoping against hope that he had remembered the coffee date. She had so been looking forward to turning him down flat.

She stared at him, going quite blank for a couple of beats.

"You want my dream counseling services?" she asked when she finally managed to pull herself together.

"Not exactly. It's your para-music talent that I need."

"I don't understand."

Rafe leaned back in the chair and stretched out his legs. There was an amused gleam in his amber-brown eyes. There was something else there as well, something Ella could not put her finger on but which she was pretty sure should worry her.

"Ever heard of Rainshadow Island?" he asked.

"No."

"It's a little dot way out in the Amber Sea."

Rafe broke off because Lorelei had hopped down from the desk. She scurried across the carpet to her basket of toys, seized her favorite—a delicate wedding veil with a crystal-studded headpiece—and bounced over to Rafe's chair.

She vaulted up onto the arm of the leather chair and proudly displayed the veil for his admiration. Ella stifled a groan when the little hussy chortled and blinked her baby-blues.

Rafe patted Lorelei somewhere near the top of her head and considered the wedding veil with an unreadable expression. When he turned back to Ella his eyes were a little too neutral. He looked like a man who was bracing for very bad news.

"Does the wedding veil belong to you or the dust bunny?" he asked.

Ella flushed. "Her name is Lorelei and the wedding veil belongs to her."

Rafe appeared oddly relieved.

"Looks like a regular wedding veil, not one that was designed as a costume for a dust bunny," he said.

"It's definitely a real wedding veil." Ella winced at the memory.

"But not yours."

"Not mine. Look, Mr. Coppersmith, if you don't mind—"

"Would Lorelei by any chance be the dust bunny you followed down into the tunnels the day we met?"

"Yes, as a matter of fact."

"Can I ask how she came by what appears to be a fairly expensive veil?"

"She went with me to a fitting at a bridal shop," Ella said coldly. "There was an accident."

"What sort of accident?"

Ella sighed. "Lorelei fell in love with that veil. She sort of helped herself to it."

"She stole it?"

"Dust bunnies don't have the same nuanced understanding of the law that humans do. She just couldn't resist the sparkly headpiece, I guess. The owner of the shop threw a fit. I had to pay for the veil."

Lorelei chortled again and waved the veil so that the netting floated gracefully in the air. It settled over her like a gossamer circus tent. She went ecstatic, hopped off the chair, and dashed around the room, the veil fluttering around her.

"Cute," Rafe said. "Until you see the teeth."

Ella raised her brows. "I gather you know something about dust bunnies."

"I've met a couple recently."

"Where?"

"On Rainshadow Island," Rafe said.

Lorelei returned to Rafe's chair and once again offered him the veil. He took it from her and touched some of the sparkly green crystals in the headpiece. Ella sensed energy shift in the atmosphere. The dull gray ring on his hand flashed, quicksilver-like, with a little energy.

"These crystals are good stones," Rafe said, sounding surprised. "There's a little heat in them. A pricey toy for a dust bunny."

"It was worth it," Ella said. "Lorelei loves it."

She decided not to mention that one night a week ago—just for fun—she had tried on the veil in front of her bedroom mirror.

A tingle of awareness skittered through her. Rafe was still a little jacked from testing the green crystals in the veil. She could see his dreamlight quite clearly, as sharply as if she had physical contact with him. That was unsettling enough, but there was something else about the dream fields of his aura—something that had not been there three months ago. She caught her breath, genuinely shocked.

Rafe was running a psi-fever.

Strong, healthy auras tended to be stable over time unless they were altered by some form of serious trauma. Physically, Rafe looked as strong and vital as the last time she saw him, but she was pretty sure that something very bad had happened to him in the past three months. Her low-burning anger and hurt were abruptly tempered by unwilling concern. She warned herself that she did not want to feel sorry for this man.

He must have sensed her scrutiny because he looked up abruptly, his gaze trapping hers. His jaw hardened and his eyes narrowed. He knew that she had sensed the unusual vibe in his aura. Swiftly he lowered his talent but it was too late. She had seen the fever.

Part of her—the smart, intelligent, secret-keeping Siren part—informed her that she should be reaching for the little emergency button embedded in her telephone control panel. When you dealt with unusual and/or eccentric clients with major dream issues, you took a few security measures. If she pressed the button, Darren would come through the door in a matter of seconds. Members of the Crystal Center building security team would follow close behind.

But she did not push the emergency button. She told herself it was because Lorelei did not appear alarmed. But Lorelei was a dust bunny. What did she know about humans who burned with psi-fever?

What did humans know, come to that? The condition was extremely rare, although the experts believed it was underreported. Very little research had been done on the problem if, indeed, it was a problem. That murky situation had allowed a lot of urban legends and bad press to develop over the years.

In the popular imagination, a psi-fever was a strong indicator of dangerous psychic instability.

The only certainty about psi-fever was that it was not contagious.

She folded her hands together on her desk. Rafe had kept her secret. She would keep his. They were both strong talents and among powerful talents there were a few unspoken rules. So long as Rafe refrained from showing any signs of being seriously deranged, she would pretend that she had not noticed any weirdness in his aura. It was, after all, not the first time she had dealt with an off-the-charts talent who presented with an aura that had some peculiar things going on in the dreamlight region. The clients who came through her door tended to be out of the ordinary.

She smiled as if nothing unusual had occurred.

"Why don't you tell me a little more about Rainshadow

Island and why you think you need a dream counselor," she said, employing her best professional tone.

Dark amusement came and went in Rafe's eyes. She knew then that as long as she pretended nothing had happened, he would play the same game—at least for now.

He reached inside his leather jacket and removed a small sapphire-blue crystal. He offered the stone to Lorelei, who accepted it with her usual enthusiasm for anything sparkly. She retrieved her veil and bounded off the chair with her prize. Vaulting up onto Ella's desk, she carefully placed the blue crystal in the cigar box.

"I hope that rock wasn't valuable," Ella said. "Might not be easy getting it back."

"It's a gift," Rafe said. "Plenty more where that came from. Let's get down to business. I'm not looking for a private dream counselor. I'm representing Coppersmith Mining today."

"What happened to your FBPI consulting gig? Still doing odd jobs for the Bureau?"

"I've been a little busy with other things since I saw you last."

Something in his voice told her that he did not want to discuss the other things. She wasn't going to get an excuse or an explanation for the three months of silence.

"I see," she said. "Please continue."

"Like I said, I'm here today because of a Coppersmith venture. I've been tasked with troubleshooting a big project on Rainshadow. We can usually fill our field operation's manpower requirements from the ranks of our employees.

But something has come up in the jobsite that requires a strong music talent. We don't have one in-house."

"So you immediately thought of me."

For the first time in three months, no doubt, she added silently. Another flash of anger sparked through her. She suppressed it with Siren control.

"I immediately thought of you," Rafe agreed. But he looked a little wary now.

"I'm sure you're aware that music talents aren't particularly rare," she said. "There are probably hundreds, if not thousands of them available throughout the city-states."

"Sure. Anyone who can play air-rez-guitar thinks he's a music talent. But I need someone who can handle paranormal music," Rafe said. "That type of ability is rare, at least at the high end."

She unfolded her hands, picked up a pen, and absently tapped the tip against the small crystal figurine of a dust bunny that sat on her desk. She listened to the faint, melodic *ping* ring gently out across the spectrum from the normal into the paranormal.

So Rafe Coppersmith wanted her help. Now, wasn't that interesting? And just exactly how did she feel about the situation? she wondered. It was not as if he had finally remembered their coffee date. All the evidence indicated that he would not be sitting here in her office today if not for the fact that he wanted to hire her.

Face it, when it comes to relationships, Sirens never catch a break. You know that.

"I'm a dream counselor," she said finally. "It's true I

can hear Alien music, but I really don't see how I can help a company like Coppersmith."

"Coppersmith signed a contract with the Rainshadow Preserve Foundation, which controls a recently discovered sector of the Underworld on Rainshadow Island. We've got the exploration and mining rights but first we have to secure the sector."

"The Guilds secure the various territories of the Underworld."

"The Rainshadow Guild lacks the in-house expertise needed so they've contracted out that work to Coppersmith."

"In other words you've got a contract for the mining rights and another one for security," Ella said. "Sounds complicated."

"*Complicated* pretty much describes business as usual in the Underworld," Rafe said. "The first priority is securing Wonderland."

"Wonderland?"

"That's the nickname the locals on Rainshadow have given the new sector." Rafe paused. "You'll see why if you take the contract."

If she was wise, she would decline the offer outright, she thought. But she was intrigued in spite of herself. The chance to employ her talent in a new and unusual manner was almost irresistible. Nevertheless, she had to consider her long-term career and her social commitments. She could not afford to be away from her office or from Crystal City for an extended period of time.

"How long would this job last?" she asked.

"Depends. I think we'll find out real fast whether you can handle the work. If it turns out you can, it shouldn't take long to come up with the data the lab techs need to create a permanent fix."

"Are you absolutely certain that this contract does not involve the FBPI or the illegal weapons trade?" she asked. "Because I really do not want to go there again."

"This is the Underworld we're talking about. It's not inconceivable that we might come across some danger-ous antiquities, and if that happens, it's possible the FBPI might step in. It's also possible that some pros in the ille-gal artifacts trade might pick up chatter about Wonder-land and put out a few feelers."

"Hmm."

"But I can promise that you'll have several layers of protection between you and the FBPI and also between you and any bad guys who might decide to come sniff-ing around Wonderland. Coppersmith takes care of its people."

She narrowed her eyes. "Let me be perfectly clear. If I take the contract I would not be one of your people. I'm an independent consultant."

"Okay, I can respect that. But the company will take responsibility for your welfare while you're under con-tract. That's how we do things."

Ella tapped the pen against the crystal dust bunny again. She listened to the paranormal echoes fade away.

She had some personal issues with one Raphael Cop-persmith but there was no getting around the fact that his family's company was a prestigious firm. It would be very nice to add Coppersmith Mining to her list of clients. Also, she would be involved in opening up a new sector in the Underworld. The prospect was exciting.

She told herself not to consider the fact that she would also be working with Rafe.

"I'm probably going to regret this, but keep talking," she said.

"To date, we have hired four consultants, all of whom claimed to be able to handle paranormal music energy. The results have been . . . disappointing."

"Define 'disappointing.'"

"All four nearly got eaten."

For a split second she thought she hadn't heard him correctly.

"I'm sorry," she said. "Did you say *eaten*?"

"By dinosaurs."

She stared at him. Maybe she should take the psi-fever in his aura a little more seriously.

"You're joking," she said.

"Unfortunately, no. It looks like, back in the day, the Aliens engaged in some reverse bioengineering in Wonderland. The monsters they created look a hell of a lot like the reconstructions the paleontologists have created from fossils found here on Harmony. We think the creatures the Aliens created were frozen in a state of suspended animation for the past few thousand years."

"Some sort of living museum?"

"Maybe. But recent paranormal activity on the island has evidently destroyed the mechanism that kept the animals in stasis. They have begun to wake up and the first thing they do, naturally, is go looking for food."

"What, exactly, do these creatures eat?"

"Some eat foliage but most are predators," Rafe said. "The only thing that is keeping them under control at the moment is that they require a heavy psi-ecosystem. That means they can only hunt inside the Preserve, which is an area aboveground on the island that is laced with a lot of strong paranormal energy. And they only hunt at night. Evidently they can't handle normal sunlight, even the limited amount that reaches the surface inside the Preserve. They go back underground to Wonderland during the daylight hours."

"Creatures of the night," she said softly.

"We've got two problems. First, as I'm sure you know, standard-issue hunting rifles and other high-powered weapons don't work in the Underworld. They don't work in the thick paranormal atmosphere of the Preserve, either, so we don't have a practical way to hunt down the dinosaurs."

"I see."

"Unfortunately, they've got a damn good way of hunting us."

"How?"

"They sing."

She blinked. "What?"

"The critters hunt with psychic energy," Rafe said. "They use it the same way predators in the deep ocean use bioluminescence to draw their prey. There's no way to know how their animal prey interpret the psychic lures, but the human mind translates the energy as music—hypnotic music. It's damn near irresistible."

She caught her breath. "Sirens."

She didn't realize that she had spoken aloud until she saw Rafe smile a little.

"The dino version," he said. "We need to figure out what wavelengths the dinos broadcast on and then we need to develop defense mechanisms that can neutralize those wavelengths."

"This is all quite . . . fascinating," she said.

"I had a feeling you might be interested in the job." Rafe glanced at his watch. "But if it turns out I'm wrong, I need to find someone else and fast. Every day spent looking for talent is a very expensive day lost in Wonderland. We've got research teams on site and ready to go down but they can't make a move until we've cleaned out the monsters."

She cleared her throat. "My fees are quite high."

"Not a problem. Coppersmith will double them, plus add a bonus if you give us the para-physics data we need to solve the dinosaur problem."

She tried not to show her surprise. But the truth was that no matter how much she charged, it would be a mere drop in the bucket to Coppersmith Mining.

Singing dinosaurs. Alien technology. The chance to help open up an uncharted sector in the Underworld. The Knightsbridge Dream Institute could not turn down such a golden opportunity, she thought. A successful outcome would put her one-person firm at the top of the dream analysis world. The Wilson Parsons Agency could go suck untuned quartz.

There was a great deal to be said for the pleasures of payback.

"When would you expect me to start?" she asked, trying not to let her excitement show; going for a cool, calm, and professional demeanor.

Rafe checked his watch again. "I've got a company jet sitting on the ground at a private airfield here in Crystal. If we leave today we can be in Thursday Harbor this evening. We'll spend the night there and take a boat to Rainshadow at first light. Can't fly a plane near the island even on a good day. Too much paranormal interference. Messes up the instruments. It's possible to take a boat in after dark but it's risky. Only the locals have the experience needed to navigate the area at night, and they do it only if it's a flat-out emergency situation."

"You want to leave this afternoon?" Shock and dismay cascaded through her. Well, she had known the offer to work for Coppersmith Mining was probably a little too good to be true. "I'm afraid that's not possible. I've got a very important business reception tonight."

"Cancel."

She glared at him. "Easy for you to say. This is an important business affair held by a new client—the Dreamlight Research Department at Crystal City College. Coppersmith Mining may pay well for a one-time job but I have to think of future business."

Rafe's jaw twitched but she could see the frustration in his eyes. She held her breath.

"Okay," he said. "We'll leave tomorrow. Does that work for you?"

She glanced at her calendar again. "Yes, I can reschedule my appointments. I will have to be back here in Crystal by the twenty-fifth, however."

"That's cutting it kind of short. Might not work."

"You said we would find out right away whether or not I could do the job."

"All right." He didn't look happy but he appeared resigned. "Mind if I ask what's so important that you can't put it off if necessary?"

She flushed and cleared her throat. "A friend is getting married. It's a Covenant wedding. I'm a bridesmaid. As a member of the wedding party I can't just bow out at the last minute—certainly not for something as superficial as business reasons. This wedding has been nearly a year in the planning stages. You know as well as I do that I'd have to be at death's door in an intensive care unit to get out of it."

"Huh."

He was not pleased but he was stymied and they both knew it. Covenant weddings were major life events. One did not casually RSVP with regrets—not if one wanted to maintain friendships.

"A return date by the twenty-fifth is nonnegotiable," she said, not bothering to conceal the frosty edge on her words. "Now, do we have a deal?"

"We've got a deal. I'll push the project timeline back another day. We'll leave first thing in the morning."

"Excellent." She exhaled, trying not to show her relief. "I'll have Darren bring in the papers."

"One more thing," Rafe said. "Do you have a date for the reception this evening?"

She stiffened. "I don't think that's any business of yours."

"Doesn't matter to me. Just makes things simpler if you don't have to explain me to your date, that's all."

"And why would I need to explain you?"

"Remember what I said about Coppersmith providing you with a bodyguard? That service kicks in as soon as you sign the contract."

She tapped the pen against the crystal dust bunny one more time and listened to the *ping* fade away.

"Okay, I can understand why I need protection down below in that place you call Wonderland, but surely that's not necessary here in Crystal City."

"Probably not but I can't be certain of that," Rafe said. "Everyone involved in this project has tried to keep news of Wonderland from leaking out to the media, but maintaining airtight secrecy just isn't possible in this day and age. Stories about monsters and speculations about an ancient Alien bioengineering lab on the island have begun to appear in the tabloids. The conspiracy buffs are coming out from their caves. Coppersmith Security has received some threats."

"There's nothing new in that. The cranks are always all over new tales of the Underworld. I hardly think a few vague threats rise to the bodyguard level."

"You may be right, but these particular threats have been coming from an outfit that calls itself the Do Not Disturb movement," Rafe said. "They are more specific than the usual vague warnings we get from the fringe crowd. There have been a couple of incidents at the jobsite on Rainshadow.

Small stuff, but we've tightened up security in response. Coppersmith doesn't want to take any more chances than necessary. Rainshadow is dangerous enough on its own."

"I see." She wasn't sure where to go with that.

"Very few people know I'm in town—I sure as hell didn't broadcast the information. But after I leave here word will probably start to get around that we've signed a contract. Nothing stays secret in the business world for long, as I'm sure you're well aware. The DND crowd may get wind of our arrangement. If they do they might try to harass or intimidate you."

"I've heard of the Do Not Disturb crowd but I've never known them to be violent. I thought they were garden-variety cranks who hang out at the entrances to shopping malls and ask for donations."

"Until recently they've limited their activities to making a lot of noise and issuing warnings along the lines of *the world as we know it will end if big corporations excavate Alien ruins.* But like I said, they seem to be escalating. If they find out that you're going to a Coppersmith jobsite as a consultant they may try to convince you to cancel the contract."

"Hmm."

"Look, I'm sure there's nothing to worry about but I'd feel more comfortable if I escort you to and from the reception," Rafe said. "I won't be a problem for you. I'll just wait out in the car."

Okay, that sounded awkward. Ella considered her options.

Rafe Coppersmith was definitely a problem, but problems

sometimes presented opportunities. Wilson Parsons would no doubt be at the event.

She cleared her throat. "The reception is in honor of the new head of the Dreamlight Research Department. I was told I could bring a companion. I'm sure no one will mind if I drag you along."

"Try to contain your enthusiasm."

"But you might feel somewhat out of place. I'm afraid this event is black tie." She studied his denim and leather attire. "I suppose I could have Darren rent a tux for you."

"Forget it. I'll take care of the clothes. That's why they invented hotel concierges. What time shall I pick you up tonight?"

This was all happening way too fast, Ella thought. She did not want Rafe to get the notion that he was in charge. He was a client, not her boss. It was time to apply the brakes.

"I've arranged for my regular car service to pick me up and take me home." She paused. "I suppose I could collect you at your hotel."

"That works. What time should I be available for, uh, collection?"

He was deliberately trying to provoke her, she concluded. Okay, so she had made the offer in a rather grudging fashion. It wasn't her fault. He was the one who had insisted that she rearrange her schedule for him.

"The reception starts at seven," she said. "I'll pick you up at six thirty."

Rafe's eyes tightened a little at the corners. There was a whisper of hot psi in the atmosphere. She braced herself for an argument.

"Now what?" she asked.

"Nothing." He gave her a polite smile. "Just wondered if you always take care of the logistics on a date."

She went cold. The chill was followed immediately by the uncomfortably warm flush that she could feel rising in her cheeks. She searched Rafe's face but as far as she could tell he was not being sarcastic. Instead, he sounded genuinely curious.

There was no way he could have known that her history with men consisted of a series of painfully short-lived relationships that had all foundered on the rocks of her desire for deeper intimacy. Several months back she had finally sought refuge in celibacy.

She had learned the hard way that men were often initially attracted to a confident woman who did not hesitate to take the reins. But sooner or later they started to find her threatening. The fact that men who felt threatened by her appeared weak to her inner Siren did not help matters.

"Just to clarify, this is not a date," she said crisply. "If you insist on attending the reception with me, be ready at six thirty."

"Can we go to dinner afterward?"

"You can go to dinner anytime you like. I'll have to go straight home and pack."

"Right." Rafe smiled. "You're the take-charge type. Not a problem. I'll be ready at six thirty." He opened the door and paused one more time. "Your voice."

"What about it?" she asked, tensing a little.

"You sound exactly how I remembered."

He moved into the outer room and closed the door.

Chapter 7

HE WAS PRETTY SURE ELLA HAD SENSED THE FEVER IN HIS aura but it was clear she wasn't afraid of him. Then again, there probably wasn't much that could scare a Siren. *My kind of woman.*

He was still mulling that over when he got to Joe Harding's office. He hadn't planned to stop by but now that the trip to Rainshadow had been delayed he had some time to kill. He and Joe had worked several cases in the past couple of years. Chasing bad guys in the tunnels built a bond.

"I can't tell you how to do your job, but in my opinion, you're taking a hell of a risk hiring Ella Morgan." Joe Harding leaned back in his government-issue desk chair. The chair squeaked as if to prove that it was, indeed, government-issue and had been purchased from the lowest bidder. "I've been keeping an eye on her ever since she miraculously escaped from the two-time wife killer who took her hostage at that wedding a few months ago. I can't prove it but I'm pretty sure she's a Siren or damn close."

Rafe got a cold sensation in his gut. This was not good. Joe Harding had figured out that Ella was more than she seemed. That should not have come as a shock. The man known throughout the Bureau as Hard Joe was a very smart cop and a strong hunter talent.

Harding was a career FBPI agent with some fifteen years of experience. He had the physique and constitution that went with his paranormal nature. His lightning-fast reflexes, superb night vision, and his ability to think like the bad guys had served him well in his career.

He had climbed rapidly through the Bureau ranks and was considered a front-runner for the director's job, although, as he was the first to point out, given the political nature of the position at the top, nothing was certain.

"All I care about is that she's strong," Rafe said. He walked to the window and looked out. "I need some serious talent on the Rainshadow project."

"Those stories about dinosaurs are for real?"

"Yep."

Joe whistled. "Hard to believe."

"Trust me, the monsters are real and they hunt with some kind of music energy."

Joe's office was on the fifteenth floor of a government office building. From where he stood Rafe could see the rooftops of the low, Colonial-era structures around the massive green quartz Wall. Some of the Old Quarter neighborhoods had been gentrified in recent years. They boasted upscale condos, apartments, and trendy restaurants and clubs. But vast swaths of blight remained.

Many of the narrow lanes and alleys near the Wall were empty during the day. At night they became the hunting grounds of the most dangerous predators on the planet—the kind that walked on two feet. When the First Generation colonists had come through the Curtain they had brought their very human crime problems with them.

"It's your call, of course," Joe said. "But watch your back. I wasn't joking when I said she might be a Siren."

"I understand. Got anything else to go on besides the fact that the guy who held her hostage at the wedding had a stroke?"

"A very convenient stroke. And, yeah, there are a couple of other things. Like I said, I've kept an eye on her. She used to work at the Wilson Parsons Agency. It supplies midrange consulting talents in a variety of fields. She was a dream analyst."

"So?"

"A few weeks before she went into business for herself she was assigned a Wilson Parsons client named Gillingham. Rich old guy with a thing for antiques. She had a session with him. Afterward the housekeeper found her employer unconscious on the floor of the library. Miss Morgan was gone. Took Gillingham a couple of days to come out of the coma. When he did he reported that a valuable First Generation antique was missing from his collection."

"He thought that Ella Morgan had stolen it?"

"That was his theory but the antique later turned up somewhere in the house and everyone involved agreed that it had been misplaced. Gillingham withdrew his complaint. I don't have all the details. The Crystal City police handled the case."

Disdain dripped in Joe's voice. He considered the Crystal City PD to be incompetent and he didn't seem to care who knew it. The fact that the police lacked the high-tech resources that the Bureau took for granted was no excuse in his book.

On the other side of the equation, the chief of the Crystal City PD wasn't exactly a fan of Joe and the Bureau. It seemed that every time there was a high-profile case in the city, Joe was the one who wound up standing in front of the cameras, taking credit for the bust. Chief Truett, grim-faced, could generally be seen standing in the background and off to the side.

It was ever thus, Rafe thought. The various branches of law enforcement had always fought turf wars. It was one of the many reasons why he preferred to remain a part-time consultant.

"A missing antique wasn't exactly a case for the FBPI," he pointed out mildly.

"I don't give a damn about the antique. It was Gillingham's mysterious collapse that interests me. Looked a lot like Bellamy's collapse at the wedding except that the results were not as severe. Gillingham recovered. But immediately after the incident, Ella Morgan handed in her resignation to Wilson Parsons. A month later she opened up a small shop in the Quarter. Less than a week after that, she changed the name of her business to Knightsbridge Dream Institute and signed a lease in the Crystal Center business tower."

"You're wondering how she financed the move to the Crystal Center."

"It does raise some interesting questions. So does the name change."

"Well, you know she didn't use Gillingham's antique to underwrite her new office space. You said it turned up at Gillingham's house."

"Maybe because Gillingham went to the cops and Ella Morgan got nervous and arranged to have the antique reappear. She was going into business for herself, after all. The last thing she needed was a charge of theft from an old client. But Gillingham was just one of a number of clients that she worked with at Wilson Parsons. Some of the others may not have had such good memories after they woke up."

Rafe wondered if Ella had any idea that Joe was watching her so closely. The FBPI liked to keep track of very strong talents, especially those that fell into the dangerous category.

At least Joe didn't seem to know that Ella had been present in Adam Vickary's underground black-market salesroom the day that the task force had picked up Vickary, Trent, and the enforcers. Luckily, none of the perps had remembered exactly what had happened that day. They had all assumed that one of the Alien weapons had exploded. Which was not that far off the mark, Rafe thought.

He could still remember the flash fire that had swept through him when he put his hand on Ella and activated the artifact. Rezzing Alien tech had always jacked up his senses. But making physical contact with Ella while they were both running hot had taken the concept of *rush* to a whole new level.

The disaster three months ago had destroyed his ability to resonate with Alien technology. But this afternoon when he walked into Ella's office he had been hit with the same electrifying thrill that he'd gotten the day he'd found her in Vickary's lair. She had greeted him in the same beautiful voice that he had heard in his dreams, the voice that had pulled him out of the worst of the nightmares. Evidently, not even the fever could change the effect she had on his senses.

Focus, Coppersmith.

He pushed his personal issues aside—noting with some surprise that he was getting better at doing just that—and contemplated what Joe had told him about the Gillingham incident. It certainly raised some questions. How the hell had Ella financed the move into the Crystal Center?

Joe sat forward. His chair squeaked again. "Look, I'm the first to admit that I don't have anything solid on Ella Morgan. I just wanted to give you a heads-up."

"Thanks. But I'm out of options. I need a strong music talent."

"I understand. Just be careful."

"Sure."

Rafe started to turn away from the window but he stopped cold when a familiar chill iced his senses. The fever was spiking again. Anger flashed through him.

Not now. I'm a little busy at the moment. Things to do. People to see. Not now, damn it.

But the interior of the office was already blurring at the edges of his vision. He gripped the windowsill and braced himself against the vision, fighting it with all his will. He focused on the view of the Dead City ruins and tried to maintain an outward calm. He was getting better at the acting job. Hell, he'd had three months of practice. If he was careful Joe would never know what was happening.

He did not lose his sense of orientation completely this time but the vision whispered through all of his senses. He experienced the hallucination the way he did a dream—a waking nightmare.

. . . The monster emerged from the cave in which it had been hiding. It looked a lot like a serpent but it propelled itself on six legs. A forked tongue darted out of its mouth. The fangs dripped venom. It started toward him.

"You're not real," Rafe said in the silent language of dreams. "I know you're not real and I'll be damned if I'll let you try to convince me."

"Whatever," the monster said. "It's kind of funny, though."

"What is?"

"This is exactly what makes us monsters so dangerous. No one believes we're real."

"Rafe?" Joe's voice shattered the small trance. "Are you okay?"

Rafe willed away the last of the hallucination. He inhaled cautiously and did a quick internal check. All systems were normal again, at least as normal as they got these days. He released his death grip on the windowsill and rubbed the back of his neck.

"I'm fine," he said. "Been busy lately. Haven't been getting much sleep." That much was certainly true. "My dad dumped the Wonderland job on me a few days ago and I've been working around the clock to get up to speed."

"Mind if I ask where you've been for the past three months? Maybe it's none of my business but you and I go back a ways. Figure I've got some rights. There were rumors going around that you'd been burned on a Coppersmith job."

"There was some trouble at one of the exploration sites. I did get burned. Had to take it easy for a while. No big deal." Now that was a flat-out lie. "I spent most of the time hanging out at my family's compound on Copper Beach Island."

"Huh." Joe nodded but he didn't look entirely satisfied. "You're okay now, though, right? Can't see the company assigning you the troubleshooting job on Rainshadow if they thought you still had problems."

"No," Rafe said. "They wouldn't have sent me to Rainshadow if they had any doubts. There's too much riding on the project. Wonderland is the most important site Coppersmith has opened up in twenty years."

But it wasn't the board of directors or a high-ranking executive who had assigned him to the Rainshadow job. His father was the one who had sent him to the island. There had been some grumbling within the management hierarchy—rumors about the disaster that had left him psi-burned were rampant within the company. But Orson Coppersmith was the president and CEO of the family empire. His decisions were law.

"Good to know." Joe relaxed a little. "In that case, can I count on you for more consulting work in the future? When it comes to the illegal Alien-tech trade, I've never had anyone else as good as you on my team."

"I'll think about it," Rafe said. He was not in the mood to explain that he had lost his talent. "But I've got to clean up the problems on Rainshadow first. It's a family job. You know how it is."

"Family first." Joe glanced at his watch. "It's almost five. Want to grab a beer and some dinner?"

"I'd like that but I've got a date."

"Didn't know you knew anyone that well here in Crystal."

"I'm Ella Morgan's plus one for a business reception at a local college tonight. We're not leaving for Rainshadow until tomorrow."

Joe raised his brows. "You two must have hit it off well today. Congratulations on the fast work."

An unfamiliar tension gripped Rafe. For some reason he was suddenly consumed with the need to protect Ella's reputation.

"Strictly business," Rafe said. "If the DND crowd figures out that I'm in town and that I've hired Ella, they'll try to convince her to rethink our contract. I don't want to take the risk of losing her. Not a lot of strong music talents around."

"Got it. But remember what I said, pal. She may be more than just a high-end singer. If she's a for-real Siren, she's dangerous."

Chapter 8

SHE HAD SEEN THE FEVER IN HIS AURA BUT SHE WASN'T afraid of him.

Rafe thought about that again as he walked toward the sleek black limo waiting in front of the hotel. Actually, he'd been thinking about it almost constantly since the meeting in her office.

He knew that she was harboring a lot of mixed emotions about seeing him again; knew that she was more than a little pissed. She had a right to be mad given the way he had gone off the grid for the past three months. Still, she was not afraid of him.

If only she knew how often he had thought about her; how often he had relived that moment of intimate connection when they had weathered the storm of Alien energy unleashed by the crystal weapon.

When the nightmares struck—and they were always there, lying in wait for him if he allowed himself to sleep deeply—it was Ella who sang him through the storm. He woke up feeling battered and exhausted after foundering on the jagged rocks of his dreams, but at least he woke up. He knew that there had been nights when his family had feared that he might not.

I've dreamed about you, Siren. You don't know it but you saved my sanity and probably my life.

The hotel doorman opened the passenger door of the limo. Rafe slid into the darkly cushioned depths and opened his senses a little, anticipating the rush. It hit him the same way it had earlier when he had been ushered into Ella's office. The only difference then was that he had not been ready for it.

But this time he was ready; more than ready—he was hungry for the intoxicating frisson of sensual awareness. And the rush hit hard.

This afternoon he had been oddly surprised to discover that she was just as he had remembered her; just as he had seen her in his dreams. She was on the small side with an interesting, intelligent face and mysterious green eyes. There was a feline edge to her that aroused all his senses. He reminded himself that his sex life had been nonexistent since the diagnosis. What with one thing and another, he had to allow for the possibility that it probably wouldn't take much to get him hard. Still, Ella Morgan was different and the sensations he got when he was near her were different, too.

The driver spoke from the front of the vehicle. "Ready, Miss Morgan?"

"Yes, thank you, Bill," Ella said.

Bill pressed a button. The glass privacy screen slid into

place behind the driver's seat. The passenger compartment was transformed into an even more intimate chamber. It seemed to Rafe that the heat in the atmosphere climbed another degree or two. The energy swirling in the back of the limo wasn't coming just from his fevered aura, he thought. Ella was running a little hot, too.

She was the picture of a powerful talent who was also a cool, self-confident professional, but he was pretty sure that she was aware that they were striking sparks off each other.

"Thank you for being on time," she said. "When he picked me up, Bill told me that traffic was bad this evening. It will take a little longer than usual to get to the college."

"No problem," Rafe said. "I'm good about being on time. One of my virtues. Possibly my only virtue."

She smiled at the weak joke, gave him an appraising look, and nodded once in approval. "I see the concierge came through."

"The tux was delivered to the hotel about forty-five minutes ago."

"I'm surprised a rented tuxedo fits so well."

It was his turn to be amused. "It fits because it's not rented."

That got a reaction. She stared at him, mouth open in shock.

"You bought a new tux?" she managed. "Just for tonight?"

"Don't worry about the tux. I can afford it."

"I'm sure you can. That's not the point. You don't even know the people we'll be meeting this evening. You'll never see any of them again. Buying a tux was a complete waste of money."

"Okay, worry about the price of the tux if you really want to, but I'm not."

"Okay." She took a breath and let it out with control. "It's just that it seems rather extreme to invest in some obviously very expensive formal attire—"

"Would you mind if we changed the subject?" he asked gently.

"Sorry," she said stiffly. There was a beat of silence. She cleared her throat. "You look very nice."

"So do you," he said, keeping his tone equally polite. "Thank you."

She was still radiating tension but at least she was no longer carrying on about the damn tux. She sat in the shadows on the far side of the seat, giving him plenty of space. Her whiskey-gold hair was no longer in a severe bun the way it had been that afternoon. It was still up but now it was in a twist that was secured by an amber-studded clip. A few tendrils had escaped confinement, falling around her neck in a charming, sultry, subtly sexy manner. He did not know if the effect was intentional or if she had been in a hurry when she did her hair. Whatever the case, the style certainly worked for him. It was all he could do not to lean over and kiss the back of her neck.

Her shoulders were draped in a soft, dark wrap. He could not be sure of the color—black, or maybe a midnight blue. The hem of a slim skirt in the same color hit at a discreet yet sexy place a couple of inches above her knees. High-heeled sandals framed dainty ankles and elegantly arched feet.

The thought that his charged reaction to her might be a weird side effect of the fever crossed his mind but he decided to ignore it. He had too many other problems to worry about. Besides, the realization that he was alone in the back of a limo with the most interesting woman he had encountered in a very long time, maybe in forever, was too good to mess up with overthinking. So what if she was running Alien weapons on the side and had used her talent to steal a valuable antique. No one was perfect.

Maybe he really was losing it because of the fever, but at that particular moment he did not give a damn.

"Where's Lorelei?" he asked.

Ella seemed to relax a little at the question. "Out. She frequently disappears at night. I think she goes hunting with her dust bunny pals. I've concluded that I probably don't want to know all the details."

"So she stuck around after you rescued her buddies from Vickary's little shop?"

"That evening Lorelei appeared on my balcony. We've been pals ever since."

"Okay, that answers that question."

She smiled, coldly amused. "What you really want to know is how I managed the move from my first low-rent office space to the sixteenth floor of the Crystal Center."

"That would be interesting," he conceded.

"I thought so. The answer is that Lorelei paid her bill. She brought me a chunk of very valuable ruby amber. A friend of mine who happens to be in the antiquities trade sold it for me. A collector paid a bundle for it."

It was a good story, Rafe thought. And one that could never be easily proved or disproved. But he didn't give a damn. Tonight he was prepared to accept it at face value.

Ella could have told him that she had won the lottery or inherited a fortune and he would have been willing to accept the explanation. He was content to be in the car with her. At long last they were alone together. Except for the driver, Bill, of course. But Bill was minding his own business in the front compartment. With luck, traffic would be bad and it would take quite a while to get to the reception.

"Mind if I ask why you changed the name of your business to the Knightsbridge Dream Institute?" he asked.

"I thought it sounded more upmarket. Image is everything in my line."

"Image is important to any business," he said.

There was another short pause.

"Actually, there was another reason why I decided to rename my business," Ella said after a moment.

"Yeah?"

"I was fairly certain that you would keep quiet about your theory concerning the exact nature of my talent."

"Only fairly certain?"

"Well, it's not like I knew you well enough to know if you could be trusted, now did I?"

He thought about that. "No, I guess not."

"But even if you kept silent about your, uh, theory, I couldn't be sure that you would be able to keep my name out of the investigation. Special Agent Joe Harding is a real glory hound. If he did figure out that I was there in Vickary's underground shop that day, I don't think he would have hesitated to blab that little fact to the media. I thought it would be wise to come up with a new name for the business."

"The image thing."

"Exactly."

He settled back for the ride through the dark streets, savoring the invigorating energy of Ella's aura and her scent. The combination was more effective than an energy pill.

He had been battling the low-level miasma of nagging exhaustion brought on by sleep-deprivation for the past three months. Most of the time he could hold the tide at bay with a judicious mix of psi, caffeine, and short catnaps, but every so often he was forced to give in to the demands of his body. Sleep—the deep kind—came with a high price tag these days. He had been pushing himself ever since he had been tasked with troubleshooting the Rainshadow job. The bill was going to come due and payable soon. When that happened he needed to be alone and in a secure environment, a place where he could be assured that no one would witness his descent into the hellish realm of fever nightmares.

Ella stirred a little in the seat, crossing her legs. "You kept my secret."

"And you're going to keep mine, aren't you?"

"If you're talking about that little heat issue you've got going on in your aura, of course. I'm a dream analyst, remember? I'm very good at keeping other people's secrets."

"Okay," he said. "We've got a deal. We keep each other's secret."

She watched him intently for a while. "Something bad happened to you three months ago, didn't it?"

"Yes," he said.

"Care to talk about it?"

"No," he said. "I don't want to talk about it."

Chapter 9

ELLA WATCHED WILSON PARSONS MAKE HIS WAY THROUGH the crowded reception hall. Everything inside her tensed in battle-ready preparation for what she knew would be an unpleasant encounter. She was reasonably certain that Wilson would not make a scene—like her he had his image to consider. But that didn't mean he wouldn't try to stir up trouble.

Earlier she had assured herself that attending the prestigious affair with Rafe by her side would enhance the Knightsbridge reputation. But now, with Wilson closing in, she was having misgivings. Wilson had not forgiven her for walking out on that last assignment. He had predicted doom and disaster for her if she dared to leave him. The fact that she was rapidly making her way up through the highly competitive ranks of dream analysts was probably not sitting well with him.

"Who's this coming toward us?" Rafe asked in low tones. "He looks like he's got an agenda with you right at the top."

"That is very perceptive of you," Ella said. "His name is Wilson Parsons and I'm quite certain that he has an agenda. But I think it's very likely that you're the one at the top, not me."

"Wilson Parsons. Your old boss?"

"I see you've done a little research on me," she said.

"I'll bet you did some on me."

"Okay, you've got me there. Although, in fairness, I couldn't find much. Your family does a great job of maintaining a low profile."

"All the Coppersmiths are good at keeping secrets. We've had some experience."

"You're not the only family with that sort of experience. There's not much to tell you about Wilson Parsons. As you know, he was my former boss. Now he's one of my competitors. Also, in my opinion, he is ethically challenged."

"I see."

The reception to honor the new head of the Dreamlight Research Department was at its peak. The low roar of voices raised in loud conversation reverberated in the high-ceilinged room. The hall was crammed with members of the faculty in their purple-and-green caps and gowns, and wealthy alumni dressed in formal black and white. In addition, Ella spotted the mayor and several other city officials as well as businesspeople such as Wilson and herself, who had connections to the department.

She was drinking sparkling water because she always

stayed away from alcohol at social events that were business related. Rafe was also holding a glass of water. She wondered if that was because he was following her lead or if it had something to do with the psi-fever.

He was standing very close to her, so close that she was intensely aware of the controlled energy in his aura. He wore the tux—the original power suit—with cool authority. She remembered her sense of shock earlier when she had watched him emerge through the glass doors of the hotel lobby and walk toward the limo. The man who had been at ease in boots, denim, khaki, and leather in her office was clearly just as comfortable in formal black tie.

"Do you and Parsons have some serious personal history or was your relationship strictly business?" Rafe asked.

"Trust me, there was nothing of a personal nature between Wilson and me."

"Got it."

"Wilson Parsons took over the agency when his father died. I liked Mr. Parsons senior and enjoyed working for him. He always sent me out on interesting assignments. But the son is a very different proposition. I knew I would have to leave sooner or later, but when I walked out in the middle of an assignment Wilson was furious. He still is. If he can find a way to ruin my career, he'll grab it. He never expected me to get this far, this fast, you see. He was sure I was doomed to run a low-rent storefront dream-psychic operation forever."

"I assume you had your reasons for ditching that last case?"

"I certainly did. The client tried to rape me."

Wilson was almost upon them. She turned up her brightest *screw you, Wilson Parsons* smile.

He was in his early thirties, tall, and endowed with the reassuring, square-jawed good looks that stopped just short of too handsome. There was a strong vibe in the atmosphere around him. Wilson might have some problems when it came to ethics, but there was no denying that he had some serious talent. Wilson's abilities lay in the realm of marketing and sales. In Ella's opinion he could probably sell cold, untuned amber to a ghost hunter.

"Ella," Wilson said. "So good to see you."

His tone was rich and plumy but there was icy assessment in his eyes. She was sure she knew exactly what he was thinking. He was wondering if she and Rafe had signed a contract or if there was still time for him to make a move.

He returned her polished smile with equal firepower and had the nerve to try to top it with an air kiss. She pivoted toward Rafe at the last instant as if oblivious of Wilson's intent. The result was that Wilson found himself trying to kiss the glass of sparkling water in her hand.

"Have you met Rafe Coppersmith?" she asked. "Rafe, this is Wilson Parsons of the Wilson Parsons Talent Agency."

Wilson recovered from the botched air kiss and extended his hand to Rafe.

"Pleased to meet you, Rafe," he said. "Rumor has it that Coppersmith is looking for some highly specialized talent."

The handshake between the two men was quick and

minimal, the kind of handshake two fighters exchanged when they got into the ring.

"I was looking for some good talent," Rafe said. He smiled at Ella. "Fortunately, I found it."

"I see." Wilson glanced at Ella. "You needed a mid-level dream analyst, then?"

"I needed someone exactly like Ella," Rafe said. There was a mag-steel edge in his voice.

Wilson blinked and took what looked like an unconscious step back.

"I see," he said. He did not look convinced but he did look a little more cautious.

"Rafe and I signed the contract this afternoon," Ella said.

"Is that right?" Wilson raised his brows. "I'm surprised he had heard about your little one-person firm, Ella."

She considered emptying her glass of sparkling water on his shoes but she managed to restrain herself.

"Knightsbridge may be small but our reputation is growing," she said.

Wilson switched his attention to Rafe. "Your company is into mining. Mind if I ask why you need a dream analyst?"

"Coppersmith is involved in a wide variety of research projects." Rafe smiled a thin blade of a smile. "We employ an equally wide variety of consultants."

Wilson recovered quickly from the setback. He bestowed a patronizing grin on Ella.

"I understand that a contract with a company the size

of Coppersmith is a big deal for a little operation like Knightsbridge," he said. "If you find you're in over your head, feel free to contact me. Wouldn't be the first time Wilson Parsons has had to come to the rescue of one of our competitors."

Ella gave him a bright, shiny smile. "You bet. If I need help, Wilson Parsons will definitely be on my call list."

Wilson blinked a couple of times. He was obviously having trouble figuring out how to take her response. It finally must have dawned on him that she was being sarcastic.

"There's Dr. Flanders," he said, looking past Ella's shoulder. "I need to have a word with him about his new dream research project. If you'll excuse me?"

"Certainly," Ella said.

"Remember, Parsons will be happy to step in if you find you need our insights," Wilson said. But he was speaking to Rafe.

He melted into the crowd before Ella could respond. Rafe watched him go.

"What happened when you told Parsons that the client tried to rape you?" he asked.

His cold voice sent a chill through Ella.

"Wilson tried to convince me that it was my imagination. When that failed, he claimed that I had made a mistake in the course of the therapy."

"In other words, the attempted assault was your fault."

"Yes. That's when I handed in my resignation."

This was a dangerous topic, Ella thought. She needed to change the subject. Luckily, a familiar face emerged from the crowd. "Good evening, Professor Suarez. Thank you so much for inviting me this evening."

"Ella, dear, I'm so glad you could make it. And how many times must I tell you to call me Marlene?"

Marlene Suarez was a petite, silver-haired woman with a vivacious vibe and a sharp, analytical mind. She gave Rafe a speculative look.

"Who is your plus one this evening?" she said to Ella.

"I'd like you to meet Rafe Coppersmith," Ella said. "Rafe, Marlene is a professor in the Dreamlight Research Department."

"Coppersmith." Marlene's brows rose. "As in Coppersmith Mining?"

"That would be the family business," Rafe said. "Technically speaking, I'm an outside consultant."

Marlene chuckled and winked at Ella. "Congratulations, my dear. It's about time you started dating again."

Ella choked on the sip of sparkling water that she had just swallowed. She sputtered and coughed.

"Mr. Coppersmith is a client," she wheezed.

Rafe gave her a couple of bracing slaps between her shoulder blades and smiled at Marlene.

"Ella and I are still in the getting-to-know-each-other phase of things," he said.

Chapter 10

FORTY MINUTES LATER ELLA SAID HER GOOD-BYES AND walked out into the mist-bound night with Rafe.

A little buzz of energy tingled through her. She loved the streets of the Old Quarter after dark, especially when they were laced with fog. The lightly roiling mist was infused with the eerie green energy of the ruins, creating a fascinating chiaroscuro. She had always enjoyed the otherworldly atmosphere, but tonight the sensation was enhanced because of the man at her side.

It would have been a wonderful night for a stroll through the safe, gentrified streets of the Quarter with a real date, Ella thought. But Rafe was not a real date.

She was very aware of him at her side as they made their way through the well-tended gardens of the faculty club.

"You're sure there's nothing more I need to know about your relationship with Wilson Parsons?" Rafe asked.

"Positive," Ella said. "He's just mad because I left his firm and went out on my own."

All of which was the truth, as far as it went, she thought.

"What about the son of a bitch who attacked you?" Rafe asked. "What happened to him?"

"That part is a little more complicated," Ella said.

"This may surprise you, but I can be a good listener."

She had told herself that it would not be a good idea to discuss the Gillingham affair, but Rafe already knew a lot about what she could do with her talent. What was one more secret?

"Harold Gillingham had a thing about dream analysts— a sexual thing." She shuddered at the memory. "He seemed to think that just because I could analyze his aura and manipulate some of the dreamlight currents, I must be eager to have sex with him. When he came on to me, I informed him I didn't do that kind of therapy and tried to leave. He was furious. Said he'd paid a lot of money for me and he wanted his money's worth. There was a struggle. He was very strong."

"I assume you fought back using your talent."

"Yes. I only intended to make him fall asleep, but as it turned out he slept for two days. When he woke up he tried to convince everyone that I had knocked him out with a drug and stolen one of his First Generation antiques. But he had no proof, of course. He was furious, not just with me but with Wilson. He blamed the agency for sending him a therapist who had turned out to be a thief. Wilson blamed me for mishandling the client and creating the problem in the first place."

"What happened?"

"Gillingham went to the police. I called Jones and Jones."

"Arcane's investigation agency?"

"Cost me a small fortune but one of their investigators was able to direct the cops to the missing antique in about five minutes and that was the end of the matter."

"Where was it?" Rafe asked.

"Right where Gillingham had hidden it—in a secret closet in the library. The accusations were all about revenge. He was furious with me and wanted to punish me so he made up the theft charge."

"You resigned from the Wilson Parsons Agency because Parsons took the client's word over yours," Rafe said.

"That's it."

"Think Parsons knows that you can sing a man to sleep?"

"No, of course not. I don't go around advertising that little fact. You're the only person outside my family who knows what I can do with my talent." She stopped short at the edge of the drive, searching for the correct limo. "I don't see Bill and the car," she said.

A young, uniformed valet attendant hurried toward her. "Miss Morgan?"

"Yes," she said. "I had a driver tonight."

"Yes, ma'am, I know. He went home sick. Something he ate. Your car service sent another vehicle. The driver is waiting for you. I'll let him know you're here."

The valet raised a hand to signal. In response, a sleek black limo identical to the one Bill drove pulled out of the line of waiting vehicles.

"Poor Bill," Ella said. She unfastened her small evening

bag to take out some tip money for the valet. "I hope he's all right."

"I've got this," Rafe said quietly.

He slipped the cash to the valet before Ella realized what he intended to do. Irritated, she closed her bag with a sharp snap.

"That was not necessary," she said stiffly.

Rafe's mouth curved slightly at one corner. "You're welcome."

The long black car rolled to a halt in front of the valet stand. The attendant opened the door of the passenger compartment.

Ella discreetly hitched up the hem of her skirt and slipped into the car. She scooted hastily across the leather seat, making room for Rafe. He eased in beside her.

The valet closed the door and rapped on the driver's window a couple of times to let him know the passengers were safely on board.

The driver spoke from the front seat. "Good evening, Miss Morgan. I'm Briggs. Sorry about the change of cars. Your regular driver reported in sick. I'm the replacement. We're going to 321 North Wall Lane, right?"

"Eventually," she said. "But first we're going to drop Mr. Coppersmith at his hotel. The Colonial Inn on Quartz Drive."

"Yes, ma'am, I understand. I'll give you both some privacy."

There was a soft hum as the glass shield that separated the driver and passenger compartments slid into place. Ella was once again enfolded in the sensual intimacy of black leather and low lighting with Rafe. She tried to focus on the fog swirling in the neon-and-psi-lit streets.

"When, exactly, are we leaving in the morning?" she asked.

"As early as possible, but since we'll be on a Coppersmith jet we don't have a precise timetable," Rafe said. "Six o'clock work for you? I'll instruct the pilots to pick up some takeout for breakfast on the plane."

She winced. "Okay. Six o'clock." She still had some packing to do. Might as well not even bother to go to bed, she thought.

Rafe seemed satisfied. "That should put us into Thursday Harbor by midafternoon. Time enough to get to Rainshadow before dark."

"I apologize for that little scene with Dr. Suarez," she said quietly. "I'm sorry she assumed you were my date for the evening."

"So what if she leaped to the wrong conclusion about us?" Rafe turned slightly and settled deeper into the corner. He rested one arm along the back of the seat and watched her with unreadable eyes. "No big deal. You set her straight. I'm just a client."

She could not decide if he sounded irritated, bored, or simply unconcerned about Dr. Suarez's assumption.

"Right," she said briskly. "I will admit I took some pleasure showing off my new high-end client to Wilson. But, then, I'm probably shallow that way."

Rafe surprised her with a grin. "Where I come from that kind of thing is called good business. Never let the competition think it's got the upper hand."

"Good to know." She frowned. "The question is, how many other people in that room assumed you were my date for the evening?"

"My advice is, don't worry about it."

"Easy for you to say, but this is my business reputation we're talking about. There's a fine line between being seen at a public function with a prestigious client and having everyone think I'm—"

She broke off sharply, horrified at what she had been about to say.

Rafe finished the sentence for her. "Having everyone think you're sleeping with your client. I get that."

She tightened her grip on her little purse, grateful for the deep shadows. She was sure she was turning bright red. "Mmm."

"Don't worry so much. We're leaving town tomorrow. By the time you return everyone will be talking about something else."

"I hope you're right."

There was a long pause from Rafe's side of the car.

"Would it be so bad?" he asked eventually.

She glanced at him. There was a little heat in his eyes. For a moment she went quite blank.

"What?" she said.

"Would it be so bad if a few people leaped to the conclusion that you and I have something more than a client-consultant relationship?"

Anger crackled through her. "Well, of course it would be bad."

She adjusted the wrap around her shoulders and turned

her attention back to the nightscape unfolding on the other side of the window.

The limo had left the gentrified neighborhoods behind and was moving deeper into the Quarter. The trendy, fashionable restaurants and nightclubs disappeared. There were fewer people on the streets now and most of them looked like the sort who preferred to hide from the light.

Garish neon signs advertising bars and low-rent eateries with dark windows glowed briefly and then disappeared back into the night. It was not, she thought, the route she would have taken if she had been driving, but the driver seemed confident.

She was chagrined to realize that the intimacy in the back of the limo was starting to affect her nerves. She was feeling edgier by the minute. Her pulse was kicking up, too, and it seemed to her that it was getting harder to take a deep breath.

She was alone in the limo with a man who had a psi-fever burning in his aura.

She really did not know much about Rafe Coppersmith, she suddenly realized. Sure, she'd researched him online, but the Coppersmith family was reclusive and powerful. It obviously controlled much of what showed up in a routine search. There had been nothing about a scion of the clan suffering from a dangerous fever of the paranormal senses, for example. Who knew what else had been concealed from the media and the public?

"Something wrong?" Rafe asked.

"No," she said quickly. "I'm fine. Just making a mental list of the things I need to pack for the trip."

"The climate on Rainshadow is semitropical. You won't need a heavy coat, just something for the rain and maybe a light jacket or sweater for the evenings. As for Wonderland, it's like the rest of the Underworld—comfortably warm night and day. The temperature never varies."

"Good to know." She tightened her hand on her shawl.

"Are you sure you're all right?" Rafe asked.

"Yes," she hissed.

But she wasn't all right. She was starting to feel a little light-headed. Just nerves.

Rafe shifted slightly in the seat, leaning toward her a little as if to get a better look at her face. Her throat tightened. She was not alone in the car, she reminded herself. If she screamed for help the driver would hear her. The glass partition was not that thick.

But what if she was unable to scream? What if Rafe slapped a hand over her mouth and tried to overwhelm her para-senses just as Gillingham had done? Memories of the moments of shock and panic flooded over her. Her talent spiked in response. But this was Rafe. He would never try to overpower her like that.

She glanced at him again. Alarm flashed through her when she realized that his fever was spiking. She could see the wild heat in the shadows of his dreamlight. It was much stronger now than it had been that afternoon. A chill iced her senses.

In the low light she could see that Rafe's forehead was damp. As she watched, he wiped his eyes with the back of his hand and blinked several times.

"Damn it, something *is* wrong," Rafe said. His voice

was tight and grim, the voice of a man who was using everything to hang on to his control.

She flinched and retreated as far as she could into the corner of the seat. She was overreacting; allowing her imagination to get the better of her. She was losing it. She could not afford to do that, not with the most important client to come her way since she had opened her business.

She pulled hard on her jittery senses.

"I told you, I'm fine," she said. "Just a little tired."

"Do you always take this route home?"

"What?"

She stared at him, bewildered by the question. But he was not looking at her. He was focused on the view through the heavily tinted rear window.

She turned back to the side window, trying to orient herself.

"No," she said. "I always take Blue Amber Street through the Quarter. So does Bill."

"But Bill isn't driving tonight."

Rafe slipped a small phone out from under his jacket. "Can't get any reception."

"We're too close to the Wall."

"Do you know where we are?"

"No, not exactly."

Rafe seemed cooler now. The fever spike was settling down in his aura. But her own senses were frazzled. She searched for familiar landmarks but she could not seem to focus on the street scene. She was well acquainted with the renovated and gentrified sections of the old Colonial sector, but there were vast stretches of urban dead zone still waiting for developers and their money. Most of those bad areas bordered the West and South Walls. No knowledgeable professional limo driver would take his passengers into such dangerous neighborhoods.

Still, the big car hummed along, as if Briggs was very certain of his path.

She glanced at her watch. By now they should have been nearing the hotel. She started to turn in her seat to speak to Rafe.

"The driver is lost," she said. "I'm sure of it. He must be new—"

She broke off because Rafe wasn't paying attention. He pulled down the control panel that was suspended from the roof of the vehicle and flipped the intercom switch.

"Stop the car," he ordered.

There was no response from the front seat. Instead of trying again, he eased off the rear seat and made his way forward, crouching to avoid the low roof.

When he reached the partition he rapped sharply on the tinted glass. There was no reaction from the front seat. If anything, the car picked up speed.

A faint, cloyingly sweet scent stirred Ella's senses—not in a good way. Her first thought was that it was an air freshener. But the interior of the limo started to melt around her.

"Rafe."

"Gas," he said. "It's coming through the air-conditioning system. Cover your nose and mouth and get down on the floor."

She pulled her wrap across the lower portion of her face, unfastened her seat belt, and rolled off the seat. She reached up and pressed the button to lower the door window to allow some fresh air into the car. The window did not move.

She tried the door handle. It was locked.

It was getting harder to breathe through the wrap. Or maybe she was having a panic attack, she thought. She held the fabric a couple of inches away from her mouth and inhaled sharply, desperate to fill her lungs.

She got a full breath but at a price. The limo once again started to dissolve. The disorienting effect left her dazed and vaguely nauseous. Hastily, she drew the wrap across her nose and mouth again.

She turned her head and saw that Rafe was breathing through a white handkerchief. As she watched he reached inside his jacket. She barely had time to adjust to the realization that he had a gun in his hand before he used the butt of the weapon to hammer the glass partition.

Glass exploded into the driver's compartment. Briggs yelped and reflexively hit the brakes.

"What the fuck?" he shouted.

An instant later he trod heavily on the accelerator. The big car lurched forward.

"Stop the damn car," Rafe ordered.

He leaned through the jagged opening and put the barrel of the gun against Briggs's neck.

"I said stop the car," Rafe repeated evenly.

Briggs obeyed. He took his foot off the accelerator.

"You're crazy," he said. "They never told me you were fucking crazy."

"Surprise," Rafe said.

He aimed the small gun at Briggs's shoulder and rezzed

the trigger. There was a muffled crack of sound. Briggs screamed.

Ella was so stunned she forgot to breathe. Rafe had just shot a man at point-blank range.

Briggs slumped in the seat.

"Rafe?" she managed.

"He's not dead. Para-shock pistol. Coppersmith lab device designed for law enforcement. Knocked him out but the effects are temporary."

Rafe used the butt of the gun to knock the remaining shards of glass out of the partition. Leaning into the driver's compartment, he pressed a button.

"Try the door," he ordered.

She yanked the handle. "Still locked."

"I was afraid of that. They're overriding the locking system."

"What? Who is overriding the system?"

"Whoever arranged for you to get a new car and driver tonight."

He made his way back to the rear seat and slammed the butt of the gun against the window. The glass did not even fracture.

"High-tech glass," he said. "The damn stuff probably came out of a Coppersmith lab. Can't even put a hole in it with a mag-rez pistol. Good thing they didn't bother to install it in the partition." He slipped the gun back inside his jacket. "Help me pull out the backseat. We can get out through the trunk."

"Wait," Ella said. "Let me see what I can do with the window. It will be faster."

She planted one palm flat against the glass and drew hard on her talent. It took a precious few seconds to find the right notes but glass was glass. There was always an inherent instability where it was not quite a liquid and not quite a solid.

"Got it," she said.

She sang the silent, destabilizing song. The bells on her bracelet chimed. The glass resisted at first and then melted like butter in a hot pan.

Rafe flashed her a quick grin. "You are one killer soprano." He motioned with the gun. "Out."

With some forceful assistance from Rafe, she scrambled out through the window. There was a sharp ripping sound at one point. She knew the narrow skirt of her dress had been torn.

When her high heels touched the ground she straightened, gripped the roof of the limo, and drew a deep breath of fresh air into her lungs. Her head cleared.

Rafe followed her through the opening with the agility of a rock climber slipping through a narrow crevasse. He raked the street with an assessing gaze while he breathed deeply.

"Let's go," he said. "Whoever is running this operation will know by now that things have gone wrong."

"What in the world is happening? None of this makes any sense."

"This is an ambush," Rafe said. "The pickup team will be along any second."

She wanted to ask more questions but it was clear that this was not the time or place for an in-depth discussion. She looked around, still a little woozy from the effects of the gas.

Abandoned, boarded-up buildings that dated from the Colonial era loomed on either side of the narrow street. The pavement dead-ended at the towering green-quartz Wall.

"Are we going back the way we came?" she asked.

"No, this is a classic box-canyon setup," Rafe said. "The rest of the crew will come straight down this street any minute now. We don't want to run into them."

"I take it that means we're going to break into one of these buildings?"

"It's our best chance."

He was already moving toward the doorway vestibule of one of the darkened buildings. She hurried after him.

"Stand back," he ordered.

She stumbled to a halt. Rafe grasped the edge of a sagging board and hauled it away from the doorway. The old door was still in place but transients or vandals had smashed the lock long ago.

"This will have to do," Rafe said.

He moved into the deep shadows. Ella heard the low whine of a big engine just as she followed him into the dense darkness.

"Why are they doing this?" she asked. "What do they want?"

"You, probably."

"*Me?* Why?"

"My fault. I'll explain later."

Rafe slammed the door closed behind her. She turned to look at him. With her own senses jacked up she could see his dreamlight. The psi-fever had kicked up again. It burned with laserlike intensity in his energy field.

Chapter 11

THIS WAS A HELL OF A TIME FOR THE FEVER TO SPIKE, Rafe thought. He had been fighting it for several minutes now, ever since he had realized that the car had been hijacked. The visions were getting stronger.

He struggled to suppress the surge of heat and energy that was rushing through him. Maybe the knockout gas had triggered the latest spike. No telling what had been in it, obviously some crap that affected the para-senses as well as the normal senses.

Every day brought a new and more unwelcome discovery concerning the nature of the low-burning fire that was ravaging his senses.

Note to self: In future, avoid toxic fumes of unknown origin.

He focused on the only job that mattered now. His first priority was to get Ella safely out of Crystal City and into the protective custody of Coppersmith Security. He had brought the devil down on her tonight. He could not allow the fever to get control of his senses until he made sure that she was out of reach of whoever was trying to grab her.

His senses were still jacked, enough so that he could see Ella standing in the shadows, watching him, just as she had watched him in his dreams for the past three months. He could sense her fear and feel the jumpy vibe of her heightened talent. But she was in control. Hell, even after having been dosed with some unknown gas, she was still powerful enough to melt glass.

A man could get used to having a woman like this around.

He opened the door an inch and watched the street. The heavily shadowed vestibule provided ample cover for the moment. The pickup team would not immediately notice the door slightly ajar.

A heavy Resonator 600 slammed to a halt directly behind the limo. Two men dressed in head-to-toe black, ski masks covering their faces, leaped out of the big SUV and ran toward the other vehicle. Their outfits were identical. The only visible difference between the two thugs was that the driver was a few inches taller and heavier.

He reached the limo first.

"Briggs is here but the targets are gone," he announced. "Looks like one of them got through the partition and took out Briggs. Must have been Coppersmith. Shit. The glass in the door window in back is gone."

"How the hell did that happen?" Shorty demanded. "That stuff is bulletproof."

"Coppersmith must be armed with something that

came out of one of the company labs." The driver took a small device out of his jacket. "There hasn't been enough time for them to get far. We'll track them down. We've got the woman's frequency."

Rafe heard Ella suck in a sharp breath.

"My amber," she whispered. "It's all tuned. They know the freq. They can follow me anywhere, even Underground."

"Strip," Rafe said.

He did not have to explain. He could hear Ella rustling around, removing her earrings, the amber hairclip, and a few other items from locations he knew would not have been obvious to the casual observer.

"Got her." Tall Bastard looked hard at the dark vestibule. "She's inside that building."

"Coppersmith's probably with her," Shorty said. "He's armed. If we charge that doorway we're going to make really good targets."

"I removed all of my amber," Ella whispered. "Now what?"

"Just leave it on the floor," Rafe said. "We're not hanging around here for long. But before we leave, I'd really like that pair to come out from behind the Resonator. I can't shoot through the steel on that vehicle."

The driver opened the cargo bay door of the Resonator.

"You're going to use the damned bell?" Shorty asked. He did not sound thrilled.

"You volunteering to rush the door and take a chance on getting shot with whatever shit took out Briggs?"

"Hell, no."

"Then we use the bell."

"I hate that thing. Alien tech gives me the shakes."

"Alien tech is going to make you rich," the driver said. "Put on the headphones. The boss says this thing will take care of anyone in the vicinity who isn't geared up."

"So much for hanging around for a good shot," Rafe said quietly. He closed the door and shoved a chair under the handle. "No way to know what kind of Alien tech they're about to use, so we're getting out of here."

He pulled out the flashlight.

"You wore a gun *and* a flashlight to the reception?" Ella asked. "I'm impressed."

"Helped myself to the flashlight. It was in the limo console. And don't be impressed. I'm the guy who let you get into the car even though there was a different driver."

"Yes, well, I'm the one who booked the service."

"We can argue about it later."

He rezzed the flashlight. The narrow beam speared the darkness, revealing a jumble of small round tables, cushioned banquettes, and a stage.

"Looks like an old nightclub," Rafe said. "With luck, that means there will be a hole-in-the-wall in the basement. Clubs in the Quarter always like to feature a little extra psi to go along with the booze and other assorted drugs being served."

"I can sense it," Ella said. "Somewhere down below."

"Yeah, I can feel it, too."

She looked at him quickly. "You can still sense that kind of energy? Even with a fever?"

"Yes, damn it." He did not mention the hallucinations.

It would only make her more nervous. Besides, he had them under control. Sort of.

She flinched.

"Sorry," she said. "Didn't mean—"

"Never mind. Let's move."

Wonderful. Now he was snapping at her.

The whiff of catacomb energy floated up from somewhere behind the bar. He started toward it. Ella followed.

The tattered remnants of a black velvet curtain loomed in the beam of the flashlight. An ancient sign hung above the arched doorway: INVITED GUESTS ONLY.

He pushed aside the curtain and started down the stairs into shadows lit with green energy.

"We're in luck," he said.

He was listening intently for the sound of the front door being forced open when he heard the eerie tolling of a terrible bell. It rang with mind-destroying force, freezing him on the stairs.

Ghostly energy threatened to ice his aura. Mortal dread slammed through him. A tsunami of nightmares and hallucinations surged out from the depths of his unconscious mind. He somehow knew them to be different from the visions he'd been experiencing. These dreams could shatter his senses and stop his heart.

His first thought was that the psi-fever was spiking higher than ever. This time it would kill him. He could not let that happen until he got Ella to safety.

An incomprehensible urge to rush back up the stairs and outside into the street almost overwhelmed him. Part of him was certain that obeying the summons of the bell was the only way to survive.

Except that it was not the way to survive. Responding to the hypnotic music would get them both killed. He knew that, but the knowledge did not seem to have any meaning. It was just a fact, and not a particularly important fact, at that.

"Rafe?" Ella called to him from the top of the stairs. "Are you all right?"

"That bell," he said through clenched teeth. "Alien tech."

"Yes. It's some kind of mesmeric device but it works on music frequencies like a lot of Alien tech. I think I can handle it."

Her musical voice was a flame in the night, briefly pulling him out of the trance. He used all of his willpower to heighten his senses. For a moment he was able to refocus.

"I'm not sure I can handle it," he said. He undid his cuff links. "Take some of my amber. It's tuned. Judging by what they said, they have your frequency but not mine."

"Rafe, listen to me."

"Go down into the tunnels. Pick a random exit point. When you come out, don't go home. They'll have your place staked out." He tugged his wallet from the inside of his jacket and extracted a business card. "Call this number. It's Joe Harding's private line. He'll take care of you. Understand?"

"Listen up, Coppersmith. I am not about to call the FBPI. I'm pretty sure Harding doesn't trust me."

The nightmare bell tolled again, smashing against his senses in waves of darkness.

"Shit," he whispered.

"Give me your hand," Ella said.

"Just go, damn it. I'll cover you."

But she grabbed his hand. He felt the rush of her talent. Her aura enveloped him.

. . . And mercifully the sound of the bell receded.

He managed to take a deep breath.

"Okay, I can suppress the energy of the bell," she said. "No problem. I can't give you complete protection but I should be able to shield you from the worst of the effects."

The eerie bell tolled again, sending out another wave of terrifying energy—but the summoning effect was oddly muted. Ella shuddered.

"Good grief, how did you manage to handle the first wave?" she asked. "Most people would have lost consciousness."

"You're good," he said.

"Like Mom says, we all have a talent."

He could hear the lilt in her voice and knew that she was getting a little buzzed because she was using her paranormal senses. Some of the thrill she was experiencing was affecting his aura due to their physical contact. He suddenly felt more confident. His senses steadied.

"Can you keep this up long enough for me to deal with those two?" he asked. "Because I'd really, really like to know who they are and who sent them."

"I think so."

"Then we have a change of plans. Stay behind me. Whatever you do, don't let go."

"I won't."

He threaded his fingers through hers and drew her back up the basement steps. They took cover behind the bar.

The driver kicked the door open. Shorty was right behind him. For a moment they were clearly silhouetted against the green psi-light emanating from the ruins. The driver was clutching an object the size and shape of a small, graceful flower vase in both hands. Even Alien weaponry was ethereally beautiful, Rafe reflected absently. But the device glowed with a hellish light.

He got a fix and took the first shot. The driver grunted and went down. The artifact fell to the floor with a thud. The nightmarish tolling ceased abruptly.

"Shit," Shorty muttered.

He tried to retreat back through the doorway but he wasn't fast enough. The shot caught him in the shoulder. He flung out his arms and collapsed in the vestibule.

Rafe waited a beat to be sure that neither man made a move toward the Alien device. Then he released Ella's hand.

"Are they unconscious?" she asked. "Like the driver?"

"Yeah." He went forward, crouched beside the driver, and ripped off the headphones and the stocking mask. He aimed the flashlight at the man's face. "Know this guy?"

Ella moved closer. "No. I'm sure I've never seen him before in my life."

Rafe rose and bent down to take off Shorty's mask. Ella shook her head again.

"No, I've never seen him, either," she said.

"Neither have I."

He did a quick search of both of the fallen men.

"No ID," he said. "Not even a driver's license."

"Maybe in their vehicle?"

Rafe shook his head. "Doubtful. Whoever sent them did not want to take the chance that they might fail and wind up leaving a trail."

"I can't imagine why anyone would send a bunch of thugs to kidnap me. It makes no sense."

"And why now?" Rafe went to the door and studied the expensive Resonator. "There has to be a connection between what almost happened here tonight and that contract you and I just signed. Otherwise the timing is just too damn coincidental."

She blew out a small breath. "I see what you mean."

"Maybe Coppersmith Security can get something off the equipment these bastards are carrying and their locators. I want to get that damn bell into a vault as soon as possible, too."

He stripped off every piece of gear he could find on the unconscious men, including the odd earphones. It was a large haul—far too much stuff to carry in his hands. He decided the easiest way to transport the assorted devices would be in a sack made from a shirt.

He saw the first tattoo when he unbuttoned the shirt of the man who had worked the bell.

"Well, damn," he said softly. "This is interesting."

It wasn't much as tats went—certainly not exotic artwork—just a small tornado or waterspout done in black ink on the upper chest.

Ella came to stand on the other side of the fallen man. "A lot of people have tattoos."

"Yes, but usually the artwork is more elaborate."

He got to his feet and went to Shorty. He unfastened the jacket and opened the shirt.

"Same tattoo," he said.

"Gang markers?"

"Probably. Definitely some sort of identification tag."

He took out his cell phone and snapped pictures of the two men and their tattoos.

"That's it," he said. He clipped the phone to his belt. "Can't risk staying here any longer. Let's go."

She looked down the empty street. "It's going to be a long walk out of this neighborhood."

"We'll use the tunnels."

"Okay, sounds like a plan."

"More like half a plan. We'll work on the other half after we're underground." He slung the makeshift sack of gear over one shoulder and started toward the door of the old nightclub. "But I'd like to get one thing clear between us going forward."

"What's that?" she asked.

"Next time we go out on a date, I'm driving."

Chapter 12

RAFE WAS IN TROUBLE—PSI-FEVER TROUBLE. ELLA COULD sense it but she could also tell that this was not the time to question his ability to control the heat in his aura. No strong talent welcomed that kind of very personal inquiry, and in her experience, that usually went double for talents who happened to be of the male gender. It was right up there with questioning their manhood.

The critical thing at the moment was that Rafe appeared to be in control of his talent and the fever.

They made their way back downstairs into the night-club's cluttered basement and wove a path through the long-forgotten evidence of more prosperous days. Extra chairs, unopened cases of glassware, broken stage equipment, and empty liquor cartons littered the floor. Faded banners and decorative streamers celebrating New Year's

Eve dangled from the ceiling. The date on the decorations was three decades earlier.

The entrance to the catacombs lay behind a door in the wall that sagged on its hinges.

She followed Rafe into another stairwell. This one featured a spiral staircase made of glowing green quartz that descended deep into the Underworld. The wide steps were designed for feet that were not quite human in shape.

Once inside the quartz stairwell, she breathed a small sigh of relief and opened her senses. The walls sang to her in elegant, exhilarating harmonies that originated far out on the paranormal spectrum. Other people experienced the catacombs as a slightly intoxicating, refreshing tonic that induced a certain buzz—frequently a buzz with sexual undertones. She got that effect, too, but she also heard the kind of music that no human-made instrument could ever produce.

The First Generation Colonists had been terrified of the tunnels with good reason. Until they had discovered how to use tuned amber to steer a path through the heavy-psi environment, the Underworld had been a lethal maze for humans. Like the vast oceans, the underground rainforest, and other natural hazards, the catacombs were still deadly for those who did not have proper navigational equipment.

At the foot of the staircase, Rafe checked his amber locator and turned left into an illuminated green hallway that was identical to the three other green corridors that branched off in various directions. Ella knew that he had selected coordinates for an exit.

"Any idea who wants you badly enough to risk grabbing you off the street?" he asked.

"Good heavens, no," she said. "I've got some odd clients but none who would resort to kidnapping and attempted murder—at least, none that I know of. I'm very careful when it comes to clients."

"Until me?"

His tone was a little too even.

"I was ready for dinosaurs—not kidnappers."

"Yeah, same here. I keep thinking about those tattoos."

"One of your competitors maybe?"

"The mining business can get rough," Rafe said. "People play hardball. But I can't see any of Coppersmith's corporate competitors risking this kind of action. There is another, more likely possibility, however."

"What?"

"I think those guys who tried to grab you tonight are probably linked to the crazies who have been sending us warnings about how Harmony will be doomed if we keep digging up Alien secrets."

"The Do Not Disturb crowd?" She thought about that. "The Alien return whackjobs are certainly out there. But mostly they seem like harmless crackpots."

"Until now, I've never heard of them using Alien tech to make their point, though. Hell, they're against Alien tech."

"Wouldn't be the first time someone picked up the same weapon that the enemy is using," Ella said.

"True. And there's no question but that DND has been escalating lately. You know, I'd tell you to bail on the contract but I'm not sure that would keep you safe. Not now. I've led the bastards straight to you. Even if you tear up the contract they might not leave you alone."

"Which means there's no point terminating our arrangement," she said briskly. "I'm not going to pull out, Rafe. One thing has been bothering me, though."

"Just one thing?"

She ignored that. "With the exception of the DND cult, most of the conspiracy buffs I've heard about are loners with no visible means of support. Whoever ambushed us tonight obviously has some serious financial backing— enough to put a fancy limo and a big Resonator on the street, not to mention all that high-end equipment those men were carrying. The bell, alone, is worth a fortune."

"We're dealing with someone who can afford some very expensive Alien toys." Rafe paused. "It's a damn good thing that you can suppress para-music frequencies."

She glanced at him. "Can't you?"

"No."

"But you can activate Alien weapons," she said. "You did it that day when the mob guy, Trent, and his enforcers tried to kill us. You fired the artifact as if it were a gun. You channeled that energy."

"I can rez the trigger of a pistol, too. But I can't stop the bullet once it's been fired."

"Oh, I see what you mean."

"Being able to rez Alien tech is not exactly a common ability, but it's not all that rare." Rafe glanced at her. "Can you do it?"

"No. I can send out dampening wavelengths to suppress the paranormal forces in Alien tech but I can't channel those forces and focus them the way you can. I'm a singer, not an Intuitive Power Channeler. That's what you are, isn't it? Technically speaking?"

"That's what I was."

"Why the past tense?"

"Things change," Rafe said.

She might not be a high-level intuitive talent, but she could tell when someone had just shut down a conversation.

"What happened to those two Alien weapons that Vickary was trying to sell?" she asked. "They didn't show up in the media accounts of the big bust."

"Currently they're in a special underground vault at FBPI headquarters."

"Ah-hah. So, at least some of the conspiracy theories in the *Curtain* are right."

Rafe glanced at her. "What?"

"Never mind."

"Both of those men in the Resonator had to put on some sort of earphones before they used the bell. What do you think that was all about?"

"I think it's safe to say that they needed the earphones to shield them from the effects of the weapon." She looked at the makeshift sack Rafe was carrying. "That gear you confiscated might provide some clues. Stuff that sophisticated came out of a high-end lab."

"True. I'm damn sure it wasn't one of ours. But every para-tech engineer leaves his or her unique psychic prints, just like computer programmers leave their prints on their code. With luck our research people will be able to take these earphones apart and come up with a way to trace them back to whoever created them."

"It seems to me that the real question here isn't how those two were able to shield themselves from the effects of the bell," Ella said. "It's how did they activate it in the first place? I don't think either one of them was a music talent. If that were the case they wouldn't have had to use the headphones."

"I've been thinking about that. Same is true if they'd had my old talent. They wouldn't have needed protection from the energy waves because they would have been channeling them. You know, if someone has discovered a way for the average bad guy to rez Alien tech, the FBPI, the police, and the Guilds are going to be facing some serious new problems on the streets."

"That is not a cheery thought."

"No, it's not." Rafe tightened his grip on the shirt sack. "The last thing we need are a bunch of thugs armed with Alien weapons. It's hard enough to control illegal activity in the Underworld now."

"Well, if it's any consolation, I doubt if the man who used the bell on us could have kept the power surge going for long—a couple of minutes at most."

"But long enough to force a person to surrender."

"Or kill him."

"Without a trace," Rafe mused. "The perfect murder weapon. Most experts are aware that death by Alien tech is theoretically possible, but proving it in a court of law is usually impossible, at least with current forensic science."

They arrived in a high-ceilinged rotunda with several

intersecting corridors. Rafe checked his locator and chose a tunnel.

"I assume you have a specific destination in mind," Ella said. "There are hidden holes-in-the-wall scattered all over the city, but the main gate—the one guarded by the Guild—is inside the Great Wall."

"That won't work for us," Rafe said. "We don't know who is after us or what Guild connections they might have. We have to assume that whoever set us up tonight will be watching all the obvious locations where we might be expected to show up. That includes the private airfield where the Coppersmith jet is waiting."

"That's a depressing thought," she said. "I suppose our next move will be to call in the FBPI."

"You really don't like the Bureau, do you?"

"Nothing personal. The problem is, the Bureau tends to be innately suspicious of people like me."

"Off-the-charts talents."

"Specifically, off-the-charts talents the Bureau thinks are potentially dangerous," Ella said. "I've been living with my secret ever since I came into my para-senses. My family has been living with it, too. I've got a career to protect. The bottom line is that I don't want to end up on a watch list."

"I never told anyone that you were a Siren," Rafe said, a grim edge on the words. "But I've got some bad news for you."

A frisson of panic zapped her nerves and her senses. "Please don't tell me—"

"The head of the Crystal City FBPI has some suspicions

concerning your talent based on what happened at that wedding."

"Oh, damn. *Damn.*" She clenched her hand around her little purse. "Joe Harding has been watching me?"

"From a distance," Rafe added hurriedly.

"Damn." She shot him a quick look. "How long have you known?"

"I just found out today when I dropped by his office to see him. He asked why I was in town. I said I had come to Crystal to hire you. He warned me that he suspected you might be a full-on Siren."

She wanted to hurl something at the nearest wall but all she had available was her small evening bag.

"Damn," she said. Again.

"I'm sorry," Rafe said. He watched her with an expression that contained a mix of sympathy and wariness.

She sighed. "It's not your fault."

"Joe's suspicions were fueled by the fact that you moved up so fast in the business world."

"Do you believe my story?"

"I admit I had a few questions at first," he said. "But I believe it now."

"Wow, thanks for the vote of confidence," she muttered.

"Are you sure you don't want to terminate our contract?"

She glared at him. "Do you want me to terminate it?"

"No. I need you and I don't know anyone else who can do the job. But it's obvious you're a little upset."

"Oh, shut up," she said. "I'm not upset, I'm stone-cold furious. There's a difference."

"Right. But not mad enough to end our arrangement."

"It wouldn't make any difference as far as my problems with the Bureau are concerned."

"True," he agreed.

She gave him a steely smile. "From the sound of things, I need you as much as you need me. Nothing like having Coppersmith Mining on my list of clients to give me some credibility in case the FBPI comes calling."

Rafe thought about that. "Good point. We'll have your back."

"Fine. In that case we've still got a deal."

"Good." Rafe exhaled slowly. "That said, I don't think we'll contact the local office of the Bureau or anyone else here in Crystal City."

"I'm delighted to hear that, of course." She narrowed her eyes. "But I need to ask, why not?"

"Too many people are aware that I hired you today. We don't know who sent those guys with the bad tats and this isn't the time to find out."

"Sounds like you may be working on a conspiracy theory."

"Maybe. Bottom line is that I can't afford any more delays. I want to get you to safety, which means that we need the second half of that plan you were asking about."

"Got the second half?"

"I think so. To begin with, we're going to stay out of sight until we get clear of Crystal City. Once we're airborne and on our way to Rainshadow, I can dump the problem of the tattoo crowd into the lap of Coppersmith Security. You and I can focus on the singing dinos."

"Okay."

"I sense a lack of enthusiasm."

"Well, it's not like I have a better plan."

"Definitely a lack of enthusiasm."

"Don't read too much into my response. I'm not at my enthusiastic best at the moment." She gave up on the stiletto heels and came to a halt. "Hang on."

She stepped out of the shoes and carried them, dangling, by the thin heel straps.

She didn't have to look in a mirror to know that her hair had come undone in the course of the mad scramble to avoid the kidnappers. Somewhere along the line she had lost her wrap. The center back seam of her skirt had ripped several inches up her thigh and now she was barefoot.

Rafe also looked a little the worse for wear but in a dashing, sexy way. She studied him, somewhat resentfully.

His collar-length hair, which had been sleeked back behind his ears earlier in the evening, now hung in dark wings, framing his predatory features and dangerous eyes. He had opened the collar of his crisp white shirt. The black silk tie was draped around his neck. The tux jacket was unfastened, revealing glimpses of his shoulder holster.

They looked like they'd had a very hard night on the town, she thought.

"We've still got a few logistical problems," Rafe said.

"We certainly do." She was aware that her tone was decidedly sharp. Not her fault, she thought. The evening had been stressful. And now she had confirmation of her mother's greatest fear. She was on an FBPI watch list. She had a right to sound short-tempered. "For starters, how am I going to get my things before we leave town?"

"I'll arrange to have whatever you need picked up at your place and sent on to Rainshadow by overnight courier," Rafe said, dismissing the problem.

"Let's get something straight. I can go to Rainshadow without a change of underwear, but I'm not leaving town without Lorelei."

"I'll make sure someone feeds Lorelei."

"You don't understand." Her temper rose another notch. "Lorelei is not a pet. Lorelei is a companion. She's a good hunter and she's quite capable of feeding herself. That's not the issue. The issue, Rafe Coppersmith, is that I am not going anywhere without her."

"You didn't mention Lorelei in the contract."

"Damn it, Rafe—"

"Okay, okay." Rafe thought for a moment. "What if we send someone to pick her up and take her to Rainshadow?"

"I doubt that she'd go with a stranger." Ella paused, thinking. "Lorelei might get into a car with Pete."

"Who is Pete?"

"He's a business associate of mine. My old office was next door to his. It was his sled I borrowed the day I rescued the dust bunnies that Vickary was going to use for target practice. Pete's the one who handled the sale of the ruby amber for me. Lorelei knows Pete and likes him. He gives her sparkly things for her collection."

"You trust this Pete?" Rafe asked.

"Absolutely. I trust him a hell of a lot more than I do the FBPI." A familiar chortle brought her to a halt. *"Lorelei."*

The dust bunny came tearing around a corner, all four eyes wide open. She was running on four paws because she had the headpiece of her wedding veil clutched in one of her two front paws.

Ella leaned down to scoop her up. She buried her face in Lorelei's fluffy gray fur.

"How did you know we were in trouble?" she asked.

Lorelei chortled again. Evidently satisfied that Ella was all right, she greeted Rafe.

Rafe looked at Lorelei and then at Ella.

"Satisfied now?" he asked.

"Have dust bunny, will travel," Ella said.

"That's good, because I've nailed down the rest of the plan."

"What does it involve?"

"Road trip."

Chapter 13

ELLA WATCHED THE HEADLIGHTS CONSUME GREAT GULPS of the mostly empty highway that stretched out to the midnight horizon. Rafe was behind the wheel of the car he had rented from an all-night agency in Resonance. She was in the passenger seat, although she was growing more convinced by the minute that she ought to be driving. She could tell that Rafe was using a lot of psi to stay alert at the wheel.

Lorelei was perched on the back of the seat, fully fluffed and munching on the chips that Ella had purchased from a vending machine at the car rental agency. Her precious wedding veil was in the rear seat.

Lorelei was the only one who appeared to be enjoying the midnight run to an unknown private airstrip.

In the faint glow of the dashboard lights, Rafe's profile was hard and determined. When Ella heightened her senses she could see the low-burning fever in his dream-light. At least it was no longer spiking, she thought.

"You know," she said. "When you mentioned that a road trip was involved I didn't think you meant it quite this literally."

"The private airstrip is a few hours' drive from the city. It should be safe. Belongs to a retired executive who owns her own plane, Gabriella Cremona. She was with the company for over forty years. Dad always trusted her, so we can, too."

"I'm not arguing with you. I agree that getting out of town without alerting whoever is trying to kidnap me is the best bet at the moment. But I think you should let me drive."

Rafe's hands tightened on the wheel. "I'm okay. I can drive."

"I don't doubt that, but you need rest. I'm fully capable of driving."

"I know, but it's not necessary."

"Are you really going to argue with me about this? Look, I can tell you're running a psi-fever. You need to allow your aura to rest and recover. When was the last time you got some decent sleep?"

For a moment she wasn't sure he would admit that he needed sleep or even that he had some issues with his aura. His hands flexed and he renewed his fierce grip on the wheel.

"Sleep doesn't work well for me these days," he said finally. "Best I can do are short naps."

"All right, let me drive while you take a nap."

"I'll get some rest on the plane."

"You need to sleep now. Be reasonable, Rafe. What if something goes wrong at the airstrip? You'll need to be fully functional, and that's not likely if you exhaust yourself driving for the next three hours."

That bit of logic evidently broke through the wall of masculine pride. He hesitated and then, somewhat to her surprise, he took his foot off the accelerator. The car slowed. He pulled over to the side of the road and brought the vehicle to a halt.

Without a word he got out of the driver's seat and walked around the front of the car. He had removed his tux jacket. In the glare of the headlights the shoulder holster and gun made for an odd counterpoint to his elegant, formal white shirt and black trousers.

She jumped out of her side of the car and hurried around to the opposite side to get behind the wheel. Lorelei chortled a welcome to Rafe when he slid into the passenger seat. She graciously offered him a few chips.

"Thanks," he said.

He fastened the seat belt and munched a few chips while Ella got the rental back on the road.

"Sleep," Ella ordered.

"You've known about the fever right from the start, haven't you?" he asked.

"Yes," she said.

"I've got it under control."

"I know. I wouldn't have signed a contract with you if I thought you were about to go rogue in the immediate future."

He crunched another chip. "You're wondering if I know what caused the fever."

"I'm curious, of course. Psi-fevers are not very common. The experts don't know much about them."

"And what they do know is that they usually end either in a severely damaged talent or the development of an unstable new talent." Rafe sounded grimly resigned. "Either way the results are unpredictable and, therefore, dangerous."

"I take it you're quoting one of those so-called experts who hasn't had much experience with psi-fever?"

"Yeah."

"Hmm." She thought about that. "What's your take on what's going on with your aura?"

"What do you mean?"

"You're the one running the fever. What effect do you think it's having on you?"

"So far, the main problem is that it has burned out my talent for resonating with hot rocks and crystals. I'm no longer any good on exploration teams and I'm useless to the FBPI because I can't rez Alien tech."

There was cold acceptance in his voice. Shocked, she glanced at him. His face was a hard mask. The loss of a paranormal talent was uncommon but when it happened it was invariably traumatic. The stronger the talent had been, the more devastating the loss. Victims often felt as if they had lost a key aspect of their core identity.

It was not uncommon for burnouts who had previously been strong talents to disappear into the tunnels without tuned amber. That kind of hike was a death sentence.

"I don't understand," she said carefully. "You are still powerful. I can sense it in your aura."

"The para-shrinks think that the burnout is still going on even though my talent is all but gone. That's why I'm running a fever. The symptoms of the ongoing destruction are hallucinations and nightmares. If I sleep more than twenty minutes or so I . . . dream."

"Everyone dreams."

"Not like I do. The dreams are nightmares. Bad enough to bring me wide awake in a cold sweat. For a short time after I wake up I feel like I'm still locked in the dream. I know I'm dreaming, but I can't wake up."

"Lucid dreaming," she said.

He turned his head sharply to look at her. "One of the experts mentioned that term but said there wasn't much data on the phenomenon."

"Probably because there isn't much data on any kind of dreaming. After all the centuries of research back on Earth and here on Harmony, we still don't know a lot about dreams—except that they can provide a pathway between the normal and the paranormal."

"No offense, but you're a music talent."

"A music talent who does dream analysis, remember? The reason I'm good at dreamwork is because music energy travels on the currents of dreamlight."

"I didn't know that," Rafe said.

"Not many people, including the researchers, have figured it out. But for me, it's obvious. I see the connection every day in my work. Think about it—music takes a direct paranormal path to the senses. It can give you chills or make you cry or induce a kind of euphoria or a sense of transcendence—all without having to be interpreted by logic and reason. Just like dreams."

"Huh." Rafe switched his attention back to the empty highway. "Never thought about it that way."

"No reason you would unless you were a music talent who does dream analysis. Now, about your hallucinations."

Rafe rubbed his eyes. "What about them?"

"When I first came into my talent and started telling people that I could hear Alien music, the initial assumption was that I was hallucinating. I was sent to a lot of dreamstate experts, none of whom could figure out what was going on with me. In the end they concluded that I was faking it."

"Why would you fake the ability to hear Alien music?"

"Because I came from a family of brilliant music talents," Ella said patiently. "It was obvious I had no real talent, myself, so I must have made up a talent. It was after the counselors announced that I had no talent and that the Alien music I claimed to hear was a product of my imagination that my family finally realized that I had very likely gotten the Siren gene. It's in the family tree—my mother's side. Anyhow, everyone concluded that it would be best if I shut up about the Alien music thing."

"Tough secret for a person to keep."

"Yes, it is."

Rafe gave her a considering look. "Ever register with a matchmaking agency?"

She flexed her hands on the wheel. "No, of course not."

He nodded. "Because it would have meant having to flat-out lie about your true paranormal nature."

"It's not like any of the agencies would have found me a match. It's a lot more likely that they would have reported me to the FBPI."

"All the reputable agencies guarantee confidentiality."

"Sure. And if you believe a matrimonial agency would have kept my secret, I've got a lovely bridge I can sell you. Hardly used."

"Okay, can't argue with you on that," Rafe said.

"But I guess it doesn't matter now, anyway, does it? If Joe Harding suspects I'm a Siren, I can take it as a given that I'm on some watch list."

"I can't do anything about that, but like I told you before, if the FBPI or anyone else comes after you, Coppersmith Mining will have your back."

She knew from his expression that he was serious.

"I remember," she said. "Thanks. But I've got to ask why?"

"Coppersmith takes care of its own."

"I'm not a Coppersmith and I don't work for your family's company. I'm an outside consultant."

"Semantics. You're working for Coppersmith. As long as you don't double-cross us, we'll be there if you need us."

She wasn't sure where to go with that. No one had ever offered to have her back before. She was a Siren. She could take care of herself.

"Nap time," she said quietly.

"Twenty minutes, no longer. If I wake up yelling or saying stuff that makes you nervous, don't try to shake me awake. I'm not sure how I'll respond. Just pull over to the side of the road, get out of the car, and wait. I'll come out of it on my own. I've worked out a sort of psychic alarm that trips whenever the nightmares get too intense."

"You don't have to sound embarrassed about it. You're running a psi-fever. Bad dreams would seem to be normal for that kind of thing."

"Who knows what normal is for me now."

The bleak, steely edge in his words made her realize that he was preparing himself for a worst-case scenario.

"I might be able to help you get some real sleep," she said.

He shot her a look of disbelief. "I doubt it."

"Okay if I try?"

"Not if it means I get stuck in a damn nightmare."

"No nightmares, I promise. Hey, I'm the dream analyst here, remember? Just let me try."

Rafe hesitated and then exhaled slowly. "I could really use a couple hours of decent sleep. Go for it. But like I said, if I show signs of sliding into a nightmare, pull over to the side."

"Okay."

He closed his eyes. It seemed to Ella that he fell asleep between one breath and the next. He was truly sleep-deprived, she thought. He needed a lot more than a twenty-minute nap.

Lorelei finished the last of the chips, hopped over to the back of Ella's seat, and nattered encouragingly.

"I can't go any faster," Ella whispered. "I'm doing the

speed limit. The last thing we need is to get stopped by a cop."

She heightened her senses a little, watching for the feverish energy in Rafe's aura. It was there, doing a slow burn. She kicked up her talent just enough to keep track of the fever and settled down to drive.

TWENTY MINUTES LATER, ALMOST TO THE MINUTE, SHE felt energy shiver in the atmosphere. Rafe stirred in the seat. He muttered something unintelligible, sounding agitated.

Lorelei muttered in concern and opened all four eyes.

Ella realized Rafe's dreams were turning dark. He said he had set his internal time clock to awaken him when the nightmares kicked in and that was exactly what was happening. But Rafe needed sleep desperately. His body was fighting the wake-up call.

She glanced at the car's GPS. They still had another two and a half hours of driving.

She took one hand off the wheel and rested it lightly on Rafe's shoulder. She touched the back of his neck with her fingertips. His skin was warm; a little too warm. Fever heat.

He twisted a little in the seat and muttered. The words were slurred with sleep but this time she understood.

"Ghost City."

For the first time she noticed that his gray quartz ring was heating with energy. It looked for all the world like a hot gemstone enveloped in eerie fog.

Without warning Rafe's eyes snapped open. They blazed with a hellish light. His hand clamped around her wrist.

She was so startled she almost lost control of the car. It swerved out of the lane. She struggled with the wheel and the brakes. Lorelei growled.

"Rafe, it's me. Ella."

"Siren."

She knew then that he was caught in the web of a nightmare.

"I can make it go away, Rafe," she said. "Let me make it go away."

"Sing for me," he whispered.

She raised her talent and pulled powerful, soothing harmonies from far out on the paranormal spectrum. After a few seconds they began to resonate gently with the fierce heat in Rafe's aura. The tension in his energy field eased. The fever faded from his eyes.

"Siren," he said again.

But there was no fear or disbelief in his eyes. If anything, he looked satisfied.

He slipped back into sleep.

Lorelei ceased looking alarmed and went back to enjoying the road trip.

Ella drove on into the night singing a silent, psychic song infused with peace, tranquility, and calm.

Rafe slept.

Chapter 14

HE CAME AWAKE FROM A DREAMLESS SLEEP. FOR A moment he fought against surfacing. He wanted nothing more than to fall back into the magical realm.

An enthusiastic chortle made him open his eyes. He looked at Lorelei, who was perched on his knee, watching him intently. She clutched her wedding veil in one paw and nibbled on what looked like a chocolate chip cookie.

"Hey, there," he said. Reflexively, he patted her head. "Where did you get the cookie?"

"The same place I got a cookie," Ella said. "There's one for you, too. And some coffee."

Belatedly, he realized the car was parked and the driver's side door was open. Ella was leaning into the vehicle, holding out a mug of coffee. The lights of a big house and a private landing strip glowed behind her.

"Sorry I had to wake you," she said. "But we're at your

friend's ranch and there is a very expensive corporate jet waiting for us. The pilot said we need to hurry because there is some bad weather moving in over the Amber Sea. He wants to get us to Thursday Harbor before the storm hits."

"I'm awake," Rafe said.

Reluctantly he rezzed a little psi and shook off the sweet lethargy. He unfastened his seat belt and opened the door. Lorelei jumped off his knee and onto the seat, bouncing a little.

He got out, reached back into the car, and plucked Lorelei off the seat. She chortled and vaulted up onto his shoulder, the wedding veil trailing behind her.

"Your friend Ms. Cremona is packing some food for us and the pilots," Ella said, speaking across the roof of the car.

He drank in the sight of her standing there, silhouetted against the lights. She was wearing a gray sweatshirt over what was left of her tattered dress. The night breeze tossed her hair.

She was not running hot but he was aware of the strong energy of her aura. He would know it anywhere, he thought, even in his dreams, just as he would know her voice and her scent. Her power called to him; it sang to him. The sensation was unlike anything he had ever experienced—fiercely intimate; shatteringly sexual. He had never even kissed her, yet in that moment he knew that he wanted her more than he had ever wanted anyone or anything. The knowledge dazzled him. It also depressed him. She deserved a mate who was her equal in all ways, one who could match her strength. He was no longer that man.

But at the moment he was the only one around who could protect her. He had to get her to the safety of Rainshadow where Coppersmith Security could shield her from whoever was trying to grab her.

Strange to think of Rainshadow as a safe zone, he thought. But it offered a lot of the things the urban environment could not—a trustworthy security staff, a secure compound, and a perimeter that could be patrolled. In addition, he trusted the local chief of police. He and Slade Attridge went back a ways.

"Ella." He stopped, unsure where to go next. "Thanks. That's the first good sleep I've had in a long time."

"You need more but I understand the flight to Thursday Harbor is nearly four hours so you'll have time to catch up on your rest. Looks like the fever has gone down a little."

A flicker of unease made him go still. He did not like knowing that she could sense the weakness in him. "You can detect it that clearly?"

She cleared her throat. "I think I'm especially sensitive to your aura because we've had some physical contact while we were running hot. You know how it is with strong talents."

It dawned on him that she was struggling to make it all sound very clinical. Two strong talents touch each other while each is fully rezzed and, presto, they are suddenly able to sense each other's auras more clearly.

Except it didn't usually work like that, Rafe thought. Not unless something else was going on—something like sexual attraction, which often had a strong paranormal vibe.

But he knew this was not the time to point out a few of the basic bio-psi facts of life. Ella had been affected by the link between them. Knowing that was enough—for now.

He was suddenly feeling a little less depressed.

"Right," he said. "Just one of those things."

"Yep, just one of those things."

The door of the big house opened. A woman dressed in jeans and a pullover sweater emerged. The porch light gleamed briefly on the silver in her black hair. Gabriella Cremona was a strong crystal talent who, for years, had overseen one of Coppersmith's most innovative labs.

"Rafe." Gabriella came down the steps carrying two large insulated carriers. "Good to see you again. It's been too long."

One of the pilots hurried toward her. "I'll take those, ma'am."

"Thank you." Gabriella handed the carriers to him. "Sandwiches and cookies. Should be enough to last all of you for the trip. You said you had coffee on board."

"Yes, ma'am. Plenty of coffee but we didn't have time to stock up on the food. Appreciate the sandwiches and cookies, believe me."

He looked at Rafe. "Ready when you are, Mr. Coppersmith. We won't file a flight plan until we're in the air. We need to get going, though. We should be wheels-up in the next fifteen minutes if we want to beat the weather in the Amber Sea."

"We'll be on board in a minute, Larry." Rafe walked around the car and gave Gabriella a hug. "Good to see you, too. You'll be coming to the annual company picnic this summer on Copper Beach Island?"

"Wouldn't miss it for the world," Gabriella said. She studied the wedding veil that Lorelei clutched. The netting drifted on the night breeze, floating around Rafe's head and shoulders. "Don't get me wrong—you'll make a stunning bride, Rafe—but do you mind if I ask what is going on here?"

"I hate to say this, but the truth is, I've got no idea. Coppersmith is opening up a new territory in the Underworld. We need some specialized talent."

"That would be me," Ella said.

"I see," Gabriella said.

"Someone evidently wants to prevent Ella from taking the job with Coppersmith," Rafe concluded. "They tried to grab her tonight. They were using Alien tech."

Gabriella raised her brows. "This new territory must be quite promising."

"They're calling it Wonderland," Rafe said. "That's a pretty damn good description. Maybe you'd like to come out to Rainshadow and see for yourself one of these days."

"I'd like that," Gabriella said. "I'd like that a lot."

Rafe glanced at his watch. "We've got to get in the air. Thanks for everything, Gabriella."

"Anytime. Tell your folks I said hello and that I'll see them this summer."

"Will do."

Gabriella smiled at Ella. "A pleasure to meet you. Good luck in Wonderland."

"Thanks," Ella said. "It was a pleasure to meet you, too. And thanks for the sweatshirt."

"No problem. Sorry I didn't have anything else that would fit you." Gabriella shot Rafe an unreadable glance and then smiled at Ella. "You can return the sweatshirt when I see you at the Coppersmith summer picnic."

"Oh, no," Ella said. "That sounds like a company event. I'm strictly a consulting talent."

Her absolute denial of even a remote possibility of attending the picnic was damned annoying. Rafe had to clamp down on a flash of temper.

"You never know," he said. "Summer is a ways off. Let's go. The pilots are waiting."

"Okay," Ella said. "Good-bye, Ms. Cremona."

"Good-bye, Ella." Gabriella reached up to pat Lorelei on Rafe's shoulder. "And good-bye to you, my little friend. Here's another cookie to hold you until they open the picnic coolers on the plane."

She handed Lorelei a chocolate chip cookie. Lorelei went into ecstatic mode.

Gabriella chuckled. "Doesn't take much to thrill a dust bunny, does it?"

"No," Ella said. "I guess we could all learn something from dust bunnies."

Gabriella laughed. "Definitely."

Ella turned, stuffed her hands into the pockets of the

sweatshirt, and started walking toward the jet. Rafe realized she was still wearing her stilettos.

Some bodyguard he had turned out to be. He had very
nearly allowed her to get kidnapped tonight. Then he had
run her through the catacombs, after which she had
driven them both to an isolated airstrip where they were
about to board a jet that would take them on a long flight
to a very dangerous island. She had to be exhausted, he
thought. But she had not complained or pointed out his
several glaring inadequacies.

Oblivious of his dark thoughts, she contemplated the
sleek jet sitting on the paved strip.

"You know, under other circumstances, this could be
construed as a very romantic scene," she said.

He stared at her. "What the hell are you talking about?"

"Think about it—a mysterious man wearing a gun and
a tux whisks the lady off to an exotic island in a private jet."

"You call this romantic? In case you didn't notice, you
nearly got kidnapped tonight. And Rainshadow isn't
exotic. It's an island where things get very weird and your
primary objective will be to avoid becoming a snack for
some Alien-engineered dinosaur."

"Got it."

"Whatever is going on here, one thing is for sure—
this is not a romantic scenario."

"Absolutely not. I don't know what came over me. Just
a poor attempt to lighten the situation. Sorry."

He came to a halt, snagged her arm, and forced her to
stop, too. He turned her so that she faced him.

"And stop trying to humor me," he said between his teeth.

"Why?" She smiled. "Because you have no sense of humor so I shouldn't waste my time?"

"Damn it, there are other consultants out there."

"But none of them are as good as me, not for this job. You need me, Coppersmith, so what do you say we try to get along?"

Maybe it was the psi-fever or maybe it was the lack of sleep. Whatever the case, he consigned common sense to hell and pulled her into his arms.

"You're right," he said. "I need you."

He knew her aura was spiking. He could feel it. His own was probably damn near radioactive.

"This is not a good idea," she said.

"No shit."

"You see, one of the downsides of dream analysis is that clients sometimes read things into the counselor-client relationship that are inaccurate or misleading. Dreams are so intimate. That can make clients think the relationship with the counselor is intimate, too."

"Do me a favor and stop trying to analyze me."

Evidently sensing a new adventure in transportation, or maybe bored with human drama, Lorelei chortled, jumped down from Rafe's shoulder, and bounced up the jet steps. She disappeared into the cabin, the veil trailing behind her.

Rafe tightened his grip on Ella. She did not pull away. He knew in that moment that she had decided to roll the dice with him. He didn't like knowing that she considered him a bad risk but, what the hell, she was probably right. There was no knowing where the fever would take him. All he cared about was that for now it was under control and she was in his arms.

He covered her mouth with his own.

The kiss exploded around them, setting their auras on fire. Her hands on his shoulders were suddenly clenched tight, as if she were hanging on for dear life. She made a low, hungry little sound that jacked up all of his senses.

He was burning now, not with psi-fever but with old-fashioned, primal sexual heat. Whatever was happening between them was dangerous. That fact only made it all the more compelling; all the more thrilling.

But this was not the right time and it sure as hell wasn't the right place.

"Sorry to interrupt, Mr. Coppersmith, but we really need to get this plane into the air," Larry said from the top of the steps.

Reality slammed back with the force of a hurricane.

Reluctantly, he gripped Ella's upper arms and set her a few inches away from him. She stared at him with wide, dazed eyes.

Good enough for now, he decided. He might not be the man of her dreams, but judging by the stunned look on her face, she wouldn't forget him anytime soon.

"Let's go," he said.

He clamped a hand around her wrist. They ran for the plane.

Chapter 15

IT WAS HER OWN FAULT, ELLA THOUGHT. SHE SHOULD NOT have made that dumb crack about the romantic scene at the remote airstrip.

Deep down she had known that injecting the word *romantic* into the conversation was dangerous. But she was only human, she told herself, and she had been through a lot that evening. It wasn't every night that a mysterious, sexy man saved her from a kidnapping attempt and then swept her off in a private jet to a strange island where a thrilling adventure in the Underworld awaited.

She had the expensively outfitted cabin to herself. The pilots were up front doing whatever pilots did when a plane was in the air. After the exhilarating rush of the takeoff, followed by several more cookies, Lorelei had amused herself for a time exploring the interior of the aircraft. Exhausted from all the fun, she was now dozing on one of the leather seats. She was on her back, all six paws in the air, the wedding veil draped over the edge of the seat.

Rafe was also sound asleep but he was stretched out on a narrow bed in the back. He had not needed any dream songs this time. He had gone out like a light the instant his head hit the pillow. Ella knew that he was still making up for an extensive sleep deficit.

The dream song she had sung for him in the car was still holding. She did not know if the fix would prove permanent. It all depended on the fever. If it subsided, which it seemed to be doing at the moment, Rafe's dream issues would likely go away. But if the heat spiked again in his aura, the nightmares would probably return.

And the mystery of the fever itself remained. She was very curious to know exactly what had caused it. Armed with that information, she would have a clearer notion of how to deal with it. But Rafe seemed intent on keeping his secrets.

She thought about the two words he had spoken when he had been trapped in the lucid dreamstate. *Ghost City.* A memory of a fairy tale stirred. The story had involved an ancient Alien city constructed of ice and fog. Great riches and vast powers were said to be concealed within the walls of the dead city, but it was a place of terrible danger and astonishing mystery.

According to the fairy tale, only those endowed with strong talents and a brave spirit dared to undertake the quest to find the city. Few had discovered its location; fewer still survived to tell the tale. Those who did return were not the same. Whatever they had seen or experienced inside the walls of the legendary ruins had deprived them of their talent and driven them mad.

But *The City of Ice and Fog* was a fairy tale and Rafe had been trapped in a dream when he had spoken of the Ghost City. It had all been part of his nightmare.

They were flying west into the night. Ella settled deeper into her seat and thought about the heated kiss on the airstrip. She was pretty sure Rafe would regret it when he awakened. She had learned long ago that there was a pattern in her relationships and it wasn't a good one.

Rafe would get cold feet like all the others and he would regret the kiss. But in the meantime, she was setting out on an adventure and she could do a little dreaming of her own.

Chapter 16

ELLA AWOKE TO THE STEADY DRUMBEAT OF RAIN. FOR A minute or two she lay still, afraid to move. But eventually she decided that she was once again feeling normal. A shower and some sleep had done wonders for the seasickness she had endured on the boat from Thursday Harbor.

She sat up and looked at the bedside clock. The amber-colored numerals on the face told her it was two fifteen in the morning.

Lorelei had been buzzed nonstop with excitement, both on the boat ride and upon arrival on the island. She had disappeared soon after Ella had settled into a room in the old lodge that was serving as the Rainshadow headquarters for Coppersmith Mining.

Ella pushed the covers aside, got to her feet, and found the thick, white terry-cloth robe that one of the female employees had produced from a stockpile of spa supplies. The matching slippers were on the floor beside the bed.

The previous evening was something of a blur but she remembered Rafe handing her over to a competent woman named Bethany who had identified herself as the person in charge of housing the Coppersmith personnel.

Bethany had shown her to a room and given her a key. When Ella had expressed surprise at the nicely appointed spalike accommodations Bethany had laughed and explained that the previous proprietor of the old lodge had operated a high-end corporate retreat and seminar business on the grounds. When Coppersmith offered to purchase the property, lock, stock, and barrel, and had offered a premium for vacating the premises in a speedy fashion, the owners had jumped at the offer. They had left everything behind, including the spa robes, towels, and amenities.

Evidently the corporate retreat and seminar business had fallen off dramatically in recent months. Rainshadow wasn't for everyone, Bethany had explained.

The room was decorated in a warm, rustic style with leather furnishings, a king-sized bed, and a small, cozy sitting area. A set of French doors opened onto the covered second-floor balcony that wrapped around the building.

She knew she had not made a good first impression. A consultant who arrived at the jobsite seasick and jet-lagged did not project the appropriate, can-do image. She needed to get her act together by morning.

She opened one of the French doors and stepped out onto the wide balcony. Rain dripped steadily from the eave but the night was humid and balmy, laced with an invigorating warmth that carried a whisper of psi. Rafe had explained that the lodge was not far from the mysterious, fenced-off portion of the island that was the Rainshadow Preserve.

She moved to the railing. Here and there the grounds were lit with industrial fixtures, but the illumination did not extend far into the heavy rain. From where she stood she could barely make out an old boathouse and a dock that stretched a short distance into the black waters of the lake.

If it hadn't been for the drumming rain the silence would have been downright eerie. She was accustomed to the background noise of an urban environment. Here on the island there were no sirens and no street sounds. She missed the steady nighttime glow of the green quartz walls that surrounded the ruins and illuminated the Old Quarter. What little she could see of Rainshadow looked very dark and forbidding.

She was not in Crystal City anymore, she thought.

A frisson of energy flickered through her senses.

"The place grows on you," Rafe said quietly.

She caught her breath and turned quickly. He was standing a few feet away, dressed in jeans, a dark T-shirt, and low leather boots. He had on his shoulder holster. The handle of the gun was matte black in the shadows. His hair was sleep-rumpled and his eyes burned with a little heat.

"Sorry," he said. "Didn't mean to startle you."

"It's all right. Why are you up at this hour? Did the dreams come back?"

"No." He moved closer to her. Leaning forward, he rested both forearms on the railing and looked out at the rainy night. "I got a few more good hours in, thanks to you. I feel like I've caught up on my sleep for the first time since the fever hit. What exactly did you do to me?"

"There were signs of stress in your energy field."

"No kidding."

"Probably a combination of the fever and the lack of sleep. Auras respond to music, so I sang some harmonies to calm the agitated wavelengths. The fever went down after that." She kicked up her senses and smiled when she saw the cooler energy in his dreamlight. "And it's still low. You needed sleep."

"Will the therapy last?"

"I honestly can't say. I think it depends on whatever is going on with the fever. Once that situation resolves you'll have a better idea of what you're dealing with."

"I haven't told anyone here on the island about my little fever issues."

"Don't worry, I'm not going to gossip about them." She did not bother to hide the brittle edge on her words. "Your aura is your private business." She paused a beat for emphasis. "Just as the exact nature of my talent is my business."

He winced. "Understood. We have a deal, right? We keep each other's secrets."

"Yes, we have a bargain. For the record, discretion and the ability to maintain confidentiality are the cornerstones of my business."

His jaw tightened. He straightened and turned toward her. "Damn it, I didn't mean to imply that I don't trust you."

"Why should you trust me? We've only known each other for about a day." She paused. "Well, there was that brief meeting three months ago."

"Yes, there was that meeting three months ago." His voice roughened. "But we've been through some stuff together, the kind of stuff that builds a bond between two people."

She folded her arms. "I know this is going to sound petty, but you stood me up three months ago. You said you'd call for a coffee date. That was the last I heard from you until you showed up in my office to offer me a job yesterday."

"Shit happened after I saw you three months ago. The fever happened."

"That's why you didn't call?" As soon as the words were out of her mouth she could have screamed in frustration. She had never intended to let him know that she had waited for his call. But it was too late. She could not stop herself. "Sorry, that excuse won't fly. You've still got a fever, remember? But you obviously had no problem getting in touch when you concluded that my talent might be useful to you."

"It's a complicated story."

She gave him a thin smile. "I'm sure it is. Probably much too long and way too complicated to tell me tonight, so I'm going back to bed."

She turned to head toward her room. His hand clamped around her shoulder. She froze. His touch sent her senses into overdrive. She knew that he was jacked. The intoxicating heat of his aura enveloped her.

"Wait," he said quietly. He turned her slowly around to face him. "Please."

She kept her arms tightly folded, resisting the urge to put them around his neck. "What do you want?"

"A chance to explain." He took his hand off her shoulder

and surveyed the balcony with a quick, assessing glance. "But not out here. I don't want to be interrupted."

She hesitated. "All right. We can go into my room."

She turned around and led the way back through the open French doors. Taking a client back to one's hotel room was never a good move, but in that moment she simply did not care. She wanted answers.

He followed her into the room; turned and shut the glass-paned doors. The dull roar of the rain faded into the background. She drew the drapes closed, plunging the small, intimate space into an even more intimate darkness. It took her an awkward moment to find the switch of the bedside lamp. When she did get the light on she was mildly horrified by the sight of the tumbled bedding. Hastily she grabbed the coverlet and dragged it up over the pillows.

When she turned she saw that Rafe looked grim but determined. She motioned toward a chair.

"Sit," she ordered.

He sank into the chair and glanced at the in-room coffeemaker on the dresser. "Would this be the wrong time to suggest that we do that coffee date?"

She flushed and dropped down into the small chair across from him.

"Yes," she said.

"Right." He rested both arms on the curved sides of the chair and straightened his legs out in front of him. "About the fever."

"I'm listening."

"After I turned over Vickary and the mob guys to the Bureau I got called back to Coppersmith headquarters on an emergency security matter. A company research team had disappeared into the Rainforest. I'm the unofficial Coppersmith troubleshooter, so I was put in charge of the search-and-rescue operation."

Rafe stopped. She got the feeling he was pulling his thoughts together. She sat quietly and waited.

"The team had been sideswiped by an energy river that had destroyed all of their locator equipment. That kind of disaster is often a death sentence for everyone on a project, but Coppersmith has some protocols in place. Rule number one is, don't move from your last known location. The team obeyed the rule."

"So you found them?"

"Yes. They had taken shelter in some ruins. We got everyone organized and ready to trek back out of the jungle, but there was one person missing. The others said he had cracked under the pressure of being stranded and had disappeared deeper into the ruins. There was a lot of strange energy in the area. My talent for resonating with hot rock meant that I was the one most qualified to conduct a search."

"Did you find him?"

"I did." Rafe raked his fingers through his hair, pushing it back behind his ears. "He tried to kill me."

"But you were attempting to rescue him."

"He was psi-burned. He wasn't thinking clearly. At any rate he tried to use a mag-rez pistol on me."

"While you were inside the ruins? In the Rainforest? With all those paranormal forces in the atmosphere? Good heavens, you're lucky to be alive. What happened?"

"When I realized what he was going to do I took shelter

in a chamber in the ruins." Rafe paused. "It was . . . an amazing room. Made entirely of gray quartz."

She looked at his ring. "The kind in your ring?"

"Yes."

"Go on."

"When the crazed tech fired the mag-rez there was an explosion that triggered a major chain reaction throughout the ruins. The place was literally engulfed in a paranormal firestorm. The gray quartz chamber was as hot as everything else. I thought I was a dead man. But there was a pool inside the gray room. I could sense the paranormal energy in the water. I was desperate. I wondered if the water might offer some protection from the storm."

She watched the shadows in his eyes. "You went into the pool?"

"I had some crazy plan to stay under the surface as long as I could hold my breath and come up for air only when I absolutely had to. I figured I could tolerate the energy of the storm in short bursts, at least for a while. But when I went into the water I realized it wasn't water. It was some kind of liquid crystal. I figured I really was dead then. But I thought I saw a door."

"Another vision?"

"In my delirium I opened the door and walked through it into a crazy dreamscape."

"What was on the other side of the door?"

Rafe looked at his ring. Energy shifted deep inside the quartz.

"A city of ice and fog," he said quietly.

She caught her breath. "The Ghost City in the old legend?"

"I think so, yes." He met her eyes. "It was a dream. I saw things—astonishing things—but they were all part of the hallucination. In my dream I walked through a vast walled city. I was all alone. There were no other living things. The structures looked like those in the aboveground ruins, but instead of being made of green quartz, everything in the city seemed to be built of weird crystal that was the color of fog or ice."

"Just like in the fairy tale." She thought about that for a moment. "Was it cold?"

Rafe frowned, as though he had never considered the question. "No, but you don't think about temperature and weather in a hallucination, do you?"

"No, I guess not. Go on."

"There was power—incredible power—everywhere. I didn't have a clue how it could be used but I sensed that it was potentially very dangerous."

"How did you get out of the Ghost City?"

Rafe's mouth twisted in a humorless smile. "The way you usually get out of a dream. I woke up."

"Where were you when you awakened?"

"In the gray chamber. In my dream I came up out of the liquid pool, realized that the storm had subsided, and I hauled myself up onto the floor of the chamber. The place was still hot." Rafe looked down at his ring. "I remember picking up this stone. And then I just started walking. The ruins were engulfed in a massive psi-firestorm that must have been triggered by the explosion. I got through it and just kept going. Luckily, my locator started working as soon as I got beyond the range of the storm. Somewhere along the way my brother and a Coppersmith team found me."

She nearly fell off her chair. "Wait. Hold on here. *You walked through a psi-firestorm*? How? Nothing can get through a firestorm."

Rafe contemplated his ring again. "I think this rock somehow helped me navigate the currents of the storm."

"Hmm." She considered that briefly. "What about the gray chamber and the pool of liquid crystals?"

Rafe met her eyes. "Don't you understand? I hallucinated the pool and the gateway to the Ghost City. Like the T-shirt says, I went to the city of ice and fog and all I've got to show for it is this lousy ring."

They both looked at the gray quartz in his ring. It was no longer sparking with energy.

"It seems to respond to your energy field," Ella ventured.

"Oh, yeah. It gets real hot when I'm having visions. For all the good that does."

"Yet you kept it."

He exhaled slowly. "I kept it because it tells me when I'm seeing things. It's my own personal warning light."

"Do you really believe that you dreamed the city of ice and fog?"

Rafe exhaled and rubbed the back of his neck. "That's the only explanation that makes sense."

"What happened to the ruins?"

"They're probably still there but no one can get to them because of the firestorm."

Ella eyed the ring. "No one except you?"

Rafe followed her gaze. "I might be able to get back

through it. Maybe even guide a team to the ruins. But what's the point? There's no liquid crystal pool and no portal to the Ghost City. It was all a dream."

"What happened to you after your brother found you in the Rainforest?"

"It was obvious I had been burned and that I was running a fever. No one knew what the result would be so the para-psych docs suggested that I be locked up in a nice padded room where I couldn't do any damage to myself or others. My family did not go along with that treatment advice."

"What did your family do instead?"

Rafe's mouth crooked in another wry smile. "They locked me up in the family compound on Copper Beach Island, instead. And that's where I've been for the past three months."

There was a long silence.

Ella finally cleared her throat. "You know, you could have sent a message."

"Saying what? Sorry, bad burn. Probably turning into a monster or a rogue talent so I won't be asking you out for coffee?"

Anger snapped through her. She shot to her feet. "Something like that, yes. I'm afraid your excuse doesn't fly, not with me. I'm one of the monsters, too, remember?"

He stared at her, clearly shocked by her fury.

"You're not a monster," he said.

"Neither are you."

"Look, I'm not exactly good dating material, okay? The para-genetics in my family is complicated enough. Now I've added a bad burn and a fever to the mix. So, yeah, I decided it might be a good idea to make sure I wasn't going rogue or turning into some kind of psychic vampire before I asked you out on a date."

"Excuses, excuses."

The gray quartz stone in Rafe's ring sparked with fire. In the next instant he came up out of the chair. Very deliberately, his eyes never leaving hers, he unfastened the shoulder holster and set it and the gun down on the table.

He walked toward her, his eyes heating. Her pulse was racing madly but she refused to retreat.

He clamped both hands around her shoulders.

"Do you know what it's been like being me these past three months?" he asked in a dangerously soft voice.

"How could I? You never bothered to get in touch."

"I was the crazy relative the family had to hide in the attic. Everyone around me watched me as if expecting me to explode at any minute without any warning. Every time I looked into my mother's eyes I could see her pain and fear. I knew she wasn't afraid of me. She was terrified *for* me. Every time I awoke from one of the fever dreams I'd find her bending over me, trying to calm me. Meanwhile, my brothers and my father kept pretending that there was nothing out of the ordinary going on—that I was healing."

"When did you finally conclude that maybe—just maybe—you weren't going to turn into a monster?"

"It was my father who made the decision. He realized I was going stir-crazy and his intuition told him that I wasn't dangerous. He decided that what I needed was a job. That's why I'm in charge of clearing out Wonderland. And that's exactly what I'm going to do because it's my chance to prove I'm not going rogue."

"So you decided to call me when it occurred to you that you needed me to get your precious job done here on Rainshadow."

"I was going to call, regardless," he said between his teeth.

"You expect me to believe that?"

"Yes, damn it." He tightened his hands around her shoulders. "After what we've been through together, I expect you to trust me."

"I do trust you." She paused delicately. "In some ways."

"What the hell is that supposed to mean?"

"Well, I certainly trust you to have my back in a kidnapping attempt. I trust you to pay your bill when this consulting job is done. And I trust you not to tell the world that I'm a Siren."

"I'm just damned thrilled with all that trust."

"What more do you want?"

"You." He drew her closer. "I want you, Ella Morgan, but I can't offer you any long-term guarantees."

She rezzed up a steely smile. "I'm just like you when it comes to long-term guarantees, remember? I don't come with an extended warranty, either. Women like me scare the hell out of normal men. And the not-so-normal kind scare the hell out of me."

"You don't scare me. Do I scare you?"

She looked at him, aware of the heat sizzling between them. At this rate they might set the room on fire, she thought.

"Are you absolutely positive that I don't scare you?" she whispered.

"I've never been more certain of anything in my life."

She slid her arms up around his neck. "So here we are, a couple of people who should be scared to death of each other. If we had any sense, we'd both be running in opposite directions."

"Don't know about you, but I'm not going anywhere tonight—not unless you push me out the door."

"No," she said. "Not tonight."

He pulled her hard against his chest and captured her mouth with his own. They were both running hot and the intoxicating heat of Rafe's aura clashed with her own energy field in sensual combat.

She was vaguely aware of Rafe untying the sash of her robe. The plush garment fell to the floor around her feet. The prim, plain cotton nightgown that she had purchased in Thursday Harbor followed.

And then she was stripped bare and Rafe's strong hands were gliding intimately over her body. His touch was at once fierce and achingly tender. When she shuddered with anticipation he groaned and moved his mouth to her throat.

"You are so soft," he said, his voice rough with hunger. "I knew it would be like this. You'll never know how many times I reached for you in my dreams these past three months. But you were always too far away."

"You dreamed of me?"

"Every night."

He cupped one breast in his hand, bent his head and kissed the nipple. She took a shaky breath.

"*Rafe.*"

"Sing for me, Siren."

"You don't know what you're asking."

"I told you, I'm not afraid of you."

"Oh, Rafe." She slipped her hands under the bottom edge of his T-shirt and flattened her palms against his sleekly muscled back. "This is enough. More than enough."

"We haven't even started."

He picked her up in his arms and dropped her lightly onto the rumpled bed. With a few quick, efficient moves he got rid of the low boots and stripped off his jeans, briefs, and the T-shirt. The clothes landed in a careless heap on the floor.

He was hard and erect. She caught her breath at the size and power of the man. Excitement tempered with a whisper of feminine trepidation shivered through her.

Before she could second-guess herself about the wisdom of what she was doing, Rafe descended.

It was as if he had brought the forces of the storm outside into the room. He braced himself above her, rezzed his talent, and made love to her with a passion unlike anything she had ever known—unlike anything she could have imagined.

There was lightning in his kisses and electricity in his hands. Her senses were tossed about as though caught in gale-force currents. When he found the melting core between her thighs with his mouth, she bit back a scream.

"Sing for me," he said.

The tension rising within her was overwhelming; irresistible. She felt her control start to slip and a strange panic consumed her. She never allowed herself to lose control. It was too dangerous.

As if he knew that he was winning the battle, Rafe was relentless.

"Sing," he said in a soft, husky voice that thrilled her. "It's all right. You're safe. I won't let you fall."

He slid his fingers into her, opening her, stretching her.

The storm broke over her, through her; flashing across her aura. But Rafe held her fast, savoring the elemental feminine energy he had unleashed.

And she sang.

It was a song unlike any she had ever sung before, a song that drew power from the far ends of the spectrum, a song of light and dark. A song of life.

Somewhere in the midst of the torrent of paranormal harmonies she felt Rafe glide up her body and thrust slowly, heavily into her wet, tight heat. She came again.

"Siren," Rafe said. "My sweet Siren."

He stroked deep, again and again. His climax slammed through both of them. The shock waves resonated across both their auras. She knew then that, for a few minutes at least, he had released the mag-rez grip he kept on his self-control. He was flying into the storm.

She wrapped her legs around him, holding him with all of her strength, and sang her silent, soaring song. The music would have overwhelmed another man's aura and sent him crashing into oblivion. But Rafe seemed to draw power from the wild harmonies, just as she drew power from the stormy heat in his aura.

Reality would return soon enough. For tonight she would abandon herself to a fantasy. Tonight she would glory in the pleasures of true intimacy with a lover; one who was not afraid of her.

Chapter 17

THE DAMN RAIN MADE IT IMPOSSIBLE TO SEE ANYTHING
but vague shadows.

Ken Maitland huddled in the limited shelter provided
by the roof of the boathouse and listened to the downpour.
It drummed on the opaque surface of the lake, muffling
other sounds. He hated the way it rained on Rainshadow.

He had been on the island for nearly a week waiting
for his chance. In that length of time he had come to hate
everything about the place—the rain, the weird fog, the
creepy energy that seemed to be everywhere. He could
not wait to get the hell off the rock, but he was not about
to leave until he had made the big score.

He had followed an old girlfriend into the Do Not Disturb movement. The scam hadn't deceived him, not for a
minute. He had been on the streets long enough to recognize a fellow con artist when he met one. He had recognized

Houston Radburn, the guru of DND, as a fraud right from the start. It took one to know one, Ken thought. But he had seen the opportunities immediately.

His computer skills had helped him advance rapidly within the organization. Thanks to him the donations had tripled within a few months. Ken had discreetly siphoned off some of the take into a private bank account. He deserved a commission.

Radburn had been delighted with the cash flow situation for a while, but lately he had started to become suspicious of his sharp new fund-raiser. It was time to bail, Ken thought. But not before he pulled off one last score.

He could hear the black water lapping gently beneath the boards of the dock. In the weak glare of the boathouse's light fixture he caught glimpses of the strange snakeweed plant that choked the lake. The vines coiled and writhed just below the surface.

He'd heard one of the locals say that falling into the lake was a death sentence. The weed twisted around the body and dragged it down into the depths. The lake never gave up its dead, according to the island residents.

That unnerving fact didn't seem to bother the people who called Rainshadow home, Maitland reflected. They took the scary lake in stride, the same way they did all the other bizarre things on the island. The place had once been an Alien biolab. You'd think that would be more than enough reason to make any normal person pack up and get on the ferry. But as far as he could tell, the residents accepted the hair-raising results of the ancient experiments as just part and parcel of the landscape.

But, then, having been on Rainshadow for a while, he had concluded that the locals were as weird as the island itself. He was sure that the chief of police was some kind of talent and so was his wife, the owner of the antiques shop. Maybe the energy on the island actually changed people. Maybe they were all psi-burned or something.

Maybe the Do Not Disturb outfit had a point. Maybe people shouldn't be messing around with the Aliens' secrets.

"Ken?" Angela came around the side of the boathouse. The hood of a dark blue rain slicker was pulled up over her head. "I got your message. Where are you?"

"Over here." Relief crashed through him. He suddenly realized how tight his breathing had become. The island was wrecking his nerves. The sooner he got back to civilization, the better. "I thought maybe you weren't coming."

Angela rushed toward him. He caught her close and kissed her.

After a moment she stepped back. "It's so good to see you, but what are you doing on Rainshadow? Everything is going according to plan. I've been doing what Mr. Radburn told me to do—small stuff. I started a fire a couple of weeks ago that destroyed some computer equipment and I made sure the new amber locators disappeared into the lake. I've got another idea, too—"

"I don't care about what you're doing. Angela, I'm getting out of DND."

"What?"

"I'm leaving. The movement is a scam."

"No, that's not true."

"It has been from the start. Radburn is a con. He's fooled you and the others but I know him for what he is."

"What are you saying?"

"Look, I know what I'm talking about," he said. "Who do you think has been helping him rake in the cash for the past year?"

"You?" she whispered.

"Yeah. But now Radburn is getting close to figuring out that I've been taking a cut. Time to get out. I've got one last project, though. Something really big."

"I can't believe you're doing this." Angela started to cry. "What about the cause? Doesn't it mean anything to you?"

"Not a damn thing. Get real, Angela. It's hopeless. The ruins are going to get dug up and excavated and nothing DND or anyone else does can stop that. What's more, I don't care. I was only in this for the money. And you. I'd have bailed months ago if it hadn't been for you."

Angela sniffed. "Stop talking like that."

"I'm here on Rainshadow because I've got a plan to get one last big donation—from Rafe Coppersmith, no less. Figured you'd like that part. Think about it—Coppersmith is going to finance our future. Serves them right for being in the ruin business, huh?"

"Are you crazy?"

"No, listen, this will work but I need your help. I want you to get a message to Coppersmith. Slip it under his door or something. I can't risk communicating with him online. I think someone is eavesdropping on me."

"Who?"

"Probably Coppersmith Security. I've got to be very careful."

"You're going to sell information about DND to Rafe Coppersmith, aren't you?"

"It's bigger than DND. I've got some very specific intel that he'll pay a fortune for, believe me. So, are you coming with me or not?"

She shook her head very slowly. "You're not the man I thought you were, Ken. You have the nerve to call Mr. Radburn a con but you're the real scam artist. No, you're worse than that. You're a traitor."

Chapter 18

THE URGENT SCRATCHING SOUNDS ON THE GLASS PANES of the French doors pulled Rafe out of a deeply luxurious state of near total relaxation. He lay still a moment, reluctant to move. He had one arm wrapped around Ella, cradling her spoon-fashion. Her bottom was snugged up against his new erection.

"It's Lorelei," Ella mumbled into the pillow. "She's back."

There was more scratching on glass followed by muffled chortling.

Rafe groaned. "I'll let her in." He sat up and glanced at his watch. "Three fifteen. Damn. I'd better get back to my room before people start waking up."

He swung his legs over the side of the bed and stood. He padded across the carpet, pulled the drapes aside, and looked down. In the low light from the balcony lamp he saw

Lorelei. She blinked and made pitiful squeaking sounds. Her bedraggled wedding veil trailed out behind her.

"She's drenched," Rafe said. "Doing her best to look pathetic."

Ella pushed aside the covers. "I'll get a towel."

She grabbed a robe and disappeared into the bathroom.

Rafe opened the door. Lorelei bustled into the room and paused just long enough to give herself a brisk shake. Water sprayed across Rafe's bare feet. Fully fluffed, Lorelei bounded up onto the bed with the limp veil.

Ella reappeared with a large spa-sized towel. "Where did you go tonight? Meet some new friends?"

She bundled Lorelei into the towel and rubbed briskly. Lorelei chortled with delight.

"Everything is a game to you, isn't it?" Ella took the veil. "I'm not sure this will ever recover but I'll hang it up in the bathroom to dry."

Rafe glanced toward the lake as he started to close the door. From where he stood he could just barely make out the weak halo of hazy light that illuminated the area around the boathouse. The rest of the scene was masked with rain and darkness.

"It's still pouring out there," he said.

"I can hear it." Ella unwrapped Lorelei and disappeared back into the bathroom with the wet towel. "I've never seen rain like this."

"Everything, including the weather, is a little different here on Rainshadow."

He started to close the balcony door but stopped when

he caught the faint shift of spectral light at the edge of his vision. The stone in his ring sparked with a little gray energy.

The fever was spiking again.

Not now, damn it.

Rage and despair splashed through him. Not another hallucination. Not now after the best night of his life. Not now when he was just beginning to hope that he might be healing. *Not now.*

He fought back with all of his will and the vision weakened but it did not disappear. In the murky dreamscape a door opened. A ghostly figure, the face invisible, started to enter a gray chamber where another person waited.

It was all he could do not to shout a warning. *Don't go into the room.*

The damn visions were getting more real by the day. How much longer did he have before he could not control them at all? How much longer until even his family had to admit that he needed to be warehoused in a parapsych hospital? How much time did he have with Ella until the visions destroyed any hope of even a short-term relationship?

In the hallucination the mysterious figure walked through the door.

"Rafe?" Ella spoke from the far side of the bed. "Are you okay?"

"Yeah, sure. Fine."

But he could not take his eyes off the boathouse and the vision. They merged into one dream fragment. There was something there at the edge of the dreamscape. If he had just a bit more light . . .

A gunshot cracked in the night, echoing for what seemed like forever. The second shot followed a heartbeat later.

"What in the world?" Ella whispered. "That wasn't thunder."

Rafe blinked away the remnants of the hallucination. Time to get real.

"Sounded like a mag-rez," he said. "I think it came from somewhere near the boathouse. Hard to tell with gunshots."

He concentrated on the boathouse. A shadowy form appeared briefly in the small aura of light that illuminated the boathouse and dock. Running fast, the figure disappeared into the dark rain almost immediately.

Rafe started to turn away to grab his clothes. But another ghostly shadow appeared in the boathouse light. It, too, vanished into the night.

He closed and locked the door. "Stay here." He pulled on his jeans and T-shirt and grabbed his holster. "I'm going to take a look." He shoved his feet into his boots and headed for the door.

There were muffled shouts from outside on the grounds.

"That will be the security team," Rafe said. "Good. They're on it."

"Maybe someone took a couple of shots at one of the dinosaurs," Ella said. "They come out at night, right?"

"Yes, but they can't escape the Preserve."

"That might not be true any longer." Ella crossed the

room, coming toward him. She had Lorelei clutched in the
crook of her arm. "Who knows what's going on down below
in Wonderland, or inside the Preserve for that matter?"

Her eyes were heated with anxiety. With a flash of pleased
surprise he realized that she was worried about him.

"It's okay," he said. "Just give me your word that you'll
stay here in the lodge until I figure out what's happening."

Her lips tightened into a stubborn line but she nodded
once. "All right. This is your operation. I'm just the consultant. But promise me you'll be very, very careful."

He brushed his mouth across hers. "Promise."

He unlocked the door and moved out onto the interior
balcony that wrapped around the atrium lobby of the rustic lodge. He nearly collided with a balding, middle-aged
man dressed in a bathrobe—John Hayashi.

"Sorry, Dr. Hayashi," Rafe said. He kept moving,
heading toward the staircase.

More room doors opened along the hall. Men and
women in robes and slippers moved out onto the balcony.

"I thought I heard gunshots," John said.

But he was not looking at Rafe. His attention was on
Ella, who stood in the doorway. Other people were taking notice now as well. Rafe was pretty sure it wasn't the
sight of Lorelei in Ella's arm that was drawing everyone's
attention.

Ella seemed unaware of the picture she made. Her hair
was tumbled around her shoulders and her feet were bare.
There was a rosy flush on her cheeks and something sultry

and sexually compelling about her eyes. *Or maybe that's just me,* Rafe thought.

Lorelei chortled, breaking the small spell. Sensing a new game or maybe just excitement, she wriggled out of Ella's grasp, scampered out of the room, and hopped up onto the balcony railing. From there she vaulted neatly onto Rafe's shoulder and made enthusiastic noises, which he translated as the dust bunny equivalent of "*Let's ride, partner.*"

John blinked and hurriedly looked away from the sight of Ella in the doorway. His gaze snagged Rafe's. *Nope, not just me,* Rafe thought. Hayashi was at least two decades older but he had read and interpreted the scene with acute male accuracy. Hell, a man would have to be dead and buried to be immune to the sight of Ella fresh from a bed.

There were other eyes analyzing the scene now. There was nothing he could do about it, Rafe thought.

He went quickly down the stairs. So much for Ella's professional reputation. The news that he had spent a portion of the night in her room would be all over the jobsite by dawn.

He was not sure how he felt about that. Part of him wanted the world to know that she belonged to him, at least for now. But the realistic part of him was only too well aware that she would be pissed when she realized that she had become the subject of gossip. He did not want her to be hurt by the relationship.

Boots pounded down below on the timbered floor of

the lobby. Rafe heard the head of the security detail, Arthur Gill, calling orders to his crew.

"Secure the main lodge first," Gill said, pitching his voice so that it cut through the commotion. "Then we'll figure out what we're dealing with."

Rafe reached the foot of the stairs and caught up with Gill.

The head of Coppersmith Security on Rainshadow was a formidable presence. Gill was short but he looked as if he had been constructed out of solid granite. He had a weightlifter's bulk, tough, dark eyes, and a bald head that gleamed in the overhead lights. He nodded brusquely when he saw Rafe.

"Mr. Coppersmith," he said.

"I saw two people in the vicinity of the boathouse immediately after the shots were fired. Both were running but they didn't appear to be together."

Gill gave Lorelei a wary look and then refocused quickly on the more important problem. "Don't suppose you got a good look at the running guys?"

Someone handed Rafe a rain slicker. He put it on and moved outside into the driving rain. Gill and the security people followed.

"Can't even be certain of the gender," Rafe said. "Just shadows. Both looked like they were dressed in dark rain slickers. Coppersmith field-issue, I think. The hoods were pulled up."

"That's not real helpful." Gill turned to his team. "We'll start the search down at the boathouse. And remember, at least one of the guys we're looking for is armed. Lee, round up all the employees on site and get them into the lobby. I want everyone accounted for as soon as possible."

AT FIRST GLANCE THERE WAS NOTHING TO BE SEEN ON the dock or the grounds around the boathouse. Lorelei was a soggy blob of wet dryer lint on Rafe's shoulder. She was no longer chortling. Instead, she had gone uncharacteristically quiet, all four eyes open.

"Boathouse door is still locked," Gill said. He took a master keycard out of his pocket. "We closed up the place after we took over the lodge. Didn't want anyone trying to take out one of the old rowboats. The snakeweed growing in that lake is just too dangerous. Anything that gets snagged in the stuff disappears damn quick. The weed drags it under and the weird currents carry it to the bottom."

He opened the boathouse door and played the light around inside. Rafe looked over his shoulder. Two aging rowboats were tied up at the dock. Neither appeared to have been disturbed.

Gill closed and locked the door. He surveyed the dock. "No bloodstains."

"Not likely there would be any," Rafe said. "Not with this rain."

"Got that right."

Rafe walked along the dock, shining a light into the obsidian water. There was little to be seen. The thick mass of malevolent snakeweed lurked just under the surface, forming a mat of vegetation. The stuff grew so thickly that here and there it pushed twisted vines up out of the water. The snaky-looking creepers loomed in the beam of the flashlight like the tentacles of some giant water monster.

"That damn lake is worse than quicksand," Gill said. "If someone did get shot and the body was dumped in the water, we'll probably never find it. Unless someone turns up missing when we do a head count we may never know what went down here tonight."

"Two shots fired and two people running from the scene," Rafe said. "Something bad happened."

"Yes, sir." Gill hesitated. "How about this for a scenario—someone comes down here to meet a girlfriend or a boyfriend, saw something in the lake or thought he saw something in the lake, panicked, and fired a couple of shots. The couple runs from the scene."

"Very few of the Coppersmith employees are armed, Gill. Most of the people here on site are scientists and techs. They don't have any need for serious firepower."

"Doesn't mean someone didn't bring his or her own gun to this assignment," Gill said. "Rainshadow has acquired a bit of a reputation for being downright weird, not to mention dangerous."

Lorelei rumbled. It was a low, disturbing growl, not quite a warning. Rafe watched her out of the corner of his eye.

"What do you see?" he asked softly.

Lorelei hopped down from Rafe's shoulder and scuttled to the edge of the dock. She looked over the side.

Rafe aimed the flashlight into the vegetation-choked lake. A narrow length of metallic chain glinted just beneath the surface. The necklace was snagged on a snakeweed vine.

"Got something, Gill."

"Whatever you do, don't put your hand into that water," Gill ordered. "I'll get the boathook."

Rafe took the hook from him, threaded the tip through the long necklace, and drew it up into the light. There was an amber pendant attached to the metal chain.

The chain was still secured around the neck of the dead man.

A SHORT TIME LATER RAFE, GILL, AND TWO MEN FROM the security detail stood on the dock, looking down at the body. It hadn't been easy retrieving it from the snakeweed. In the end, the task had required some wicked-looking jungle knives, the boathook, and a lot of muscle.

"The chain got tangled in the snakeweed," Gill said. "That held the body close to the surface."

The victim was in his early twenties, his blond hair cut very short. He was dressed in dark clothes from head to toe. He had been shot twice, once in the chest and a second time in the head.

"Probably not the first time the killer has done this," Gill observed. "Son of a ghost, looks like we're dealing with a pro."

Rafe crouched and played the flashlight across the body. "This guy isn't wearing a Coppersmith uniform and he's not carrying Coppersmith gear. Anybody recognize him?"

There was a chorus of *no*s and *never-saw-him-before*s from the members of the security team.

Rafe found a wallet in one pocket and went through it quickly. "Resonance City driver's license. The name is Kenneth Maitland."

"Definitely not one of ours," Gill said.

Rafe pulled the dead man's shirt aside to get a look at the chest. There was no tornado tattoo.

He picked up the amber pendant that was attached to the end of the chain. A little tingle of energy told him the amber was tuned. The design on one side was a pyramid etched against rays of sunlight. On the opposite side the letters DND were inscribed.

"Looks like someone murdered a member of the Do Not Disturb movement," he said.

"No one on the Coppersmith team likes those guys," Gill said. He exhaled heavily. "If I were the local chief of police I'd assume everyone here on the jobsite is a suspect."

"Including me," Rafe said quietly. He got to his feet.

"Nah, you don't have to worry, sir," Gill said. "You've got an alibi. You were with the new consultant when the shots were fired. Half the staff saw you come out of her bedroom."

Chapter 19

NEWS THAT A BODY WEARING A DND MEDALLION HAD been found in the lake spread swiftly through the lodge. Ella dressed in the jeans and black pullover she had purchased in Thursday Harbor and went downstairs to join the rest of the staff. A roll call was taken. No one was missing.

For the most part, techs and other employees huddled in small groups in the lobby, talking quietly. The cook brewed large quantities of coffee and tea and disappeared into the kitchen to start working on an early breakfast. It was obvious that no one was going back to bed.

Vividly aware that many of the people present had seen Rafe emerging from her room at three fifteen in the morning, Ella chose a big leather chair in a quiet corner and sat by herself. She sipped strong coffee from a thick mug and tried to ignore the curious glances and occasional flat-out stares.

Rafe eventually returned. He stood in the lobby entrance, dripping water on the wooden floors. Lorelei was perched on his shoulder.

There was a grim vibe in the air around Rafe but Lorelei spotted Ella and bounced down to the floor. She gave herself a shake and scampered across the room. She was once again in full adorable mode. She hopped up onto the arm of Ella's chair and chortled a greeting. Ella patted her gently.

"What have you two been up to?" she asked softly. Lorelei mumbled cheerfully.

Rafe looked across the lobby, saw Ella in the corner, and nodded once. He immediately turned back to his conversation with a lot of serious-looking people. Someone gathered up the wet slickers and disappeared. Someone else produced mugs of coffee.

A short time later the island's chief of police arrived. Ella heard someone identify him as Slade Attridge. He was a dark-haired man with cop eyes. Even from across the room it was clear that he had some sort of talent. He vanished into an office with Rafe and all the other serious-looking people.

"Doughnut?"

The voice was male, pleasantly gruff, and friendly. Ella turned her head and saw the cook standing beside her chair. He was in his forties with thinning hair, broad features, and warm brown eyes. He was attired in a clean white apron and a pristine white paper cap. His face was a little flushed from the kitchen heat. He held a commercial-sized serving tray piled high with freshly made doughnuts. There were some small paper plates and napkins on the tray.

Lorelei went very still at the sight of the tray. Her blue eyes were rapt with wonder.

The cook looked at Ella and raised his brows. "Name's Bob. Okay to give the little dust bunny a doughnut?"

"Sure." Ella smiled. "I'm Ella Morgan. The dust bunny's name is Lorelei."

"Pleased to meet you, Ella." Bob selected a doughnut covered in powdered sugar and handed it to Lorelei. "Here you go, Miss Lorelei."

Lorelei was thrilled with the gift. She gurgled exultantly, bounced up and down a few times, and devoured the treat with delicate greed. Powdered sugar flew everywhere, much of it dusting her fur.

Bob winked at Ella. "Figured everyone could use a little comfort food and caffeine right at the moment."

"Good thinking." She helped herself to a plate, a napkin, and one of the doughnuts. "What have you heard?"

"They're saying they found a body in the water near the dock. Shot twice. Not one of the Coppersmith team. A DND guy."

"Yes, I heard that."

"Doesn't make sense." Bob shook his head. "I mean, everyone knows the DND folks are irritating, but it's not like they're a serious threat. They just make a lot of noise. No reason to shoot one."

"Rafe said something along those same lines."

Bob squinted a little. "I hear tell you're the consultant Rafe Coppersmith brought in to clear out the dinosaurs. You're some kind of music talent, right?"

"Right."

Bob grinned. "What do you plan to do? Play the piano for the monsters?" He broke off, wincing. "Sorry. Bad joke."

"No problem." Ella took a bite out of her doughnut. It was still warm. It was also incredibly good. "But just so you know, and strictly between you and me, I'm lousy on the piano so I'll probably have to come up with something else."

Bob chuckled. Then he grew more serious. "I heard the techs talking. They're looking for an answer they can translate into tuned quartz—some kind of anti-dino gadget everyone on a team can carry."

"I'll do my best." Ella eyed her half-eaten doughnut. "This is absolutely fabulous, by the way."

"Thanks." Bob beamed. "Well, a pleasure to meet you. I'd better circulate these so that I can get back to the kitchen. Got to get breakfast on the table. You wouldn't believe how this crowd eats."

Ella popped the remainder of the doughnut into her mouth and rose to her feet. "I'd be happy to take the tray around if you would rather return to the kitchen."

"Hey, thanks, I appreciate that." Bob gave the lobby a cursory glance and lowered his voice. "Everyone's a little stressed. They've been marking time here on Rainshadow for nearly a month waiting to get the all clear so that they can go down and start work in Wonderland. Thing is, this is an island and there just isn't a heck of a lot to do at night except hang out at the taverns in town. First it was the dinos and now a murder. It's like this job is jinxed or something."

Ella took the tray. It was surprisingly heavy. Commercial kitchenware was probably built to last, she reminded herself.

"I'm sure Mr. Coppersmith and the operations people will get things on track very quickly," she said.

"Oh, yeah," Bob said. "The Coppersmiths know how to run a jobsite. And they don't like wasting time. They'll get things moving real soon."

"How long have you worked for Coppersmith?"

"Awhile now. Worked a few different exploration and mining camps in my time. One thing about my line— there's always employment for a cook who can put out three meals a day for a hungry team. But I'm hoping to stay with Coppersmith. Best benefits in the business."

He turned and ambled off to the kitchen. Ella looked at Lorelei, who was studying the remaining heap of powdered-sugar doughnuts with a very focused air.

"Sorry, the rest of these are for the team," Ella said.

Lorelei chortled, hopped down off the arm of the chair, and fluttered away in the direction of the kitchen.

"Don't get any ideas about running off with the cook just because he knows how to make doughnuts," Ella called softly. "We're partners, remember? Besides, I'm the one who knows how to order pizza."

Lorelei disappeared through the kitchen doorway. Ella sighed and set out to make new friends with her tray of warm doughnuts.

A short time later she concluded that she was pleased with the results of her cunning plan. She could still see a lot of curiosity and speculation in the eyes of the Coppersmith employees but the doughnuts had gone a long way toward bridging the awkward space that had opened up at approximately three fifteen that morning.

Okay, so the situation was still a little complicated, she conceded. And it was true that she had broken one of her own cardinal rules. But with luck, what happened on Rainshadow would stay on Rainshadow. She would go back to the old rules when she returned to Crystal City.

She was handing out doughnuts to a couple of grateful techs when Rafe and Slade emerged from the office. Rafe raised his brows at the sight of the tray in her hands but he did not remark upon it. Instead he beckoned her across the lobby.

"I'd like you to meet Slade Attridge," he said. "Slade's an old FBPI pal. Slade, this is Ella Morgan. She's the new music talent consultant."

"A pleasure," Slade said. He smiled. "Good luck with the dinos."

"Thanks," she said, and gave him a polite smile. "I'm hoping to get started soon." She held the tray out. "Two left. One for each of you if you're so inclined."

"I'm inclined." Rafe snatched up one of the doughnuts and took a healthy bite.

"So am I." Slade helped himself to the last doughnut. "Nothing like a murder investigation to work up an appetite."

Rafe looked at Ella. "We're going down into Wonderland with a team this morning. Slade will handle the murder investigation. He'll coordinate with the Coppersmith Security people. He also offered to do a little research on those guys who tried to grab you before we left Crystal City."

"The tats aren't a lot to go on," Slade said. "But the fact that they turned up on a bunch of guys using black-market Alien tech may give us what we in the cop business like to call a clue."

"Let me know if you get anything," Rafe said.

"Will do," Slade said.

He nodded at Ella and headed for the door.

Rafe turned back to Ella. He paused, as though gathering himself for a leap off a cliff. "About last night."

"Let's not go there," she said in her best client tones. "Breakfast is waiting."

"You do realize that half the people in this lobby saw me coming out of your room this morning shortly after three a.m. The other half have probably heard the gossip by now."

"Don't worry about it," she said. "These things happen."

"Not to me," Rafe said. "And not to you. Ella, what happened is my fault."

"It's okay," she said. "Stuff happens on a job. Let's go get breakfast."

Rafe started to protest but Lorelei appeared from the kitchen doorway. She dashed across the lobby, chortling with delight. The last time Ella had seen her she'd had a light dusting of powdered sugar on her fur. Now she looked like a small, snow-covered mountain peak.

"What the hell has she been into?" Rafe asked.

"Don't ask. By the way, do you have any pals who aren't connected to the FBPI?"

"Maybe. I'll have to think about that."

Chapter 20

"WELCOME TO WONDERLAND," RAFE SAID.

Ella stood just inside the paranormal gate that was the entrance to the newly discovered sector of the Underworld and looked at the glittering, sparking, flashing scene. She was dazzled.

"This is amazing," she said. "It's like a vast fairyland."

Wonderland was a surreal crystal-and-quartz landscape. Blue energy illuminated a world rendered in various shades of blue. A cobalt-blue crystalline creek wound through a forest of azure trees. Sapphire leaves glinted in the strange light. Masses of blue ferns sparked and flashed in the psi-heavy atmosphere.

All of it, from the silvery-blue rock formations to the cerulean-blue sky, looked as if it had been locked in the heart of an ancient glacier—frozen in time. Nothing moved.

The leaves on the trees did not flutter. The creek was still. It was a jewel box of a world.

Lorelei, perched on Ella's shoulder, chortled enthusiastically. She waved the somewhat-the-worse-for-wear wedding veil, vaulted down to the diamond-hard ground, and began rummaging among the blue pebbles.

Ella looked at Rafe. "What happened here?"

"We don't know," Rafe said. "There's a theory that this was the Aliens' first attempt at bioengineering."

One of the techs, a tall, lean, sharp-boned woman who had introduced herself as Angela Price, studied the hard, sparkling landscape with a wary expression.

"The Aliens screwed up big-time down here," she said. "They got the para-physics and the biophysics wrong. But to give them credit—they learned from their mistakes. After this they came up with the Rainforest, an elegantly balanced ecosystem that is still going strong."

Another tech spoke up. "Down here, with the notable exception of the wildlife, the whole system seems to have turned into stone—solid quartz and crystal."

Ella looked at him and remembered that his name was Jake. "Petrified, do you mean?"

"In a way," Angela said. "But like Jake said, there are some exceptions. The dinos certainly aren't stone. They evidently went into some form of long-term hibernation after the Aliens abandoned this lab. The beasts are waking up but their ecosystem has collapsed around them."

"There's nothing for them to eat down here except

each other," Rafe said. "So some of the critters are going aboveground to hunt inside the Preserve."

"How are they getting out of Wonderland?" Ella asked. She glanced back at the entrance. "You and the local Guild authorities control the gate."

"We control the one gate that was recently discovered," Jake said. "Obviously there is another one—maybe several of them, including at least one that opens into the Preserve. All we can say for sure is that the dinos have found an exit from Wonderland."

"The Rainshadow Preserve Foundation has put together a task force to try to locate the gate from the aboveground point of entry," Rafe said. "But they haven't had any luck so far. It's very difficult to navigate inside the psi-fence."

Duke, one of the Guild men who had accompanied the team, looked at Ella. "Fortunately, standard amber locators work down here in Wonderland. We can navigate this sector and that means we can map it—once we get rid of the dinos."

Tanaka, the other Guild man on the team, spoke up. "The flamers work, too. The critters are afraid of fire so we've been able to chase them off so far. But we're concerned that they'll gradually overcome their fear. The dinos are too big to bring down with flamers. They've got those mirrored scales to protect them. They don't seem to be real smart but sooner or later they're going to figure out that they're bigger and stronger than we are."

Everyone on the team looked at Ella. Nothing like a major success on this project to add luster to the reputation of the Knightsbridge Institute, she reminded herself.

She put on her best *I'm an expert and I'm here to solve your problem* smile.

"Right," she said. "Singing dinosaurs. Can't wait to hear them. Where do we find these critters?"

"That's the easy part," Rafe said. "They'll find us." He surveyed the gem-bright landscape. "It won't take long. It's daytime up on the surface inside the Preserve. That means the monsters are sheltering down here. They'll be attracted to live prey."

"The prey you refer to being us, I assume?" Ella asked.

"Yep."

Rafe checked his flamer. The rest of the team, including Ella, did the same.

Duke looked around. "Listen up, people. Only a couple of rules down here, but those who don't stick to 'em will probably get eaten. We stay together. We do not lose visual contact. If the monsters show up we form a defensive ring with the flamers and de-rez our senses."

"Remember, the critters hunt by following our psychic spore," Tanaka added. "You hear even the faintest music, you sound the alarm and go cold. We want to make the trail as thin as possible. Understood?"

Everyone muttered "yes" and searched the nearby landscape. Ella knew that none of them liked the idea of lowering their paranormal senses in the face of danger. It went against every survival instinct. All animals, including humans, intuitively jacked up all their senses—paranormal as well as normal—when confronted with a serious threat.

"What about storms?" Angela asked nervously.

"Protocol for a psi-storm is the same as that for dealing

with an energy river in the Rainforest," Duke said. "Make physical contact with the person next to you and seek shelter in one of the caves."

"The dinos seem to become as confused and disoriented in the storms as we do," Rafe said. "So as long as you're in the middle of a blast, you're not likely to become a snack. Everyone ready? Let's move out."

They set off in a tight formation, Rafe and Tanaka in the lead. Duke brought up the rear. Ella and the two techs, Angela and Jake, were in the middle.

The journey through Wonderland would have been a full-ride ticket at a world-class amusement park if it weren't for the constant threat of storms and monsters, Ella thought. The stands of crystalline trees, the senses-tingling atmosphere, the eerie blue light, the dazzling rocks and gleaming quartz streams and ponds made for a stunning landscape— a dead landscape—but stunning.

The energy infused in the jeweled world was equally enchanting. Ella paused to examine a sapphire leaf. The sparkling heat inside the quartz made her senses fizz. She looked at Rafe.

"I can see why Coppersmith bid a fortune for the rights to this place," she said.

"Oh, yeah." His mouth kicked up at the corners. "Going to make several fortunes here in Wonderland—as soon as we get the dinos under control."

They trekked through the blue forest, crossing streams and creeks made of solid crystal and quartz. At one point they paused to investigate a cave that glowed with a radiant blue energy.

"From what we can tell, the caves are the only sources of water down here," Rafe said. The ones we've explored so far all have hot springs inside. The water is clean. The critters won't enter the caverns, though—something about the interior energy seems to repel them."

They moved on, walking a grid pattern that the Guild men and the Coppersmith techs had managed to map.

The first notes struck gently at first. Ella was astonished by the sweet, haunting lullaby that seemed to float, ghostlike, through her thoughts. It was the song that every mother since time immemorial had sung to her baby, the song the child would hear on some level all of his or her life: a ravishing song of maternal love.

Tears gathered in Ella's eyes.

An instant later, shock flashed through her. She stopped suddenly and looked at Rafe.

"Oh, wow, is that it?" she asked. "Is that the dinos' hunting music?"

Angela frowned. "I don't hear anything. . . . Wait, there it is."

Tanaka took charge. "Everyone—shut down your senses and move into the cave. Now."

No one argued. Flamers at the ready, they retreated into a glowing blue cave. The Guild men positioned themselves at the entrance. The eerie music followed them, tugging at their shuttered senses.

Rafe looked at Ella. "Yeah, that's it. We're reasonably safe in here." Angela's fingers tightened on her flamer. "That music is scary strong, isn't it? Even with my senses shut down I can still hear it."

"This is what the sailors must have heard in those Old World stories," Duke said. "You know, those tales about Sirens who used hypnotic songs to make the men crash their ships against the rocks."

Ella froze.

"No such things as Sirens," Rafe said easily. "Everyone knows that."

No one responded. Ella gave him a sidelong glance and then cleared her throat.

"This is where I earn my very high fees," she said. "But to get a fix I'm going to have to move out of the cave and jack up my senses."

"I'll go with you and cover you," Rafe said. "Duke and Tanaka will stay with the techs. If we get into trouble we retreat back into the cave."

"Got it," Ella said.

Tanaka looked grim. Ella knew he didn't like the setup but he also knew that this was why they were in Wonderland in the first place. He angled his chin.

"Go," he said. "And don't get in the way of our flamers if we need to use them."

"We'll sure try to keep that helpful tip in mind," Rafe said.

The tension in the small group was palpable but everyone there was a pro, Ella realized. No one was going to panic. She reached up toward Lorelei, intending to hand her over to Angela. But Lorelei growled a warning and hunkered down.

"Okay," Ella said. "Partners."

Duke looked at her. "Don't worry, the flamers are effective, at least for now."

"It's that damn music," Angela whispered in a shivery voice. "It sneaks up on you every time."

"Creepy," Jake said. "We can't work down here until we get a more efficient defense system."

"I understand," Ella said. "Let me see what I can do for you."

She moved to the mouth of the cave. Rafe came to stand beside her.

Cautiously she heightened her talent.

The mesmerizing music exploded across her senses. The harmonies were piercingly sweet. They tugged at her, promising rapture. She knew that the beast had achieved a fix on her.

A few seconds later, mirrored scales flashed amid the crystal trees. The camouflage was so good that it was impossible to see the dinosaur clearly, but there was no doubt that it was very close.

Lorelei growled a low warning. Ella realized that Rafe was preparing to rez the trigger of the flamer. If he fired the creature would run and she would lose her opportunity.

"I've got this," she said.

"Right," Rafe said. He did not take his eyes off the stand of trees.

Lorelei perched tensely on Ella's shoulder.

The monster was a clever hunter, Ella thought. But for better or worse, humans had a long-standing and highly successful history of defending their top-of-the-food-chain status.

She got a focus on the searing music and began to resonate with the wavelengths the creature was generating. Within a few beats she sensed the elemental life-force that powered the enthralling harmonies. There was a fathomless hunger in the energy waves that rode just beneath the music. The creature was driven by a blood lust that roared forth from the deepest recesses of its primitive brain. The need to tear apart flesh and bone and gorge on the soft, bloody entrails of its victim was its sole reason for existing.

There was another thread of even darker music beneath the blood lust. Ella did not have time to analyze it. At that moment light and shadow shifted again in the stand of crystal trees. Blue sunlight danced on silvery-blue scales. Rafe swore softly and leveled the flamer.

"Ella?" he said quietly.

She ignored him. She could not talk and sing at the same time. She was locked on to her target now. She had a fix. The small chimes on her bracelet shivered with energy.

She began to sing, pulling energy from the dark and light ends of the spectrum. She composed delicate counter-harmonies designed to disrupt the powerful waves that the creature was sending her way.

She knew the feedback was confusing the monster because its musical lures began to break up. There was no way to know how its primitive brain received and interpreted the human singing, but on a primal level it got the message. This prey could fight back.

The creature's song ceased abruptly. Mirrored scales shimmered again, briefly, amid the trees. The dinosaur broke into a lumbering gallop, the sound of its heavy feet striking hard stone echoing in the eerie landscape.

Ella caught a few glimpses of a predatory head, a huge mouth filled with multiple rows of sharp teeth, and six legs that ended in big clawed feet. A heartbeat later the monster was gone.

She held her breath. She knew the rest of the team was doing the same. But Lorelei chortled, hopped down from Ella's shoulder, and resumed selecting small pieces of sparkling blue quartz.

Rafe looked at Ella, cool satisfaction in his eyes. "Nice work."

"Thanks," she said, going for what she hoped was the modest but self-confident-consultant tone. She jangled the chimes on her bracelet. "I think I've got what your lab techs need. Quartz that is tuned to certain frequencies should repel the dinosaurs."

The rest of the team emerged from the cave. They all looked at Ella.

Duke whistled softly. "That was damned impressive. I've seen the critters run from flamers before, but only after they got close enough to get singed—and that's just too close for comfort."

"All right, let's get back to the surface," Rafe said. "The techs will want to start working on this."

"Looks like my work here is done," Ella said.

Rafe glanced at her. He did not look pleased by that announcement.

Chapter 21

THE LAB WAS MODIFIED FOR FIELDWORK BUT IT CONtained portable versions of many of the critical pieces of equipment that were standard issue in all Coppersmith research facilities.

Rafe stood quietly to the side, letting Ella and the heads of the lab team, Susan Bowen and John Hayashi, talk frequencies. The operations manager, Sam Forrester, and the rest of the techs were grouped around the long workbench, eager to get moving on a prototype device that would counter the singing monsters.

The team had exited Wonderland less than an hour ago. The meeting in the lab had been convened immediately. Rafe had wanted to give Ella some downtime before she was debriefed by the eager techs, but after some coffee and a couple of doughnuts she had announced that she was fit to give her report.

Looks like my work here is done.

Rafe couldn't get the words out of his head. He had been so focused on finding Ella and getting her to Rainshadow and then on protecting her and then on taking her to bed that he had never stopped to consider what would happen once she solved the monster problem.

She would leave. That's what would happen. There was nothing to keep her on Rainshadow. Nothing to keep her with him.

Susan Bowen looked satisfied. "All right, I think we've got our dino repellent. Now to tune some quartz and see if it works."

"Shouldn't be a problem," Hayashi said.

Rafe folded his arms and propped one shoulder against the wall. "Think we could use tuned quartz to track the critters?"

Susan looked thoughtful. "Hmm."

Hayashi took off his glasses and polished them while he considered the question. "We've been thinking in terms of a gadget to repel the dinosaurs, but it might be possible to reverse the process."

Susan raised one brow. "Lure them, do you mean?"

"Technology isn't my area of expertise," Ella said. "But theoretically, yes, you should be able to use the quartz to hunt the monsters the same way they hunt you. The question is, what will you do with them after you get them to come to you? You said you don't have any serious weapons that will work in a heavy-psi environment."

"That," Sam Forrester said, "is an excellent question."

"We know that the dinosaurs can't handle daylight on

the surface," Rafe said. "From what we can tell, it's lethal to them. We might be able to use the quartz to track the beasts to the gate that they're using to move between Wonderland and the Preserve. If we find it, we should be able to barricade it so that they can't get back underground during the daylight hours."

Excitement flickered in Susan's eyes. "I see where you're going with this. If the critters get caught on the surface during the day, sunlight and the diminished psi forces inside the Preserve might finish them off."

Sam Forrester smiled a very satisfied smile. "We've got a plan. Plans are good."

Rafe looked at Ella. Her words echoed in his head. . . . *My work here is done.*

Damn.

WHEN THE MEETING ENDED HE WALKED BACK TO THE main lodge building with Ella. She had been animated during the conference with the techs, but as soon as they left the lab she went silent.

"What are you thinking?" he asked.

"I was just thinking that Dr. Hayashi and Dr. Bowen and their team will probably have a prototype of a harmonic disrupter device ready by tomorrow. We can field test it in the afternoon."

A chill flickered through his senses. "So?"

"So, that's it for me. If the test goes well, I'll be able to return to Crystal City the day after tomorrow."

The chill turned glacial.

"There's still the little problem of finding out who tried to grab you that night in Crystal," he reminded her.

"I can take care of myself," she said.

"You can take care of yourself when the odds are one-on-one. But the crowd with the tats looks like a small, private army."

"I've been thinking about that. I'm going to hire Jones and Jones to investigate. They also provide bodyguard services. They're expensive, but they're good."

"Coppersmith takes care of its own."

"I get that. But as I keep reminding you, I am not a member of the Coppersmith organization."

"Damn it, Ella. My life is complicated at the moment. I can't make long-term commitments. But that doesn't mean I'm going to let you go back to Crystal all by yourself."

"I appreciate that, but J and J can handle this—assuming there is anything to be handled. After all, I've finished the project here on Rainshadow. If the goal was to keep me from consulting for Coppersmith, they're too late."

They were nearing the entrance to the lobby. It occurred to Rafe that the last thing he wanted to do was conduct this argument in front of a lot of witnesses.

"I just need a little time," he said.

"Take all the time you need. It's not like I'm going to get married while you're off figuring out whether you're going to go crazy. Odds are good that I'll be available if you show up in Crystal City."

That was not the answer he wanted, but before he could come up with a fresh angle his phone rang. He yanked it off his belt and glowered at the screen.

"It's Slade." He took the call. "Got something on the dead guy?"

"Yeah," Slade said. "But this may interest you even more. I may have a lead on those guys with the tattoos who tried to grab Ella in Crystal City."

"I'm listening."

"I'd rather not do this on the phone. Besides, I have orders from Charlotte to invite you and your consultant to dinner tonight. Can you make it?"

"Hang on." Rafe looked at Ella. "This is Attridge. He and his wife are inviting us for dinner tonight."

"Us?"

"Slade says he's got some info on both the murder and the bastards who tried to grab you. Figured you might be interested."

"You're right," she said. "I'm interested."

Chapter 22

"FIRST, LET'S GO OVER WHAT I'VE GOT ON THE GUY YOU fished out of the lake," Slade said. He plunked his bottle of Green Quartz beer down on the coffee table and lowered himself into a chair. He picked up a folder and handed it to Rafe. "Kenneth Maitland, twenty-two years old. No close family. A few brushes with the law—drug dealing when he was in his teens but nothing after that. Looks like he got caught up in the DND movement about a year ago. Typical cult-recruit profile."

"A young man grows up without a family so he tries to find one," Ella said. She shook her head. "So sad."

Rafe flipped through the folder. "Presumably, he slipped onto the jobsite to make trouble, but why would anyone shoot him in cold blood?"

Ella was mildly surprised to discover that she was enjoying the evening. Slade's wife, Charlotte, was warm and

welcoming. She had the unmistakable glow of impending
motherhood.

She was a striking woman. Her dark hair was cut in a
sleek bob and her eyes were accented with stylish, black-
framed glasses. There was a strong vibe of talent in the
atmosphere around her. Rafe had mentioned that she owned
an antiques shop in Shadow Bay.

Ella was wistfully aware of the energy between Slade and
Charlotte. You didn't have to be psychic to know when two
people were deeply in love and bonded for life, she thought.

She wasn't the only one who was savoring the pleasure
of an evening with friends. Lorelei appeared to be having
a fine time with Slade's dust bunny companion, Rex. The
pair had evidently bonded over a mutual admiration for
sparkly accessories. Rex carried a small, rather expensive-
looking antique clutch purse that seemed to be his prize
possession. He appeared suitably impressed with Lorelei's wedding veil. The two had disappeared out onto the
porch. Ella wondered if she should be concerned about
the lack of a chaperone.

"This has all the hallmarks of a drug deal gone bad,"
Slade said. "That wouldn't be the biggest surprise in the
world, given Maitland's history. But there are other possibilities."

Ella looked at him. "Such as?"

Slade shrugged. "Black-market artifacts. There have
been some discoveries in the Preserve recently."

"But DND is against excavating the ruins," Charlotte
pointed out. "Why would they be involved in trafficking
black-market artifacts?"

"Two reasons," Rafe said. "Money and power."

"Right," Slade said. "Cults and conspiracy movements like DND are all about both. I'm guessing that the people at the top of the DND aren't exactly pure of heart."

"I'd say that's an accurate assumption," Rafe agreed. "Our security people have spent a lot of time researching DND. The recruits might be true believers, but the man at the top, Houston Radburn, has a long history of fraud and embezzlement schemes." He looked at Slade. "Coppersmith will continue to work with you on the DND case, but I'll be honest, the guys with the tattoos make me a lot more nervous."

"Maybe with good reason, because I don't think there's a connection to DND." Slade opened another file. "I didn't get anything useful from my FBPI contacts so I followed a hunch and checked with Arcane's investigation agency, Jones and Jones. When it comes to some things their files are better than the Bureau's."

"Funny you should say that." Rafe rested his forearms on his knees. "Ella suggested that we contact Jones and Jones about this problem."

Ella swirled the wine in her glass. "What I said was, I intend to contact the agency."

Rafe gave her a grim look but he didn't say anything. She was starting to get annoyed. She'd solved his dino problem for him in record time and what thanks did she get? Attitude.

"I had a long talk with Marlowe Jones," Slade said. "She's the head of the Frequency City branch of Jones and Jones. She did some research and says that the tattoos combined with the fact that the kidnappers used Alien tech might point to a group called Vortex."

Rafe sat back and picked up his beer. "Never heard of it."

"Neither have I," Ella said.

"No reason any of us should have heard of it until now," Slade said. "When Marlowe ran the facts through her online archives she found the reference. Evidently, back in the day on Earth, Jones and Jones had some serious problems with a crowd that called itself Vortex. This was long before the Curtain opened. Twenty-first century, Old World date."

"What was Vortex?" Ella asked.

"It was your basic criminal empire," Slade said. "But a very sophisticated operation, according to Marlowe. It was well hidden behind a veil of shell corporations and protected by influential people in government and business. What made it so dangerous was that the guys at the top managed to acquire some very exotic crystal-based weapons that had been developed in a government lab."

"In other words, human-made psi-ware," Charlotte said.

"Right," Slade said. "The weapons were paranormal in nature. I should add that this was in an era when most folks, including the police, didn't take the paranormal seriously. Which is why, Marlowe says, Jones and Jones took the lead on the investigation."

Ella looked at him. "What happened back on Earth? Did Jones and Jones succeed in taking down Vortex?"

"Marlowe has the private diaries of the man who was the head of Jones and Jones at the time, one of her ancestors. I think she said his name was Fallon Jones. He and his assistant at the agency—his wife—were successful in defanging Vortex. But Jones wrote that there was no way to know for certain if they had found and destroyed all of the psi-ware weapons."

"Well, one thing I'm sure of," Ella said. "The bell weapon that those Vortex guys tried to use on us in Crystal City was definitely Alien tech, not human-made psi-ware."

They all looked at her.

"You're sure?" Charlotte asked.

"She's right," Rafe said. "Coppersmith has done a lot of psi-ware research. Anything powered by paranormal energy carries a certain kind of psychic fingerprint. The Alien prints are very different from human prints."

"I agree," Charlotte said. "I tune paranormal objects in my shop, remember? Aliens and humans both leave prints and each is unique."

"So," Rafe said, "it looks like Vortex may have reinvented itself here on Harmony and it's gone into the Alien-tech business."

Slade's eyes narrowed ever so slightly. "Attempting to take you down so that they could grab your consultant was a very risky move. Vortex must be desperate if it's willing to take a chance like that."

"Yes," Rafe said. "That did occur to me."

Something in his voice made Ella look at him quite sharply. There was a little heat in his eyes. It wasn't the kind of heat that she associated with passion. She opened her senses and saw the telltale spike of psi-fever in his aura.

Rafe was fighting off another hallucination.

Chapter 23

"OKAY, YOU CAN TALK ABOUT IT NOW." ELLA SETTLED deeper into the passenger seat and watched the night landscape through the windshield of the SUV. "There's just the two of us. And Lorelei, of course. No need to explain things to Slade and Charlotte."

Rafe's hands tightened on the steering wheel. He gave her a quick, unreadable glance. "What is it you think I'm going to say?"

"I don't know. But when Slade was telling us about Vortex I got the impression that you had been slammed by one of your lucid dreams."

Rafe exhaled slowly, with control. Energy shivered in the atmosphere.

"Was it that obvious?" he asked.

"I'm sure Charlotte and Slade felt the energy shift, but, no, I don't think they realized what was happening.

You're getting good at concealing the visible side effects of the fever."

"But the visions are as bad as ever. You're right. I did hallucinate for a few seconds back there at Slade and Charlotte's place."

"Tell me about your dream. I'm the professional here, remember?"

He hesitated and then he seemed to come to a decision. "In the vision I was looking into the wrong side of a mirror. I could see a street. I think it was in the Ghost City. Shadowy figures were coming toward me. I knew that I should be able to recognize them but I couldn't. I understood that in order to see them clearly I had to look in the right side of the mirror."

She jacked up her own talent a little and thought about what he had said.

"The wrong side of the mirror," she repeated thoughtfully. "I think that's the key."

"Yeah?" He glanced at her, eyes tightening. "I figured the scene of the Ghost City was the key—assuming there is a key."

"Let all your preconceptions about psi-fever go for a minute and think about the vision without trying to analyze it. You can't use pure logic on dreams. It doesn't work. What was the emotional takeaway from your vision?"

He tightened his hands on the wheel. "I was frustrated because I couldn't identify the people coming toward me down the street."

"Because?"

"I told you why. Something to do with looking at the

scene from the wrong side of the mirror. Look, if there's some sort of message there . . . Shit." Rafe stared out the window, transfixed. "Looking at things from the wrong side of the mirror. You think that means I've been looking at the evidence the wrong way?"

"I don't know. But we were considering the facts about Vortex that Slade had pulled together when your fever spiked. What would you see if you considered those facts from a different perspective?"

Rafe's profile hardened. "I've been assuming that the timing of the kidnapping attempt meant that Vortex was after you. I thought I had led them to you. But maybe— just maybe—it indicates that they are after me."

"Hmm."

"Son of a ghost, Ella. Maybe this isn't all about you. Maybe it's about me."

"Hmm."

She reached up to pat Lorelei, who was perched on the back of the seat, clearly enjoying the night ride. The passenger door window was lowered and the night air wafted the veil in a ghostly manner.

The drive back to the old lodge was taking them through the small town of Shadow Bay. Earlier, Charlotte had explained that until recently the community had been a remote, isolated island village that rolled up the streets at nine o'clock at night. But the discovery of Wonderland had changed the vibe.

Shadow Bay had been transformed into something resembling a boomtown. Bars and taverns lined the main street. Their brightly lit signs illuminated the night in garish colors.

Slade said that most of the establishments had sprung up overnight to cater to the influx of rowdy ghost hunters who had arrived to organize the new Rainshadow Guild territory. A motley assortment of thrill-seekers, opportunists, and drifters had soon followed. And now the Coppersmith Mining employees were added to the mix.

There were Help Wanted signs in many of the windows. The inns, bed-and-breakfast places, and small motel near the marina were crammed. Rents were high for the few cottages and houses that were available.

Most of the newcomers had made their way to Rainshadow to seek work or to try to take advantage of the booming economy. But Slade had said that every ferry also brought conspiracy buffs, reporters, and the merely curious who had heard rumors about monsters and an underworld realm made of paranormal jewels.

Rafe drove to the end of the street and turned right, heading into the interior of the island. The winding road narrowed rapidly and the night seemed heavier. The forest pressed close on either side of the pavement. Fog swirled in the headlights, limiting visibility.

"If we're right," Rafe said, "the facts I've been using to explain the timing of what I assumed was an attempt to kidnap you could just as easily explain an attempt to grab me, instead."

"Go on."

"It all comes down to the simple fact that they haven't

had much in the way of options until recently. Think about it—when I came out of the Rainforest I was taken to the Coppersmith family compound on Copper Beach Island immediately. A lot of people thought I was either dying or doomed to spend the rest of my days in a para-psych ward. I was watched day and night. Furthermore, the island is a fortress. It would have been damn near impossible for a stranger to get inside the gates of the compound without being detected. My family has been into cutting-edge security for generations."

"Okay, so Vortex couldn't get at you until you left your family compound."

"After my family concluded that I wasn't going to go crazy, at least not in the immediate future, Dad decided I needed a job. I was sent straight to Rainshadow to trou-bleshoot the dinosaur situation. That was a little over a week ago. Again I was surrounded by a lot of Copper-smith security, not to mention I'm friends with the local chief of police. A kidnapping attempt here on the island would be extremely complicated."

"Vortex would have to get people and equipment in place. In addition, they would have to take you out by boat. That means they would need to find someone who could handle the local tides and currents."

"Exactly. On that first visit to Rainshadow I hung around for only a few days, just long enough to figure out that I needed to hire you."

"Then you flew to Crystal," Ella said. She drew a quick breath. "Where you were suddenly a lot more vulnerable."

"Vortex must have scrambled to get an operation set

up in a matter of hours, but in a city that size they probably had local people and local tech they could use. They made a stab at grabbing me after the college reception but it failed, thanks to you."

"But that still leaves us with one very important question—why do they want you so badly that they're willing to risk bringing the power of the Coppersmith Mining empire down on their heads, not to mention the FBPI?"

"I assumed the kidnapping attempt in Crystal was all about making sure I didn't get you to Rainshadow," Rafe said. "I figured the guys with the tats were either some serious corporate competition or the DND crowd. I thought it was all about Wonderland, but what if I was wrong?"

"What do you mean?"

"I think," Rafe said, speaking very carefully as if measuring each word, "that this is about the city of ice and fog."

"Why would Vortex chase a legend like the Ghost City?"

"Because they are convinced that it's not a legend. They must have a strong reason to believe it's real. They've figured out that I'm the only one who can lead them to the portal and unlock it."

"But you can't take them there. You said you hallucinated the city of ice and fog, and the portal pool as well."

"That's what I've been telling myself," Rafe said. "But I'm starting to think that my vision was real. Evidently Vortex has concluded the same thing."

"Okay, say you really did find a gate into the Ghost City. It certainly wouldn't be the first time someone has stumbled through a portal in the Underworld. That's how the Rainforest and Wonderland were discovered. Legends usually contain at least a kernel of truth, and there have been stories about the Ghost City since humans came through the Curtain."

"But the people who stumbled out of the Underworld claiming to have seen the city have always been considered mad," Rafe said without inflection.

"You're not mad. I don't think you hallucinated the city. Let's assume it's real and that Vortex wants you to open the portal for them. You said the ruins that contained the gray quartz chamber and the quicksilver pool were now concealed by a huge psi-firestorm."

"Right."

"But you could get through the storm."

"For the past three months I've told myself that the whole experience was a dream and that the best thing I could do was try to forget it." Rafe glanced at his ring. "But if I go with the assumption that it was all real, then, yes, I think I know how to navigate the storm and maybe, just maybe, I could open the portal."

Energy sparked in the gray stone of his ring. And suddenly Ella understood.

"That quartz is the key, isn't it?" she asked.

"Yes," Rafe said. "And there are a lot more keys where this came from. Every rock in the gray quartz chamber is a potential key, but I think each key has to be tuned to the talent who wants to use it to open the portal. Got a hunch only certain kinds of talents can work gray quartz."

"Somehow the explosion burned out your old talent and left you with a new talent—the ability to work gray quartz."

"Maybe. But if I've got a new talent, why the fever?"

"The process of developing your new talent was not immediate. It's been ongoing during the past three months. But I think it's almost complete. That's why you're able to suppress the visions when you choose."

"Crap. I can open a portal. Not exactly a cool talent. I might as well sign up to become an elevator operator."

"We're talking about a very unique portal. Nevertheless, I don't think opening the doorway to the Ghost City is the real nature of your talent—more like a side effect."

"Yeah? So what is my talent? Seeing hallucinations? I gotta tell you that is not exactly a huge improvement— Shit."

The *shit* came out very softly.

Rafe took his foot off the accelerator and hit the brake so quickly Lorelei lost her grip on the back of the seat. She tumbled down into Ella's lap, chortling with glee at the new game.

Ella peered through the windshield, trying to figure out what had caused Rafe to slam to a halt.

"What did you see?" she asked. "An animal in the road?"

"Shit," Rafe said again. Louder this time and with a sharp, frustrated edge.

She looked at him and saw that he was blinking rapidly. He released his death grip on the wheel and rubbed his eyes with the back of his hand.

"Sorry," he said. "But you're going to have to drive the rest of the way."

"Another vision?" she asked.

"Damned hallucinations."

She reached out to touch him. The muscles of his shoulder were mag-steel hard. In her lap, Lorelei, sensing the tension in the atmosphere, went very still.

Ella heightened her talent a little and studied Rafe's dreamlight. It was shot through with hot fever light. In response an uneasy frisson iced her spine.

"Rafe, what do you see?"

"The gates of Hell."

Chapter 24

HE STARED AT THE VISION, AWARE OF ELLA'S HAND ON HIS shoulder; aware that she had kicked up her talent. He could hear Lorelei muttering. But it was the scene on the other side of the windshield that riveted him.

The gates that guarded the entrance to Hell were made of fog and ice. They rose up out of the swirling mist, towering high above the dark trees. The top of the gates vanished into the deep night that clung to Rainshadow.

It was, Rafe decided, time to deal with the facts. The hallucinations were not going away.

The gates started to open. A quicksilver gray lake seethed on the other side.

"This is the worst one yet, Ella," he said.

"Damn it, pay attention," she snapped. "You had a really bad turn that night in the limo when you were nearly kidnapped. Tonight you had another vision when you realized that you may have been looking at the Vortex problem from the wrong angle. And now we're alone on an empty road in the middle of the night and you're having another waking dream. There's a pattern here, Rafe."

"What pattern? What the hell are you talking about?"

She drew a breath. "I think that your visions are being caused by your intuition. I think that you saw something on those other occasions and again tonight—something that didn't register on your conscious mind but which pinged your intuition. The result was a dream image."

The ice gates were halfway open now. The quicksilver lake was starting to spill out onto the road.

He could worry about his future in a para-psych ward some other time, he decided. Whatever else was going on, one thing was clear. Ella would be safer in town. Slade could protect her.

"Hang on to Lorelei," he said.

Ella sat back quickly, clutching the dust bunny.

He slammed the SUV into reverse, turned, braced one arm on the back of the seat, and stomped onto the accelerator.

The big vehicle reversed back down the narrow road.

"I saw a lane that intersects with this one," he said. "I'll turn around there."

But through the rear window he saw another set of icy gates looming, blocking his path. Evidently there was more than one way to enter Hell.

He braked hard, cut all the lights, and threw open the door.

"What?" Ella asked.

"Out. Now."

He did not give himself any more time to think about possibilities or invent explanations. He vaulted out of the car and raced around the rear of the vehicle. By the time he reached the passenger side, Ella was standing on the road. Lorelei was on her shoulder, sleeked out with all four eyes wide open. She was ready to rumble but she was still clutching her wedding veil.

"Where are we going?" Ella asked.

"Into the woods." He rezzed the penlight. "We've got fog and night on our side. Also, the psi-fence that surrounds the Preserve is not too far away. Feel the energy? If necessary, we'll go through the fence. That should make it impossible to track us."

"Someone is coming after us?"

"It's another ambush," Rafe said. "At least I think that's what my vision is trying to tell me."

"I thought it was very difficult to get through the psi-fence."

"It isn't a walk in the park, but Slade took me inside when I was here the first time. Strong talents like us can usually make it through if we run a little hot."

He led the way into the woods, using the energy of the fence as a beacon. The masses of ferns and other vegetation that comprised the undergrowth made it hard to move quickly. He judged they were still some distance away from the boundary of the Preserve when the rumble of heavy SUV engines reverberated through the night and fog.

"Two vehicles," he said, listening intently. He turned to look back over his shoulder. Headlights infused the mist. "They're blocking the road in each direction."

Ella glanced back. "Another ambush. You must have caught small indications of it while you were driving. Your intuition filled in the blanks with those visions of the gates of Hell. Like I told you back at the start, I'm guessing your talent is a form of lucid dreaming."

"Why couldn't I just have normal hallucinations like normal, ordinary psychos?"

"Because you're not a psycho. That is one high-end talent you're developing, Coppersmith. Now all you have to do is stop fighting it and learn to control it."

"Easy for you to say." He stopped abruptly and de-rezzed the light. "Hush."

Ella came to a halt and ceased talking.

Out on the road, brakes squealed and two heavy engines shut down. A sudden, unnatural silence descended on the nightscape. From where he was standing, he could just barely make out the foggy outline of the SUV that he and Ella had abandoned. It was pinned in the glare of head-lights, but the mist was so heavy it would take a few seconds before the ambush team realized their quarry was not inside.

"Coppersmith, we know you're there and we know you're armed. The last thing we want is a shootout. No one needs to get hurt. Look, you're in trouble. You're running a fever, aren't you? We can help."

Somewhere out on the paranormal spectrum, an eerie bell tolled, summoning Rafe into Hell. The implacable

music called to him. *Alien tech.* He braced himself against
the powerful energy.

Ella grabbed his hand and put it on her shoulder.

"I've got this," she whispered.

He sensed the heat of her talent in the atmosphere
around her. He kept his hand on her shoulder. The connection between them was stronger now than it had been
a couple of days ago. An intimate sexual bond had been
added to the vibe.

*"Come out with your hands up, Coppersmith. We don't
want to hurt the woman but we will if that's what it takes
to get your attention."*

It was the same speaker. Evidently he was in charge of
negotiations. So much for offering to fix my fever, Rafe
thought. The bastard had moved on to threatening Ella.
But, then, the crew was operating on strange turf and was
no doubt in a hurry.

The deep paranormal music of the bell rolled through
the fog but, thanks to Ella, Rafe heard it as if it came
from some distant dimension.

"It's not working," one of the men—not the negotiator—
shouted. "Shit, there's no one inside the damn car. They
took off before we got here."

The bell music ceased abruptly. The relief was nearly
overwhelming. Rafe grabbed a deep breath.

"Why would they abandon the car?" a third man asked.
"How could they know we were coming?"

"Later," the negotiator snarled. "Right now we need
to find Coppersmith."

"I've got them on the thermal sensor," the man announced. "They're over there, in the woods."

"Careful," the negotiator ordered. "Coppersmith is probably armed. Some sort of para-shock device, according to the boss. But it will take you down almost as fast as a mag-rez shot."

Rafe touched Ella's shoulder and put his mouth close to her ear. "Let's go."

"The Preserve?" she asked softly.

"That's our best bet. If we stay out here they'll be able to see us but we can't see them. Not a good scenario. They won't be able to track us inside and I may get a chance to grab one of them. This time I'll get some answers." He shoved the gun into the shoulder holster and gripped her hand. "Hold on. Crossing the fence line can get rocky."

The Alien bell tolled again, rolling through the fogbound night, echoing endlessly across the spectrum. The music tugged at his senses, but Ella kept the hypnotic pull in check.

They were both running hot when they plunged through the wall of dark, seething psi that guarded the Preserve.

The hallucinations materialized out of nowhere. Not visions infused with meaning like the kind he was reluctantly getting used to seeing, Rafe thought. This wasn't his intuition chatting with him. These were scenes from the mother of all horror movies. The dead walked and wailed, exhorting the living to turn around and go back the way they had come. Skeletons rattled their bones and whispered warnings of the terrors that lay ahead. Banshees shrieked in the night. Demons stalked the mist. The urge to flee was almost overwhelming. Almost.

But he had come this way once before with Slade. He knew the drill. Stay hot and focus on suppressing the visions.

The experience was different this time. When Slade had guided him into the Preserve, the visions had been seriously disorienting. The worst part was that he had not been able to tell the difference between the hallucinations created by the fence energy and those conjured by his fevered brain. It had required considerable effort to wade through the nightmares. This time, however, it was relatively easy to brush aside the psi-fence dream fragments.

"Okay, I can see why this fence is effective," Ella said.

Her hand tightened on his. Her voice was grim with the effort she was making to stay in control.

"Not much farther now," Rafe said. "The question is, will those bastards try to follow us?"

Lorelei chortled enthusiastically and fluffed up.

"Glad one of us is having a good time," Ella said.

Chapter 25

THEY BROKE THROUGH THE LAST OF THE PSI-GENERATED hallucinations a moment later. Rafe drew Ella to a halt and released her hand. She took a wary breath, mentally braced for more grim visions. But no ghosts or demons rose up out of the darkness.

"We're in," Rafe said. "We should be safe from those bastards but we need to find some cover and we need to stay close to the fence. This is dino hunting territory at night."

Ella looked around in wonder. The Preserve sang to her senses, just as the catacombs and Wonderland did. In spite of the close call on the road a short time ago, she was suddenly buzzed.

"This place is amazing," she said. "Like Wonderland but in a different way. Everything here is alive. And hot."

There was no need for a flashlight. It was midnight but

everywhere she looked the landscape was gently illuminated with psi. Each blade of grass emitted an eerie green light. Ferns glowed. The petals of flowers were iridescent. The forest was gently, darkly radiant.

The effect on her senses was exhilarating.

"The Aliens didn't succeed in destroying Rainshadow with their experiments, but the place is still a hot zone as a result of all the paranormal forces they were fooling around with here," Rafe said. "Come on, I see a waterfall. That'll work."

She looked across the meadow and saw radiant water spilling over a rocky outcropping and splashing heavily into a glowing pool of gem-dark water.

"Why are we interested in a waterfall at this particular moment?" she asked.

"There's power locked in water. Think about it. You can run an engine or flood a town with the force of water. It gives off a hell of a lot of natural energy, especially when it's crashing over a chunk of rock like that."

"Got it. The energy released in the waterfall will mask our psi-tracks."

"That's the plan. Even if those Vortex guys don't try to follow us, we've still got the critters to worry about."

"Does it occur to you that all we ever do when we go out is run from bad guys?"

"One of these days we'll do coffee. I swear it."

"Promises, promises."

The fierce music of the Alien bell shivered through the psi-laden atmosphere just as they reached the waterfall pool.

"The bastards did follow us," Rafe said. "They must be crazy."

"Or desperate. They seem to want you very, very badly."

"We're in luck, there's a cavern behind the waterfall. Hold tight. The rocks will be slippery."

He helped her up onto a wet, rocky ledge.

"Hold your breath," he said.

She obeyed. He drew her through the rushing waters. In an instant she was drenched. So was Lorelei, who evidently considered the waterfall trip grand entertainment. The water was warm and sparkling with energy.

Once they were on the other side, Lorelei gave herself a shake and chortled exuberantly.

Ella pushed her wet hair behind her ears and let the wild energy of the water flash across her senses.

"Okay," she said. "That was different. Maybe when we get home to Crystal City Lorelei and I will start hanging out at the local car wash on slow nights."

"Are you still cancelling out the bell vibe?" Rafe asked.

"No. That's the effect of the water that's distorting the wavelengths now, not me. Or maybe the bell just doesn't work as well inside the fence."

The forces in the muffled music were still strong but their summoning power had lessened considerably.

Rafe moved to the edge of the roaring water and looked out at the meadow.

"Looks like two of them made it through the fence," he said. "The guy with the bell and one member of the team. Perfect."

Ella frowned. "I beg your pardon?"

"Evens the odds. Two of us, two of them. Plus we've got Lorelei."

Hearing her name, Lorelei chortled agreement.

"You're going to try to grab one of them?" Ella asked, dismayed.

"That's the plan."

"Rafe, I hate to point this out but they've still got that damned bell."

"You take care of the bell," he said. "I'll deal with the two Vortex guys."

"How, exactly, do you propose that we take out two mobsters who are armed with Alien tech? Your fancy little knockout gun won't work in this environment."

"Distraction is the key in a situation like this."

She was about to ask several more questions when she heard the faint, eerie music. Not the summoning wavelengths of the bell this time—a gentle lullaby. Lorelei suddenly went still and sleeked out, all four eyes gazing intently through the waterfall as though she could see something on the other side.

"Damn," Rafe said. "Did you hear that?"

A shiver swept through Ella. "Yes."

"The bell. It drew one of the dinos."

"Maybe. Or maybe four humans running around inside the fence were enough to catch the attention of one of the critters."

"You know," Rafe said, sounding thoughtful. "This could be just the distraction I need."

Ella listened intently to the sweet harmony. The waterfall muffled some of the energy of the monster's music, just as it did the music of the bell, but the very fact that the lullaby was coming through so clearly was an indication of raw power.

"It's strong, Rafe. Whatever is coming this way is very big and very dangerous."

"Can you handle it?"

She raised her senses a little, feeling her way into the music. The process was complicated because of the water energy.

"I can probably deflect its attention from us if necessary. But it's not hunting us. I'm guessing it can't detect us because of the waterfall. We just got caught in the net that it's using to fish for the Vortex guys."

"I might be able to work with that."

She looked past Rafe's shoulder and saw two men at the far edge of the glowing meadow. They appeared to be entirely unaware of their plight. Both wore headphones. One held a familiar-looking, vase-shaped artifact in his hands.

"I don't think they know they're being hunted," she said. "Not yet at any rate."

"I'll bet the headphones are interfering. The dino is aware of them but they can't hear it."

"Either that or they simply don't recognize the music for what it is. They're going to be easy prey for the creature when it gets here. Rafe, we can't just stand by and let those two get eaten. I mean, they're bad guys, but the thought of watching two humans torn limb from limb by a monster—"

"Don't worry. I don't want to see them get eaten, either.

If that happens, I won't be able to get my answers from them."

She was about to ask him how he planned to save the pair but she was interrupted by a thundering roar. The rocks on which they were standing shuddered.

Lorelei hissed.

"It's here," Rafe said.

The great beast stalked into the radiant meadow. Ella caught her breath. The thing was twice as big as the one she had sent fleeing in Wonderland. The head was reptilian. The eyes glowed yellow. The wide mouth was filled with multiple rows of huge teeth. The creature moved on four of its six legs. The two front limbs were armlike appendages tipped with claws that were probably used to rip apart the belly of its prey.

The creature seemed to lumber forward but it crossed the meadow with unnerving speed. Its silvery scales sparked in the ambient psi-light, but in the lush, green environment of the Preserve they did not provide the camouflage that they did in Wonderland. Engineered for a very different ecosystem, the beast was plainly visible in the night light.

Not that it needed to hide, Ella thought. This was a top-of-the-line predator.

The monster's hunting cry must have finally pierced the headphones. The Vortex men ripped off the gear and whirled to confront the dinosaur. The one holding the bell dropped it and instinctively yanked out his mag-rez.

"No," the second one pleaded. "You're crazy. Run for it."

But the warning came too late or, perhaps in his panic,

the first man simply didn't hear it. He rezzed the pistol, which promptly exploded in a small fireball.

The shooter screamed. The burning weapon fell to the ground.

The second man tried to flee in the direction of the psi-fence but he froze. The first man went abruptly motionless, too. Ella knew that the creature's music had transfixed them. They could see their doom bearing down on them but they were helpless to run.

"Are you sure you can handle this thing?" Rafe asked. "Because if you're not, we're staying here, behind the waterfall."

"Those two men—"

"Shouldn't have followed us."

She listened to the monster's music. It was no longer a soft, sweet psychic lullaby. The wavelengths of a violent hunting song crashed and roared in the night, rolling across the spectrum, audible to both the normal and the paranormal senses. It was the dark music of a primal hunger; a deep, unending, desperate hunger that could only be satisfied with blood.

But it was still music, Ella thought. And she was a Siren.

"I can handle the dinosaur," she said.

She moved around Rafe and emerged at the edge of the waterfall. Bracing one hand on the wet rock wall to steady herself, she raised her talent.

Lorelei dug in her little claws and growled softly. She clearly did not approve of taking on a dinosaur but she was sticking with her partner.

Rafe gripped Ella's arm, ready to pull her back to the relative safety of the waterfall if necessary.

Ella focused on the hellish wavelengths of the killing music and began to sing.

She wove her harmonies into the thundering waves, seeking to disturb and destabilize the powerful, primitive forces generated by the monster.

Her goal was to send it fleeing in confusion when it lost its connection to its prey. She was working on the theory that disrupting the vibe would bewilder the predator. It was a theory that had worked well in Wonderland.

But this wasn't Wonderland; this was a different environment, and the creature she was trying to repel was not only more powerful physically than the first one she had encountered; its paranormal hunting senses were stronger, as well.

For a moment it seemed that it would succumb to the confusing feedback it was receiving. It stopped and lashed its spiked tale from side to side in what looked like the dinosaur equivalent of frustration and rage.

Ella increased the power of her song, sending the distorting energy in a relentless tide. The monster roared its fury and then went still. For an instant it looked like it would turn away and go in search of other prey.

Instead, it seemed to get a new, if uncertain, fix on the Vortex agents. It started to advance again, more tentatively this time. It lowered its massive head, its yellow eyes brightening with a merciless fire.

"I think it has a visual on its quarry," Rafe said. "It's

using eyesight to override whatever its paranormal senses are telling it."

"It's still generating enough energy to keep those two men pinned down." Ella pushed her talent higher. "I need to go for what Mom calls the money notes."

"Money notes?"

"Never mind. The thing is—just so you know—I've never done this before."

"Meaning?"

"You might need a Plan B."

"You're my Plan B. Sing."

She sang, going farther out on the spectrum, weaving the music of the dark and the light into chilling, spectral harmonies. She hurled the terrible waves at the monster.

She sensed she was reaching her own limits. Like a runner pushing her body to the edge, she was burning psi at an enormous rate. She was strong but she was dealing with a creature that had evolved an ability to trap its prey in a paranormal web fashioned of strands of music.

The world around her began to waver. She was getting light-headed. She could not hold out much longer.

Lorelei huddled close and muttered encouragingly into her ear. Rafe's hand tightened on her arm. She was not alone, she thought. She could do this.

It seemed to her that she was suddenly drawing energy from Rafe and Lorelei and the forces of the paranormal landscape around her. The crashing, churning water, the mysterious darkness of the pool, even the forces of the night-bound atmosphere rushed through her. She created music of shattering power.

She sensed the exact instant when the creature's life-force began to fail. It came to a shambling halt, swaying on its great clawed feet. It lifted its massive head to the night sky and howled, a strangely mournful cry that carried the irreversible wavelengths of death.

Uncomprehending of what was happening, it sank slowly to the ground and toppled onto its side. The rocks beneath Ella's feet trembled again.

The energy in the monster's strange eyes dimmed. Dark blood ran from its gaping mouth. The link between Ella and the monster snapped.

The shock washed over her in a heavy tide. She would have crumpled to her knees if Rafe hadn't steadied her. Lorelei mumbled anxiously in her ear.

"Are you all right?" Rafe asked.

"Yes." Her voice was so thin it almost disappeared. "I'm okay. Just a little tired." Sleep pulled at her senses. She could barely keep her eyes open. "Those two men—"

"Unconscious. With luck I'll be able to drag them both back through the fence before something else arrives to eat them. But first I need to get you out of here."

He picked her up in his arms. Lorelei transferred adroitly to his shoulder and fluffed up.

"Told you, I'm okay," Ella mumbled. "I can walk. Just need to nap a bit first."

"You need rest, all right," Rafe agreed. "But not here."

She tried to call up a little psi to push back against the lethargy that threatened to overwhelm her, but she had nothing left. Rafe's arms were warm and tight around her.

When he carried her past the body of the dead creature,

a tide of grief swept through her. Sensing her sadness, Lorelei hunkered close and made comforting noises.

"That poor beast," Ella whispered. "It was never intended for this time and place. They had no right to do that to a helpless animal."

"Who had no right?" Rafe asked.

"The Aliens."

"It's just a dinosaur, Ella."

"They're dying, Rafe," she whispered. "All of them, I think. I can hear it in their music."

"Maybe they were bioengineered to die off if things did not work out as the Aliens planned."

"They had no right to run their experiments on helpless animals."

She did not realize that she was crying until she discovered that the front of Rafe's shirt was damp with her tears.

HE HAD PLANNED TO TAKE ELLA THROUGH THE PSI-FENCE and leave her in a safe place some distance from where the ambush had taken place. He assumed the other two Vortex men would be waiting for their companions.

But when he emerged from the Preserve with Ella in his arms, he discovered that one of the vehicles was gone.

"The other two probably figured we all got eaten," he said to Lorelei.

With some effort and a bit of awkward maneuvering, he managed to get Ella curled up on the rear seat of the SUV. When he was satisfied that she was reasonably comfortable, he opened the door on the driver's side and angled himself behind the wheel. With one foot braced on the ground and his gun in his hand, he took out his phone.

Slade answered on the first ring.

"I could use a little help," Rafe said.

Chapter 26

SLADE ENDED THE CALL, CLIPPED THE PHONE TO HIS belt, and looked at Rafe. "My officers found the missing vehicle that was used in the ambush. It was abandoned near the marina. Looks like the fools stole a boat."

"Idiots." Rafe shook his head. "They don't know the currents around Rainshadow."

"Even experienced fishermen who have lived on the island all their lives try to avoid taking a boat out at night. I doubt the two we're looking for will get far. Probably wind up on the rocks. The bodies might wash ashore in the next day or so."

"We'll get some answers from the two we pulled out of the Preserve tonight," Rafe said.

"Maybe. But their ID looks solid."

"Bail bond agents working for a Crystal City bond outfit?" Rafe shook his head in disgust. "Give me a break.

What are they going to say? That I was a case of mistaken identity? They were after someone else?"

"Why not? It's as good a story as any other."

"Not a lot of bounty hunters are armed with Alien tech," Rafe said.

They were in Slade's office. It was nearly two o'clock in the morning. Ella was fast asleep, curled up on a bench in the outer office. One of Slade's officers, a woman named Myrna Reed, was keeping an eye on her.

The unconscious men were locked up in one of the police station's two small cells. The bell weapon and the headphones that the agents had worn earlier were currently sitting on Slade's desk.

Rafe knew that taking the chief's job on Rainshadow had not been anywhere on Slade's agenda back in the days when he had been with the Bureau. The world of a small-town police chief held little appeal for a man who was used to chasing serious bad guys in the Underworld. But things had happened and Slade had been forced to reinvent his life. The surprise was that he looked thoroughly at home here in his new office.

"Any idea why Vortex wants you so badly?" Slade asked. "Assuming whoever is behind this really is Vortex?"

"Not entirely sure yet." Rafe looked at the gray stone in his ring. "But Ella thinks it's connected to what happened to me three months ago. I'm strongly inclined to agree with her."

"You're saying it goes back to when you got psi-burned."

"I think so, yes."

Slade leaned back in his chair and went quiet for a time.

"We need some help with this one," Rafe said finally. "Okay if I call Joe Harding? This case started in Crystal City and it involves Alien tech. Joe has resources that aren't available to either of us."

Slade thought about it. "You're right. Call Harding."

There was a little more silence.

"I got burned once," Slade said eventually.

"I heard about that." Rafe paused. "Obviously you survived."

"There was a time when I wasn't sure I would. That was followed by an even worse time when I figured that I would survive but without my talent."

Rafe hesitated, not sure if he wanted to push the subject. "Did anything change afterward?"

"Oh, yeah."

"I mean, besides getting this cushy job here on Rainshadow."

"Besides that."

"Got to say you look fairly normal," Rafe ventured.

Slade's mouth kicked up at the corner. "Appearances can be deceiving."

"You're married, holding down a job, and expecting a baby. That's pretty much the working definition of normal."

"Yep, life is good. But between you and me, my talent changed after the burn."

"I suppose it would be amazing if it hadn't been affected in some way." Rafe felt as if he were walking on eggshells. Conversations like this were complicated.

"Thought I was going crazy for a while. That's a common side effect of a burn, I'm told."

"I've heard that."

"Figured I'd lose my talent entirely," Slade said. "But in the end that's not what happened."

"What did happen, if you don't mind my asking?"

"The burn changed my talent. It didn't obliterate it."

"Huh. Ella says she thinks something like that may be happening to me."

"My advice? Pay attention to Ella."

"That's pretty much what I did tonight," Rafe said.

"And you're both still alive. That would seem to indicate Ella's right."

"Good point."

Slade looked at the bell and the headphones. "You'll probably want to lock those up in that fancy tech vault you've got at the jobsite. I sure as hell don't have any safe place to store artifacts."

"I've been thinking about that damn bell and those headphones," Rafe said.

"What about them?"

"The headphones are human engineering. Whoever made one set could have made several sets—assuming he had the right equipment and a good lab."

"So?"

"The bell, on the other hand, is definitely Alien tech and very exotic tech, at that."

"No question about it," Slade said. "Hard to miss the Alien vibe and the power in the thing."

"A unique item. Yet it looks identical to the bell weapon that Vortex used on Ella and me in Crystal City. I find it hard to believe that Vortex just happened to have two such weapons. Alien devices that can be rezzed by humans are damned rare to start with. Something as sophisticated as that bell must be even harder to come by."

"Where are you going with this?" Slade asked.

"It's conceivable, just barely, that Vortex discovered a stash of identical bell weapons, but it occurs to me that there is another possibility."

"Which is?"

"They stole it."

"From?"

"The Coppersmith vault out at the jobsite. Pretty sure this is the same bell and the same two sets of headphones that I brought back from Crystal City."

Slade whistled softly. "If that stuff came out of your vault, it would seem to indicate that those four Vortex guys had a little inside help."

"Yes," Rafe said. "That is exactly what it indicates." He pushed himself up out of his chair. "Only one way to find out."

Chapter 27

HALF AN HOUR LATER, RAFE STOOD IN THE DOORWAY OF the tech vault. Arthur Gill, Slade, and two of Slade's officers were grouped around him. The lab techs had all been awakened and now formed a circle behind them. There was a very anxious vibe in the small crowd.

Everyone looked at the empty glass-and-steel lockbox on the shelf.

A murmur of shock and disbelief went through the assembled staff.

"You're right, Mr. Coppersmith." Dr. Hayashi shook his head. "The items are gone." He glanced at the bell and the headphones that Rafe held. "I swear, all of those artifacts were in that box yesterday afternoon when we ran the daily inventory check."

"I can vouch for that," Susan Bowen said very firmly.

"I believe you both," Rafe said. "Obviously someone

removed the artifacts after the last inventory check—
someone with access to the lab and the vault."

Gill nodded, his dour face sinking deeper into gloom.
"So, we're talking about an inside job."

"Looks like it," Rafe said. "Chief Attridge has requested
permission to conduct a search of the lab and the lockers of
all personnel who have entered the facility within the past
forty-eight hours."

Gill looked first surprised and then offended.

"No offense to the chief," he said, "but when it comes
to Coppersmith property, we usually handle our own problems."

"The search I want to conduct is in connection with
the murder of the DND operative who was shot to death
at the lake," Slade said.

"That puts it into Chief Attridge's jurisdiction," Rafe
said. "He's asking politely, but to be clear, he doesn't
have to ask at all. This is his island."

Susan Bowen glanced at the relics in Rafe's hands.
"You really think that young man's death is linked to those
artifacts?"

It was Slade who responded. "We don't know yet," he
said. "I can get a warrant from a judge in Thursday Harbor if you insist on going through the formalities."

"No, that won't be necessary," Gill said. "If Mr. Coppersmith authorizes the search, I'm okay with it."

THE Y FOUND THE MAG-REZ GUN LESS THAN TWENTY
minutes later when they opened one of the personnel lockers.

"Damn," Gill said quietly. "You're thinking that's the weapon that was used to kill Maitland, aren't you?"

"Can't say for sure yet," Slade said. "But it shouldn't be too difficult to find out."

Rafe looked at Angela Price. "It's your locker, Angela," he said gently. "Got anything to say to us?"

Angela stared at the weapon. Tears trickled down her cheeks.

Chapter 28

❧

EXUBERANT CHORTLING BROUGHT ELLA OUT OF A DREAM of wistful, faded music that echoed from an ancient past. It was the music of another species but it was, nevertheless, music. Her senses responded to it.

More chortling ensued. She opened her eyes. Lorelei was on the pillow. She was covered in powdered sugar. So was the pillowcase.

Ella groaned and pushed herself up to a sitting position. She was relieved to see that she was back in her room at the lodge. Everything appeared surprisingly normal, but when she looked down she noticed that she was wearing the cheap nightgown she had picked up in Thursday Harbor. She was pretty sure she hadn't undressed herself. Her last clear memory was of being carried out of the Preserve in Rafe's arms.

She looked at Lorelei. "I take it you didn't get the memo about eating doughnuts in bed."

Lorelei gave a small shake. Powdered sugar went flying. A light dusting of the stuff hit Ella in the face. She sneezed.

There was a perfunctory knock on the door. It opened before Ella could respond. Rafe walked into the room. He had a small white paper sack in one hand and a large cup of coffee in the other.

Lorelei chortled at the sight of the paper sack.

Ella yelped and grabbed the covers, instinctively pulling the sheet up to her throat.

"Sorry," Rafe said. "Didn't mean to startle you." He put the coffee and the paper sack on the table beside the bed. He took another look at Ella, frowning a little. "Did someone already bring you some fresh doughnuts?"

"All I got was some leftover powdered sugar. No doughnut was involved."

Rafe sat down on the side of the bed, leaned over, and swiped his finger lightly across her cheek. He smiled at the sight of the white smudge. Then he surveyed her with an assessing eye.

"You look good," he said. "Almost normal. How are you feeling?"

Ella managed to recover from the initial shock of having a man walk casually into her bedroom. But now she was not certain how to react. Okay, so she and Rafe had slept together one time. In her opinion that did not give a man the right to amble in and out of her bedroom without an invitation. On the other hand, the two of them had barely survived a number of near-disastrous incidents together. That sort of thing had a bonding effect.

She decided to punt. She picked up the cup, peeled off the lid, and inhaled appreciatively.

"Thanks for the coffee," she said. "Just what I need." She took a cautious sip.

"You need to eat a doughnut, too." Rafe opened the sack, removed one, and handed it to her. "Carbs and caffeine—two of the basic food groups. Sorry, I had to go with chocolate icing. The kitchen was out of powdered sugar."

"Chocolate works." She took a bite and paused in mid-munch. She looked at Lorelei. "Should I ask why there were no powdered-sugar doughnuts left this morning?"

"Bob, the cook, says they all disappeared shortly after he set them out on a rack to cool. Turned his back for just a few minutes, he said. When he came back to get the doughnuts, the tray was empty."

"Lorelei couldn't possibly have eaten an entire tray of doughnuts."

Rafe looked at Lorelei. "There is some suspicion that she may have been the ringleader of a gang of doughnut thieves."

Lorelei, aware that she was the center of attention, bounced a little and blinked her blues a couple of times.

"Nonsense." Ella popped the last of the doughnut into her mouth. "I'm sure Lorelei is innocent. More likely some hungry employees got to the doughnuts."

"Feel free to entertain that theory, but I'll warn you it is not the one that Bob and his staff are going with."

"Forget the doughnuts," Ella said. "Tell me what happened after I passed out last night."

"I hauled you out of the Preserve. One of the Vortex vehicles was gone. Slade and I think the two guys who were left on the road heard the roaring of the dinosaur inside the Preserve and figured their pals had come to an unfortunate end. Looks like they stole a boat from the marina."

"But everyone says that navigation is extremely tricky around the island, especially after dark."

"True. Slade doesn't think they'll make it. But meanwhile, I made the stunning deduction that there probably weren't two identical Alien bells floating around. Turned out I was right. The bell relic that those Vortex operatives used on us came from the Coppersmith vault here on the island."

Ella exhaled slowly, thinking. "So, they had inside help to get the relics and the earphones."

"Yeah. But here's where it gets even more interesting. Slade conducted a search this morning. He found a magrez in Angela Price's locker. He's going to have some tests run but he's pretty sure it's the same gun that was used to kill the DND guy, Kenneth Maitland."

"Angela shot him? Good heavens, why?"

"Motive is still unclear and Angela is denying everything. But she's now sitting in the Shadow Bay jail along with the two Vortex guys."

"What are the Vortex agents saying?" Ella asked.

"They woke up this morning but they're pretty traumatized from the confrontation with the dinosaur. Their memories of the experience in the Preserve are . . . disturbed, to put it mildly. All they know is that a beast was closing in on them when it suddenly collapsed and died. Two interesting things, though. The first is that both men have the Vortex tats."

"No surprise there."

"No, but this bunch was carrying ID—probably fake, but interesting nevertheless. They claim to be bail bond agents."

"Bounty hunters?" Ella stared at him. "Are you joking?"

"Nope. Their ID says they work for a company called Crystal City Bail Bonds. Slade called the number and got hold of a guy who claims to be their boss. He says it's all a horrible case of mistaken identity. He sent them out after some guy named Copperfield, not Coppersmith."

"That's ridiculous."

"Slade and I agree with you. Slade pointed out that this is clearly an FBPI case. He has a point. He contacted Joe Harding."

Ella wrinkled her nose. "I hate to think of Harding getting the credit for closing another big case, but I suppose there's no one else to call."

"No, this is way too big for Coppersmith Security or Arcane or the Guild. We're talking some serious Alien tech and a very well-organized criminal mob."

"Okay, okay. So we turn it over to the Bureau." Ella took a breath. "About last night—"

Rafe winced. "Really? You want to go there again?"

"I'm serious. Something weird occurred. I may have been the one doing the singing but I think I had a little help from the chorus."

"You mean Lorelei? Well, she does seem to have bonded with you. It's not beyond the realm of possibility that she was able to give you a little boost."

"Not just Lorelei." Ella wrapped her arms around her knees. "I felt you there, as well."

"I was there."

"I mean, I felt like I was using some of your talent to tap in to the energy inside the Preserve."

Rafe shrugged. "Maybe that's exactly what happened. Rainshadow is a paranormal nexus. There's a lot of power in the vicinity. Strong tides, underwater volcanos, geothermal activity—not to mention the forces unleashed centuries ago by the Aliens when they started experimenting with the local flora and fauna."

"Yes, I know, but I've never heard of anyone being able to channel that kind of raw power."

"There's a lot we don't know about para-physics. I'm guessing that most people wouldn't be strong enough to handle that sort of energy. But you're not most people."

She looked at him and then she contemplated the gray quartz ring on his hand. "If that's what happened—if I really did pull nexus power last night—I didn't do it alone."

"I'm good with being your backup singer. I think Lorelei is okay with that job, too."

"I vote we don't tell anyone exactly what we believe happened last night."

Rafe smiled slowly. "It'll be a secret among the three of us. Right, Lorelei?"

Lorelei, perched at the foot of the bed, chortled enthusiastically, and waved her veil.

"Yep, Lorelei's on board with the secret thing," Rafe said. He paused. "I've been thinking about what you said last night when I carried you out of the Preserve. You told me that you could hear something in the dino's music that made you think it would have died soon and that maybe the others will, too."

"Yes. It's hard to explain and I can't be positive that I interpreted the music correctly, but it was similar to the energy I picked up when I chased off that dinosaur in Wonderland. My intuition tells me that what I heard were the first wavelengths that indicate the onset of death." She shuddered. "It was as if I were hearing the music of a dying species, not just one particular individual. Something is seriously wrong with the dino DNA."

"Like I said last night, maybe the Aliens engineered their experiments to self-destruct just in case they got loose from Wonderland."

"Maybe."

"If that's true, it will definitely simplify exploration of Wonderland," Rafe said.

"And once again we humans hang on to our place at the top of the food chain."

"Second place on the food chain is not a good place to be," Rafe said. He looked at the paper sack on the bedside table. "Speaking of food, do you want the last doughnut?"

"No, thanks," Ella said. "What I really want now is a

shower and then a more protein-based breakfast. Would you please hand me my robe?"

Rafe got up, took the robe down off the wall hook, and handed it to Ella.

"Turn around," Ella ordered.

Obediently, he gave her his back.

She got out of bed and pulled the robe around herself. "Who undressed me last night?"

"Who do you think undressed you?"

"It was you, wasn't it?"

"Figured you'd rather have me do it than some stranger. After all, you and I bonded with all that dino singing, remember?"

"Never mind."

She hurried into the bathroom.

She had just turned on the shower and was waiting for the water to warm to a suitable temperature when she heard Rafe's voice rising in outrage in the other room.

"Hey, what the hell happened to the last doughnut?"

Ella was pretty sure she heard a muffled chortle. It sounded like it came from under the bed.

Chapter 29

SOMETIME LATER SHE TURNED OFF THE WATER AND TOW-
eled herelf dry. She got out of the shower, pulled on the
robe, and stood quietly for a moment, listening. There
were no sounds from the outer room. Rafe had probably
gone back downstairs. She did not know whether to feel
relieved or disappointed.

Feel relieved. The job had ended. Soon she would be
going home. Alone.

She wiped steam off the mirror and rezzed the hair
dryer she found in a drawer under the sink.

A soft knock startled her so badly that she nearly
dropped the dryer.

"Want your clothes?" Rafe called through the paneling.

She opened the door an inch or two and peered at him
through the narrow opening.

"You're still here?" she asked.

"I'm assuming that is a rhetorical question, given that I'm standing here in front of you."

She flushed. "I just assumed that you had gone back downstairs while I was in the shower."

"Is that what you want me to do? Go downstairs?"

Flustered, she tried to get her act together. "It doesn't matter. I mean, you're here now, aren't you? And I suppose everyone on the jobsite knows it."

He folded his arms and propped one shoulder against the doorjamb. "You suppose correctly. Got a problem with that?"

"Well, no, I guess not. What's done is done. Everyone knows—"

"Maybe it's time we had a conversation about the status of our relationship."

She drew a steadying breath. "In my experience, it's usually better not to have that conversation."

"Why is that?"

She raised her chin. "You know the answer. I thought I'd made it clear. Women like me do not have long-term relationships."

"Says who?"

"Family tradition and the Arcane files."

"Who did the research into the Arcane files?" Rafe asked.

"What do you mean?" she asked, feeling quite cross now.

"Just wondering if your so-called research was a do-it-yourself job or if you used one of the Society's genealogical specialists."

"I did it myself, of course. I couldn't risk asking for

professional assistance. The specialist would have wondered why I was so interested in the subject."

"Know what I think?" Rafe said.

"No, and something—call it a hunch—tells me this probably isn't a good time for you to give me your opinion on the subject."

He ignored that. "I think that you've managed to scare the living daylights out of yourself a few times when you were forced to use your talent in self-defense. You burned that killer groom so badly that he will spend the rest of his life in a locked ward at a para-psych hospital. You took down Vickary when he threatened to kill you. A few months ago your ex-boss pimped you out to a creep who tried to rape you. Once again you were forced to defend yourself, and in the process, you burned another jerk and put him into a coma for a while. Then, last night, you sang to death a creature that should have gone extinct eons ago and you found out just how strong you really are."

Tears blurred her eyes. "Every time I sing at the top of my talent, something or someone gets hurt or dies."

"Ghost shit. Every time you sing with the full power of your talent, people survive—not just you, but other potential victims. Who knows how many other women that client raped before you took him down? Who knows how many women you saved when you torched that serial wife-killer?"

"I know. And I'm not sorry about those two, really. It's just that sometimes I wonder if I really am one of the monsters, a for-real Siren. Born to destroy."

The tears were running down her face now. She knew

full well that she did not look attractive when she cried. She tightened her hands into fists.

"You weren't born to destroy people," Rafe said.

"Then why do I end up hurting people and . . . and helpless monsters?"

He smiled a little at the *helpless monsters*.

"There is always a dark side to any talent," he said gently. "You know that. A paranormal ability that is strong enough to heal is strong enough to kill. Power is power. It all comes down to how it's used."

"What good is a talent like mine?"

Rafe pushed the door all the way open and drew her against his chest. "You were born to do exactly what you're doing at the Knightsbridge Dream Institute. You were born to save people from their own nightmares. You were born to heal."

She sniffed a few times and then she was sobbing into his shirt. Again. The crying thing, she reflected, had become a very bad habit.

After a while the tears stopped. She was surprised to discover that she suddenly felt much better. She was calm and back in control. Reluctantly, she raised her head and stepped back. Rafe released her. She grabbed a tissue from the dispenser and blotted her eyes.

"That's the nicest thing anyone has ever said to me," she mumbled.

He caught her chin on the edge of his hand. "It's the truth. What's more, I'm living proof. Whatever you did when you sang to me on that road trip out of Crystal City changed everything for me."

"It was just a little tweak, really. Nothing major."

"It sure as hell felt major." He brushed his mouth against hers. When he raised his head there was a lot of heat in his eyes. "What's more, I'm damn sure that whatever we've got going between us is major, too."

She managed a weak smile. "Is that an expert opinion or a DIY conclusion?"

"When it comes to some things, I'm strictly a DIY guy."

The energy was rising in the atmosphere between them. She did not even try to resist. Their future might be blurry, but she was very sure of one thing—she did not want to look back with regret. Rafe was right; whatever was going on between them, it was major.

"There's a lot to be said for the DIY approach to certain matters," she whispered.

She wound her arms around his neck. He groaned. His mouth came down on hers.

The hunger in his kiss thrilled her senses. He wanted her and she wanted him. That was all that mattered for now.

Chapter 30

HER HEATED RESPONSE SHATTERED ALL HIS GOOD INTEN-
tions. When he knocked on the door of the bathroom a
few minutes ago and saw her bundled up in the bathrobe,
steam swirling around her, he had reminded himself that
she had been through a traumatic experience.

He needed to take it slowly, he thought. He needed to
give her some time to recover from the harrowing events
of the past few days. He needed to be understanding. He
needed to be gentle.

But his own need to answer the Siren's call set fire to
his senses.

She opened her mouth for him and tightened her arms
around his neck. He reached down and untied the sash of
the robe. The garment fell open and her warm, soft body
was his to explore.

Her scent was intoxicating and her sleek, feline curves

were irresistible. He drew his hands slowly down over her breasts. The feel of her firm nipples on his palms sent another wave of shuddering excitement through him.

"You are so perfect," he said against her throat. "You must have been made for me."

"Rafe." She framed his face between her palms and looked into his eyes. "This is such a gift—being together like this. I want you to know that it means a lot to me."

"Sex?" He grinned. "Hey, anytime. Seriously. Just ask."

"No, not sex. Well, yes, this kind of sex. I've never had sex like this."

"You think this is kinky? Honey, I've got news for you. What we've been doing is all plain vanilla. We haven't even started with the kinky stuff. But we've got time—"

She gripped the lapels of his shirt. "This may be plain vanilla to you, but it's not to me. Plain vanilla to me is sex without the big finish. I've never been able to let go and fly the way I did the first time with you the other night. It's . . . a little terrifying, to be honest."

"Let me get this straight—you're afraid of yourself, right? Not me."

"No, not you. Never you. I'm trying to explain something here. I've always held back. There has always been something missing."

"Me. I'm what's been missing. But I'm here now."

He peeled the robe off her shoulders and let it fall away. Then he sank to his knees on the bathroom rug and gently eased her legs apart. She was wet, and not just from the shower.

He stroked her until she was moaning and then he used

his tongue on her. She tasted of wild seas and hot rain. Her fingers clenched on his shoulders and she trembled at his touch.

He could not wait any longer. He got to his feet and caught her around the waist. He hoisted her up off the floor so that she dangled, helpless and hungry above him. She wrapped her bare legs around his hips.

He abandoned himself to the raw energy of the moment because this was the woman who knew his secrets and didn't care about them. She wasn't afraid of the psi-fever because her own talent was wild and powerful.

He braced her against the bathroom wall while he unbuckled his belt and unzipped his pants. He thrust into her tight body, trying to go slowly at first so that he could savor the hot pleasure of the physical joining.

But the heat in the atmosphere flashed from the normal into the paranormal and she was suddenly clenched around him, hanging on as though she would never let go. Their clashing auras began to resonate in an intimate harmony.

"Rafe."

She convulsed, her release spilling through her in waves that pulled him over the edge. His climax hit hard and deep and seemed to go on endlessly.

Somewhere out on the paranormal spectrum he heard his Siren singing.

Chapter 31

SLADE PUT DOWN THE PHONE WHEN RAFE AND ELLA walked into his office. "I was just going to call you. That was one of my officers. The boat the Vortex guys took last night went on the rocks a short distance outside the harbor. No surprise. They found the bodies on the beach in a small cove. Same ID as the two sitting in my jail. Bounty hunters employed by Crystal City Bail Bonds."

Rafe suppressed his irritation. "Well, that's pretty much what we expected. When can we talk to the two you picked up last night?"

"Now," Slade said. "But we need to talk fast."

"Why the need for speed?" Ella asked.

"Because I called Joe Harding to fill him in on what happened last night," Slade said. "We both concluded that this Crystal City Bail Bonds outfit is a cover for a criminal organization running serious Alien tech. Between that and the kidnapping attempt, it's clear this is an FBPI case. Let's just say that Joe got all excited."

"Probably can't wait to stand in front of the cameras again to announce the takedown of a violent criminal gang," Ella said. "That guy is such a glory-hound."

Rafe and Slade looked at her. Slade raised his eyebrows.

"She's not a fan of Hard Joe," Rafe explained.

"I see," Slade said. "It just so happens that Joe Harding has an excellent track record when it comes to handling cases like this."

Ella folded her arms. "I'm sure that's only because he has the sense to employ high-end consultants like Rafe."

Slade chuckled. "Knowing who to hire is pretty much what defines a good manager."

"I suppose." Ella did not look convinced.

"Moving right along," Rafe said. "What did Joe say when you told him about what happened last night?"

"What do you think he said?" Slade tossed a pen down onto the desktop. "He wants to interrogate our two guests as soon as possible. He's sending an FBPI charter plane to Thursday Harbor to pick them up this afternoon. I told him I would have the perps on the one o'clock ferry. I'll escort them, personally, and take a couple of my officers along for backup. I want to make sure the handoff goes smoothly."

Rafe glanced at his watch. "Then we talk to them before we chat with Angela Price."

"Right."

Chapter 32

❦

THE INTERROGATION TOOK PLACE IN THE LUNCHROOM of the small Shadow Bay police station. It did not prove fruitful. When it was over Rafe looked at his notes.

"They're sticking with the bail bond agent story and they've got the ID to prove it," he said.

"They expect you to believe that they mistook you for a criminal defendant who skipped bail?" Ella demanded, outraged.

"Don't know if they expect us to believe it or not," Slade said. "But that's their story. I could push them harder but, frankly, the FBPI is much better equipped to handle serious interrogations like this. We're dealing with what may be a widespread and deeply embedded criminal organization. My department doesn't even have a for-real forensics lab."

"I get it," Ella said. "But I don't have to watch Harding take credit on the evening news when he closes the case."

"No," Slade agreed. "You don't have to watch him take the credit."

"Speaking personally," Rafe said, "I won't mind watching him take the credit. Not if he manages to expose Vortex."

Chapter 33

✦

"I DIDN'T KILL KEN." ANGELA HUDDLED IN HER CHAIR
and gave Rafe a pleading look. "I swear I didn't. And I
don't own a gun. Someone put that mag-rez in my locker.
You have to believe me."

"Take me through it again," Rafe said.

Angela was wearing the clothes in which she had been
arrested. It was clear that she had slept in them. She looked
utterly miserable. Her face was blotchy from crying and
her shoulders sagged. The vibe in the atmosphere around
her was laced with fear. She was up against the power of
the Coppersmith empire and she assumed that her situation was hopeless.

They were not alone in the lunchroom. Slade stood in
the shadows near the door, allowing Rafe to take the
lead. Ella was there as well. She sat quietly in a wooden
chair, a small suitcase at her feet.

Angela released another weary sigh. "I told you, I knew Ken. We were both members of the Resonance City chapter of DND, and, yes, we had a relationship. But I swear I didn't even know he was on the island until he texted me the other night. He said he was here and had to talk to me. We agreed to meet at the boathouse on the lake."

"Go on," Rafe said.

"I went down to the lake to meet him. He said he was leaving the DND movement. He said it was a hopeless cause and that Mr. Radburn was a con. He said he was getting out and he wanted me to go with him. He planned to finance our future by selling you some information. He wanted me to take a message to you. I refused. Called him a traitor. And then I walked away. I had only taken a few steps when I heard the shots behind me. I was terrified. I ran. There was someone else there that night."

"But how did that person know that Maitland planned to meet with you at the boathouse?" Rafe asked.

"I don't know. Look, I admit I was angry with Ken, but I didn't kill him."

Rafe leaned back in his chair. "Are you absolutely certain Maitland didn't tell you anything more about the information he intended to try to sell to me?"

"Positive. All he told me was that it was bigger than DND. He said it was very specific intel and that you'd pay a fortune for it."

"You claim there was someone else at the boathouse that night," Rafe said. "Did he and Ken speak? Did you hear voices? Footsteps?"

Angela shook her head. "No, nothing until after the shots. Then I heard the running footsteps."

Slade spoke up for the first time. "Do you think that it was a man or a woman running away?"

Angela blinked, as though she had not considered the question. "The footsteps were solid. Strong. I suppose it could have been a woman but at the time I remember thinking that it sounded like a man running away."

Rafe sat in silence for a while. Ella and Slade took their cues from him. Neither of them spoke. Angela cried quietly.

After a while, Rafe got up from his chair and turned as though to leave the room. But he paused and looked back at Angela as if something had just occurred to him.

"Does the name Vortex mean anything to you?" he asked.

Angela sniffed and reached for another tissue. "No. Why?"

"Never mind," Rafe said.

"What's going to happen to me?" Angela said into the tissue.

"You're going to stay here for a while," Rafe said.

Ella got to her feet and picked up the suitcase. "I packed up some of your things," she said. "I thought you might want a change of clothes and a few personal items. The chief said it was okay to give them to you."

Angela stared at the suitcase and then looked at Ella with numb gratitude. "Thanks."

Slade opened the door. "Myrna, please escort Miss Price back to her cell."

Myrna Reed, a fit, competent-looking, middle-aged

blonde in an officer's uniform, appeared in the doorway. "This way, Miss Price."

Angela got to her feet. Myrna grasped her arm. They left the room.

Ella waited until they were out of earshot.

"I don't think Angela killed Kenneth Maitland," she said. "Why would she be dumb enough to stash the weapon in her locker? She should have tossed it into the lake."

Rafe and Slade both looked at her.

"She might have planned to use it again," Slade said patiently. "It's not like mag-rezes are that easy to come by here on Rainshadow."

"Okay, there's that," Ella said. "But I still don't think she did it. Her aura is very disturbed right now but mostly from fear. She's terrified."

"She's got reason to be scared," Rafe said. "She's facing a possible murder charge. But I'm inclined to agree with you. I don't think she killed Maitland."

"I don't, either," Slade said. "Which means that the killer must have been one of the four Vortex agents who were on the island."

"That makes sense," Rafe said. "If Vortex found out that Maitland was going to sell me information about their organization, they would have had every reason to murder him."

Slade nodded once, looking satisfied. "I like that. It works. Now you'll have to excuse me. Got to get those two fake bond agents to Thursday Harbor. If all goes well I'll be back on the four o'clock ferry. If I know Harding, he'll have signed confessions from both of those guys by breakfast tomorrow morning."

Chapter 34

RAFE CAME AWAKE TO THE SOUND OF HIS PHONE. HE opened his eyes and realized it was still dark outside.

"It's your phone, not mine," Ella said into the pillow.

"Believe it or not, I figured that out."

"You should be a detective."

He sat up on the side of the bed and picked up the phone. "It's Slade."

"At four o'clock in the morning?" Ella asked.

"The law never sleeps," Rafe said. He took the call. "It has just been pointed out to me that it's four o'clock in the morning."

"I know," Slade said. "But Harding just called me and I figured you'd want to hear the good news right away."

"Harding got his confessions?"

"Of course he did. This is Hard Joe Harding we're talking about. He was really rezzed up. Looks like we handed him the biggest case of his career. This will probably be the one that lands him the director's job. He's off and running, chasing a mysterious crime organization named Vortex."

"What about Kenneth Maitland's killer?"

"We were right," Slade said. "It was one of the Vortex agents, specifically one of the two that died in the stolen boat the night you were attacked. They used some high-tech device to gain access to the jobsite and the vault to steal the Alien tech. They also planted the mag-rez after the murder."

"So that case is closed?"

"Looks like it," Slade said. "Harding also said to tell you that Vortex was after you because they think you can lead them to some valuable ruins in the Rainforest."

"Yeah, I'd actually started to figure that out."

"You should be a detective."

"People keep telling me that," Rafe said. "What happens next?"

"Harding thinks you're no longer a target. He believes that the people at the top of Vortex are already scrambling to shut down the operation now that two of their men have been arrested, two are dead, and the FBPI is involved."

"So, it's finished?"

"It is for us. For Harding, the fun is just beginning."

"Thanks for the update," Rafe said. "I think I'll go back to bed now."

He ended the connection and looked at Ella, who was propped up against the pillows, watching him.

"We can all relax," Rafe said. "The FBPI is on the case."

"Oh, joy. I feel so much safer now."

"I detect cynicism."

"You should be a detective."

The scratching at the French doors distracted Rafe before he could come up with a response. When he opened the door, Lorelei bustled into the room. She had her wedding veil in one paw and she was dusted with powdered sugar.

"I have a bad feeling about this morning's batch of powdered-sugar doughnuts," Rafe said.

He was about to close the door but he stopped when the dream image flickered at the corner of his eye. Automatically he started to suppress it. Then he remembered the gates-of-Hell vision on the road.

He took a deep breath and let himself enter the dreamscape.

A shape-shifting ghost from the city of ice and fog appeared. It was impossible to make out the features but somehow Rafe knew that the being was capable of changing its identity. He also knew that he would pay a lot of money to learn the name of the shape-shifter.

"What is it?" Ella asked softly. "Another hallucination?"

Rafe turned toward the bed. "I keep wondering what kind of information Kenneth Maitland planned to sell to me."

"Something to do with Vortex, evidently. After all, it was one of their operatives who murdered him."

"How did a member of the DND movement learn something so important about Vortex that they felt they had to get rid of him?"

"I'm sure the famous Joe Harding will find the answer to that question," Ella said.

"You're right. Which leaves me with another question."

"What's that?"

"You're going home tomorrow."

"There's no reason for me to stay. Dr. Hayashi and Dr. Bowen are satisfied that the tuned-quartz devices will work to repel the monsters."

"Right. Which means my job is finished, too."

"So?"

"So, here's my question. Mind if I go back to Crystal City with you?"

There was a great stillness in the darkened room. Rafe realized that he was holding his breath.

"No," Ella said. "No, I don't mind at all."

Chapter 35

"HOW MANY MORE WEDDINGS HAVE YOU GOT LEFT ON your calendar?" Rafe asked.

"Four down and one more to go," Ella said. "I told you, this is my busy season."

The lavish Norton-Hickock wedding had gone off flawlessly. Ella was pretty sure the guests, and the bride as well, held their collective breath when the minister asked the famous question. *"If anyone knows why this man and this woman should not be married, let him speak now or forever hold his peace."*

But Ella's cell phone had not rung. For good reason, she thought. She glanced at the glowing bride and groom. It didn't take a professional matchmaker to know that Martha and Mark were perfect for each other. The positive energy around them seemed to circulate throughout the crowded ballroom, affecting all the guests.

The gala reception was at its height. The champagne was flowing. The musicians were playing a dreamy waltz and she was in Rafe's arms on the dance floor. Life didn't get much better, she decided.

Rafe danced with a smooth, sexy competence. He seemed to like having her in his arms. There was a little heat in his eyes and his hand on her back was warm and strong. She was starting to allow herself to hope that their relationship might last awhile. But her realistic inner Siren warned her not to think long-term. She and Rafe had shared secrets, danger, and a bed. Now they were dancing together. There was no denying that they were involved in a passionate affair. But passion was not the same thing as love.

"You do this every year?" Rafe asked. "The professional bridesmaid thing, I mean?"

"I've been in high demand for the past couple of years but I expect the rush will taper off next year," she said.

"Why is that?"

"Most of my friends will have been married by then. I expect there will be a few stragglers but you know how it is. Sooner or later everyone gets married."

Rafe watched her intently. "Everyone except you and me?"

"Oh, you'll get married," she said. "Just as soon as you're convinced that the fever is a symptom of a new, rising talent; not an indication that you'll be checking into a para-psych hospital."

"But until that happens you'll sleep with me, is that it? Or at least you'll sleep with me until you get bored and decide to move on to another client you think you can fix."

Outrage sparked through her. So much for the romantic dance.

"I didn't fix you, damn it," she said. "You weren't broken. You were healing just fine. All I did was speed up the process."

"Just so you know, your voice is rising." Rafe smiled. "Are you going to sing?"

"That is not funny, Rafe Coppersmith." Uneasily, she looked around. The room was still buzzing with conversation and laughter and music but the heads of a couple of nearby dancers had turned her way. Mortified, she clenched her hand on Rafe's shoulder. "Why are you doing this?"

"Doing what?"

"You're trying to provoke me. You seem to be in the mood for an argument."

"Maybe I am in the mood."

There was more heat in his eyes now and she was pretty sure it wasn't the sexy kind.

"Why, for heaven's sake?" she asked.

"Because I'm feeling used, that's why. Every time I try to talk about our relationship, you change the subject."

"Do you mind if we talk about something else?" she asked in a low hiss.

"It's a wedding. What the hell else should we be talking about? And that's exactly what I mean. You're trying to change the subject."

They were both on edge, she thought. It had been this

way since they had returned from Rainshadow three days ago. Oh, things had gone smoothly enough for the first forty-eight hours because both of them had been on their best behavior. But the uncertainties had been lurking like snakeweed just under the surface. So much for any hope of a long-term relationship.

You knew this wasn't going to work out, her inner Siren said.

"Do you know what your problem is, Rafe?" she asked.

"You tell me."

"You're experiencing a lot of stress because you don't know what to expect now that you've acquired a new talent."

"I don't think you can call lucid dreaming a talent. As far as career paths go, I'll be lucky to set up in business as a storefront psychic in the Quarter."

"That's ridiculous," she said. "You're a Coppersmith. Your family will find you a good job in the company. You did excellent work for the firm on Rainshadow."

"I got lucky. Singing dinosaurs were involved and I just happened to know a strong music talent. What are the odds that the next troubleshooting job will involve music?"

"I'm sure Coppersmith Mining will find a position for you."

"Yeah? And just how the hell do you think that makes me feel? I don't want my family to *find a position* for me. I'm not some charity case."

"You're afraid to make any long-range plans for yourself because you can't figure out what you want to do with the rest of your life. Talking about our relationship is a diversion for you, a way of not having to contemplate your own personal future."

"I'm not the only one who isn't into long-range planning. You're the one who keeps reminding anyone who will listen that she's never going to marry."

"I told you, I'm just being realistic," she shot back.

A few more heads turned.

"Ghost shit," Rafe said. "You know what I think? I think you like having an excuse to hop from one man to the next, no strings attached."

She was horrified. And furious. "That's not true."

"Isn't it? Seems to me that every time I turn around you're telling me that you aren't looking for long-term commitment."

"I've explained that my talent—"

"Forget your talent. I'm tired of that excuse."

Outrage splashed through her. She stopped cold, forcing him to stop, too.

"How dare you accuse me of inventing an excuse not to get married," she said. "If I didn't want to get married, I would just come straight out and say I didn't want to get married. Have I ever said that? *Have I?*"

"Well, now that I think about it, maybe not in so many words. However—"

The music ended with a flourish.

"Shut up," Ella said. "They're going to toss the garter and the bouquet."

The wedding host grabbed the microphone. "Let's

have all the unmarried men on this side of the stage and all of the single ladies on the opposite side."

Grateful for the excuse to end the argument, Ella hoisted her skirts.

"See you later," she said in her breeziest tone.

She whisked across the dance floor to join the crowd of bridesmaids and other single females. When she arrived in position she peeked at the herd of men on the other side of the stage. Rafe was there but he was standing several steps to the rear. He probably considered it a risk-free zone, she thought. She wondered what he would do if the garter came his way. Ignore it, probably.

The groom knelt in front of the bride, and amid much giggling and slightly off-color comments, he reached up under the voluminous skirts of the wedding dress and retrieved a blue satin garter.

Turning, he tossed it into the throng of men. It went nowhere near Rafe. He had chosen his location well, Ella thought grimly. Probably used his new talent for lucid dreaming to intuit the safest position.

The best man caught the garter and, with a cheesy grin, held it aloft and looked right at one of the bridesmaids. She blushed. A cheer went up.

"And now the bouquet," the wedding host intoned.

Laughing, Martha stood at the top of the stage steps and turned her back to the group of single women.

At the last instant—on pure impulse—Ella maneuvered into the middle of the small crowd. From that position she had a good shot at grabbing the bouquet out of midair. It would serve Rafe right if she caught it, she thought. Exactly why, she wasn't sure.

The bride flung the bouquet over her shoulder. It sailed wide to the far right—nowhere near where Ella was poised to seize it out of midair.

Probably an omen, she decided. Over the course of her career as a bridesmaid she had been very careful never to catch the flowers. Today marked the first time she had ever made a deliberate effort to snag the bouquet and the result had been abject failure.

Not that she was superstitious.

The bride collected her skirts and descended the steps. Her attendants gathered around her.

Avoiding Rafe's eye, Ella joined the laughing, happy group of women. They floated down a hallway toward the room that had been designated as a dressing chamber.

A waiter stood at the entrance. There was a tray of full champagne flutes decorated with ribbons on the console beside him.

One by one he handed each of the bridal attendants a glass of champagne as she entered the room. The door closed behind the women.

"A toast to Martha," someone said. "May she always be this happy."

There was a chorus of "to Martha."

Everyone took a couple of sips of champagne and then set their glasses aside. The process of getting the bride out of her elaborate gown and veil began.

The first wave of nausea and dizziness hit Ella a short time later. She tried to shake off the sick sensation. Instinctively, she rezzed a little psi, and for a moment or two her head and her stomach settled down.

"Ella?" Martha spoke from the center of the room where she was surrounded by bridesmaids. "Are you all right?"

A small dose of panic hit Ella. She could not spoil Martha's big day.

"Yes, I'm fine," she said. She managed a smile. "I may have had a bit too much champagne."

Martha laughed. "Maybe your date had something to do with that? Congratulations on finding a plus one, by the way. And a very interesting plus one at that."

Giggles sparkled in the room.

Ella kept her smile in place. "Thanks for letting me drag him along."

"Is he any relation to the Coppersmiths of Coppersmith Mining?" one of the other bridesmaids asked.

"There may be a connection," Ella said, deliberately vague.

"I saw the way he looked at you." Martha winked. "I wouldn't be surprised if you're the one wearing the fancy dress a few months from now."

There was a flurry of activity and then the wedding host was in the doorway announcing that the limo was waiting. Everyone except Ella rushed out on a bright tide of laughter and good wishes.

Ella stepped out into the hall just long enough to wave farewell to Martha and Mark and then she ducked back into the room and closed the door.

She sank down onto one of the red velvet stools in front of the makeup counter. Clutching her tiny beaded bag, she stared at her reflection. She looked like she was going to faint, she decided. This was not good.

The champagne glasses that they had been handed at the door were now standing on the counter in front of her. Most were still nearly full. She had taken only a single sip or two from her own glass.

There was something different about her flute— something about the ribbon tied around the stem.

It took her a few seconds to process the fact that the bow was pink. All of the other bows were purple. The waiter at the door had handed out each glass. She had not selected the one tied with the pink bow—it had been very deliberately placed in her hand as she entered the room.

No one else seemed to have had a problem with the champagne.

She had been poisoned.

She needed to get help but she could no longer trust her balance. She did not think she could even get to her feet.

Phone.

If she could just open her small handbag and take out her phone, she could call Rafe. He would know what to do. Rafe was good at stuff like this.

A side door opened just as she pried open her little bag with trembling fingers. She looked up quickly—too quickly. The slowly spinning room went into overdrive. Nevertheless, she recognized the figure she saw in the mirror.

"You," she said.

She tried to rez her talent but her paranormal senses did not respond. Her phone tumbled out of her handbag and landed on the carpet. It might as well have been a million miles away.

A great weariness came over her. She braced herself against the makeup table and leaned over, resting her hot forehead on her arm. She realized she still had one hand inside the handbag. Not that it mattered, she thought. Her phone was gone.

Her fingers closed around her lipstick.

"Strip her amber and then take her out through the side door," Bob Luttrell said. He was no longer wearing the chef's whites that he had worn for his role as the jobsite cook on Rainshadow. Today he was dressed in the uniform of a delivery service company. "The van is in the alley."

Chapter 36

THE HALLUCINATION STRUCK WHILE HE WAITED FOR ELLA to return to the ballroom. Having seen the bride and groom on their way, the bridal party was trickling back.

The skaters skimmed across the ice, whirling faster and faster in what looked to be random patterns. They were all dressed in formal black and white. Each carried a silver tray . . .

"Damn." Rafe shook his head, trying to clear his vision.

As usual, his first instinct was to suppress the hallucination. But the waking dream was screaming to get his attention.

Ella appeared on the ice. Her mag-rez skates flashed ominously. She was dressed as a bride, not a bridesmaid, and she spoke to him in the language of dreams. "Stop fighting your talent. You're now a spectacularly good lucid dreamer. Get over it."

It seemed vitally important that he follow her out onto the ice. But she was gliding away from him now. As he watched, the skating waiters formed a circle around her, shielding her from view.

But one of the waiters was missing. There was an empty spot in the circle . . .

He turned to study the waiters who were working the long bar. Earlier, one of them had gone past him carrying a tray of full champagne flutes decorated with ribbons. The bride and her attendants had soon disappeared down the same corridor.

The waiter had never returned.

Neither had Ella.

Rafe sliced through the crowd, drawing startled looks.

The door of the bridesmaids' room was locked from the inside. He lashed out at it with the heel of his shoe a couple of times. Wood splintered. The door flew open.

There was no sign of Ella but he found her amber jewelry in the trash can. Her dainty, strappy sandals with the tuned amber embedded in the heels were under a sofa.

He started across the carpeted room, heading toward a side door that stood wide. A small, shiny metallic object glinted on the floor beneath the long makeup table.

He started to crouch to pick up the lipstick but he stopped when he saw the wobbly drawing on the polished stone countertop.

Someone had used the lipstick to make a small, somewhat smeared sketch. It looked like a doodle.

Rafe's talent spiked again. His phone pinged just as he

started to put it all together. He glanced down and read
the text message on the screen.

> She's safe as long as you cooperate. Instructions
> will follow.

He took another look at the lipstick drawing. This time
he deliberately opened his lucid dream talent. His new psychic ability flashed through all the possibilities and settled
on the most likely interpretation of the little drawing.

"Got the message, sweetheart," he said. "I'm on my
way."

Chapter 37

SHE OPENED HER EYES TO THE FAMILIAR GREEN-QUARTZ glow of the catacombs. The arched ceiling overhead was inscribed with the graceful symbols and designs that the Aliens had used to decorate many of their structures. The experts had made little headway in deciphering the strange writing. Some had concluded that the inscriptions were merely decorative, not a written language.

Instinctively she closed her right hand into a small fist, feeling for her amber ring. The first thing she noticed was that her hands were bound in front of her.

The second thing she discovered was that her ring was gone. If they had taken it, they had stripped her of all her amber. Rafe would never find her. Even if he got the message she had tried to leave with her lipstick, which was not very likely, he would have no way of tracking her now. She was on her own.

Tentatively, she tried to raise her talent. There was nothing at first. She tried harder and thought that maybe— just maybe—she heard a little Alien music shiver in the atmosphere. But the quartz harmonies locked in the walls were very faint.

"Sorry about the drug," Bob said. "I didn't have much choice. You're a strong talent. I was pretty sure we couldn't get you out of that wedding party unless we put you under all the way."

She realized that she was lying on the floor. The quartz was not cold—it was never cold down in the tunnels—but it was hard. She sat up cautiously, curling her legs mermaid style. The skirts of her purple and pink bridesmaid dress foamed around her.

Absently, she noticed that both of her shoes were missing. Just like Amberella after the ball, she thought. But her prince didn't need a shoe to find her; he needed a signal from her tuned amber. Her amber was gone.

All she could do now was try to buy time and hope that her talent awakened before Bob gave her another dose of the drug.

He lounged on a stool near the vaulted doorway, a flamer resting on his thigh. He was not the only one guarding her. The waiter who had given her the drugged champagne stood at the entrance of the chamber, watching the hallway outside.

Ella fixed her attention on Bob. He was clearly the most dangerous of the two men.

"Did you bring any doughnuts?" she asked. "I could really use a doughnut about now."

Bob whistled, amused. "You're one tough lady, aren't you? But, then, I figured that out right away after you solved the dino problem in Wonderland and then took down that monster inside the Preserve. You're not just a standard-issue music talent, are you? Figure you for a genuine Siren. Scary."

"You're Vortex, aren't you?" Ella asked. "Also scary."

"I'm Vortex and so is my associate, Hodson, here."

Hodson did not acknowledge the introduction.

Bob studied Ella with a considering look.

"I see you know something about Vortex," he said. "That means Coppersmith is aware of it, too."

"Arcane and the FBPI are also investigating Vortex," Ella said. "Oh, yes, and the Guilds. Rafe has kept them all informed. No stuffing that genie back into the bottle."

"The board of directors won't be thrilled to find out that this particular operation has drawn so much attention, but that's not my problem. The people at the top will find a way to stay hidden in the shadows. Arcane, the FBPI, and the Guilds will never find them."

"Vortex is involved in the illegal Alien-tech business, isn't it?"

"You think Coppersmith isn't conducting research on some very exotic Alien tech as we speak? Give me a break. You can't be that naïve."

"Coppersmith takes contracts with the government. It works with law enforcement."

Bob snorted. "Here's a bulletin for you, Ella. So does Vortex—under a different corporate logo, of course. There's a very thin line between legal and illegal when it comes to Alien-tech research. At times that line is damn near invisible. It disappears completely when there's a lot of money and power involved."

"What do you want with me?"

"You are our last hope for saving the Ghost City operation. We've had a hard time getting Mr. Raphael Coppersmith's attention. We're betting you can do it for us."

"You certainly got his attention after two botched kidnapping attempts."

"Well, we didn't bungle this one, did we?" Bob said.

"Because you went after me, not Rafe. You can forget the Ghost City project. It's going nowhere."

Bob raised his brows. "I see Coppersmith told you something about what happened to him three months ago."

"I know that the venture was a disaster. Rafe almost died."

"Did he tell you that someone went missing? A man named Roger Jay."

"The rogue tech Rafe tried to rescue? The one who caused the explosion in the ruins?"

"Jay was working for Vortex," Bob said. "He made it out alive, barely. He was badly burned and hallucinating like crazy. He didn't survive long. But before he died he said he'd seen Coppersmith vanish into a pool of crystal."

"Jeez. Coppersmith Security really needs to get its act together. Sounds like they've hired a bunch of Vortex spies."

"Don't blame Coppersmith Security," Bob said. "They're good. But Vortex is better. Everyone in the high-tech-quartz business has been searching for those ruins for decades— ever since the first miner stumbled out of the catacombs with wild stories about a hidden city of ice and fog. When word leaked that Coppersmith Mining was going to lead an expedition to search for it, Vortex managed to embed an operative on the team. That man was Jay."

"That's called corporate espionage."

Bob smiled. "I believe it is."

"What made Vortex think that Rafe's team would find the Ghost City when all the other expeditions had failed?"

"You don't know much about the mining business, do you?"

"No."

"It's a small world at the top, and inside that small world, everyone knows that no one is better than Rafe Coppersmith when it comes to locating hot crystal and quartz deposits."

"But he got burned," Ella said. "He lost his talent. He has no clear memories of the venture."

"My employers don't believe that. They think Coppersmith put out the psi-burn story to convince competitors that the search for the Ghost City was a failure."

"Your employers are either crazy or unbelievably stupid because they're taking a huge risk for nothing."

"No, Miss Morgan, they are very, very smart and quite ruthless." Bob's eyes heated with something that looked a lot like lust. "And they pay very, very well for successful outcomes. I intend to deliver one tonight. When this is over I will get a lot of money, a new identity, and a new position inside Vortex. Eventually, I'm going to be sitting on the board."

Unwholesome excitement shivered in the atmosphere around Bob. He was serious, she thought, deadly serious.

"You're the one who shot that poor DND guy, Kenneth Maitland, aren't you?" she asked.

"I wouldn't waste too much pity on Maitland if I were you. He was looking to score. He found out about me, you see. That's the information he planned to sell to Rafe Coppersmith."

"How did Maitland discover that you were working for Vortex? Are you saying that DND and Vortex are connected after all?"

"Why would Vortex want to get involved with an unsophisticated scam operation like DND? But like Vortex, DND wanted to embed one of their people inside the Coppersmith jobsite on Rainshadow. Wonderland promises to be worth several fortunes, after all. At the time I was inserted into the project, Vortex had abandoned the Ghost City operation because we figured Rafe Coppersmith really was a total burnout."

"Imagine your surprise when you found out that his father had sent him to troubleshoot the Wonderland project."

"As soon as I saw him I knew he wasn't a burnout. No question but that he's still a hot talent. Not sure what kind of talent, but he's obviously sane and powerful. The fact that he had survived in good shape meant that the original Ghost City project might still be viable. I was in charge because I was the man on site."

"It was your big chance to prove to your bosses that you were destined for management, is that it?"

"Pretty much," Bob said. "We went back to Plan A. But by then Maitland had found me. He was DND's fund-raiser for a while but he was good with the tech stuff. He hacked into the personnel files of all the Coppersmith employees on Rainshadow in order to figure out how to get Angela Price a place on the team."

"In the process he stumbled over something in your file that raised a red flag?"

"You got it," Bob said "It was probably an accident. But he got curious. Followed the leads straight to one of the Vortex shell corporations. Luckily, when he got that far he hit a couple of tripwires that I had out on the reznet. He left his own prints and I followed him back to DND."

"That's how you discovered his relationship to Angela Price."

"That worried me for a while. Thought I might have to arrange an accident for her. But Maitland kept the info about me to himself. I don't think he trusted Angela completely. He knew that she was a true believer in the DND movement. He was smart enough to realize that, in the end, she might choose the movement, not him. He was right."

"How can you be sure that he didn't tell anyone else about you?"

"Because Coppersmith Security hasn't tried to throw me off the jobsite." Bob shrugged. "Besides, why would he tell anyone? There's no logic in that. He planned to use the information to finance his early retirement. The only person he might have confided in was Angela. But I was there at the boathouse that night. I heard their argument. He never once mentioned my name."

A faint, muted flicker of awareness touched Ella's senses. Hope rushed through her. Maybe her talent was rising. But in the next moment something small and fast scuttled past the doorway. Ella caught a glimpse of four bright eyes and then Lorelei was gone.

"Shit." Hodson jerked abruptly, straightened away from the quartz wall, and rezzed the flamer. A bolt of fire lanced the atmosphere in the corridor. He fired another blast from the flamer, aiming toward the floor.

Bob was on his feet, flamer pointed at the doorway. "What the hell?"

"A rat," Hodson muttered. "Startled me. Those things are creepy."

"There are no rats down here." Bob glanced over his shoulder at Ella. His eyes narrowed. "Must have been a dust bunny."

"Whatever it was, it's gone now," Hodson said. "That thing was fast."

Bob shook his head, looking grim. "I don't like this. If her damn dust bunny found her—"

"The dust bunny isn't exactly a big problem," Hodson said, disgusted. "It just startled me, that's all. If it comes back, I'll zap it."

"You don't understand and I don't have time to explain," Bob said. "We're moving." He reached into his pocket and took out a syringe. "On your feet, Ella."

Panic arced through her. If Lorelei tried to attack the men by herself, she was doomed. Given her small size and the close quarters, a blast of fire from the weapon could easily prove lethal.

But Lorelei *had* found her. That meant there was hope that Rafe might eventually find her, too.

Pretending to stumble awkwardly to her feet, Ella focused what little energy she could summon on trying to send a message. *Find Rafe.*

The experts claimed that there was no such thing as telepathy, but there was some kind of bond between Lorelei and herself. And Lorelei was a natural-born predator. All predators had instincts for strategy. Surely such a small creature would realize she needed backup in a situation like this.

Hope, even the weak sort, was powerful stuff. Another little pulse of energy whispered through Ella. She was pretty sure that the music in the walls was getting louder. *Just keep buying time,* she thought.

She was on her feet now. Bob reached out to grab her arm and hold her still while he readied the syringe. Realizing his intent, she stepped back. He lunged toward her.

There was another scuttling movement in the doorway.

"It's back," Hodson growled. "I'll get it this time."

He rezzed the flamer and moved out into the hallway to get a clear shot.

Ella heard a sharp, very short yelp. Not Lorelei, she thought.

"What the hell?" Bob glanced toward the doorway. "Hodson?"

Ella decided she might not get a better chance. She still couldn't pull any killer music but she had options.

She lashed out at the side of Bob's leg with one bare foot and managed a direct hit on his kneecap. He grunted, released her, and staggered backward. The syringe dropped to the floor.

"Bitch," he shouted.

He lunged toward her again but she was running for the door. She braced for a flamer burn on the back. She could probably survive a single shot, she thought. The flamers were designed to take down bad guys, not incinerate them. All she had to do was get out into the hall. Once she was free she could get lost in the tunnels. Lorelei would find her.

She nearly collided head-on with Rafe. He materialized in the doorway, a flamer in his hand.

"Drop it, Luttrell," he said.

Ella stumbled to a halt and spun to the side so that she was not in Rafe's line of fire. She caught a glimpse of Hodson. He was stretched out on the floor in the hallway, unconscious.

Lorelei came scampering down the hall, fully fluffed once more. She chortled and bounced up into Ella's arms. Ella hugged her close.

There was a thud and a clatter as a heavy object hit the floor. Turning, Ella saw that Bob had dropped the flamer.

"Coppersmith." Bob stared at Rafe in openmouthed disbelief. "How the hell did you find her? I know she wasn't carrying any amber. I made certain of it."

"Ella isn't carrying amber," Rafe said. "But you are. And naturally, Coppersmith Security has a record of every employee's personal frequency. The company is very big on jobsite safety, you know. All it took to get your number was a quick call to Security on Rainshadow."

Bob's disbelief turned to open speculation. "You came down here alone? No backup?"

"Don't worry," Rafe said. "The FBPI is here, too."

"That's right," Joe Harding said from the doorway. He moved to stand directly behind Ella. "I'm from the Bureau and I'm here to make this problem go away."

"I called Special Agent Harding before I came down here to find you," Rafe explained.

Ella glared at Harding. "It's about time you got here. What's with letting Rafe take all the risks? And how come there's only you? This is a major crime. You should have brought along a full team of agents."

"Like I said, I'm here to make this problem go away," Harding said. He switched the flamer away from Bob and aimed it straight at Ella's face. "Drop the gun, Coppersmith. You know what one blast will do to her at close range?"

"I knew it," Ella said. "You just can't trust the FBPI, at least not the Crystal City branch."

Lorelei sleeked out and tried to wriggle free.

"No," Ella whispered to her. "Please. Don't move."

Rafe put the weapon on the floor. Bob collected it quickly and stepped back.

"Sure glad to see you, Harding," Bob said. "For a few minutes there, I thought the plan was not going well."

"What happens now?" Rafe asked.

"Once again we are going back to Plan A," Harding said. "You and Luttrell will proceed to those coordinates you were given on your phone. The Vortex team will meet you there. You will take them to the ruins. You have twenty-four hours to open the portal. If I don't get word that the venture has been successful before the deadline—"

"Yeah, yeah, we know," Ella said. "You'll send me on

a long walk through the tunnels without amber. You thug types really ought to get a new script."

"As it happens, I am using a new script," Harding said. "If Coppersmith doesn't lead the Vortex team to the ruins within the deadline, I'm not going to send you into the catacombs without good amber. There's a chance you might find your way out. So, I'm going to kill you and leave you in the Underworld. No one will ever find your body."

Ella took a deep breath. "Okay, that's new."

Rafe glanced at the doorway. "Heard enough?"

"More than enough."

A formidable man walked through the doorway. He was dressed in Guild khaki-and-leather and he looked very familiar. It took Ella a couple of beats to realize where she had seen him before—on the rez screen and in the papers. He was Fontana, the boss of the Crystal City Guild. More to the point, he was the man who had cleaned up the once-corrupt organization.

Fontana was followed by four other men, two of whom wore Guild attire. One of the others was dressed in the uniform of the Crystal City police. The fourth man was Chief Truett.

"Put the flamer down, Harding," Truett ordered.

Harding hesitated. Ella felt the panic rising in the atmosphere and knew that he was debating whether to try to use her as a hostage. But the music was back. She got ready to sing.

"Harding, you might as well put the damn thing down,"

Rafe said. "It's inoperative. I de-rezzed the amber in the firing mechanism when we got into the sled."

Harding stared at him, blank-faced with shock. "How?"

Rafe fished a small device out of his pocket and held it up so everyone could see it. "A little gadget from the Coppersmith labs. Get a focus, push a little energy through it, and you've got melted amber. Did you really think I'd risk bringing you down here if you were armed with a hot flamer?"

Harding grunted. He dropped the flamer.

Bob looked at Rafe. "I don't get it. How did you know that I'm the one who took her?"

"Ella left a note," Rafe said. "Didn't you, Ella?"

"I tried," Ella said. "But they drugged me and I was going under fast. I was afraid you wouldn't understand."

"There was no note," Bob insisted. "I would have seen it. She was trying to put on her lipstick when I found her. She didn't have time to dig out a pen and a piece of paper."

"My note was written with lipstick," Ella said. "A circle within a circle."

Bob scowled. "I saw the smears on the counter. I thought you were hallucinating. What the hell was the circle within a circle supposed to mean?"

"A doughnut," Rafe said.

Bob winced. "Shit."

Ella gave him her most blinding smile. "Your doughnuts aren't that bad. Lorelei loves them."

Chapter 38

"DO YOU THINK HARDING AND BOB LUTTRELL WILL talk?" Ella asked.

"They may try to trade some information in a plea-bargain deal but it's doubtful that they can give the authorities anything that will help us find the real powers-that-be at the top of Vortex. According to Marlowe Jones, the organization is evidently structured in a series of independent cells. If one is exposed it can't be used to identify the others."

"Well, at least Chief Truett gets to take full credit for busting a major black-market operation dealing in Alien tech." Ella smiled. "I thought Truett looked good on the news this evening. You could hardly tell that he was gloating."

Rafe laughed. "Payback. Gotta love it."

Ella contemplated the view of the Dead City. A very

long day had transitioned into an even longer night. She and Rafe were both too rezzed to sleep so they were sitting on her balcony, having a drink. She was still wearing her purple and pink bridesmaid dress, and Rafe was in his formal attire, although he had removed the jacket and loosened the tie. They had both been too beat to bother changing when they had arrived at her apartment a short time ago.

It was nearly two o'clock in the morning and the eerie green glow of the ruins enveloped the Old Quarter. The gentle vibe in the atmosphere was oddly soothing.

She took a sip of wine. It was not her first glass. Earlier they had ordered in pizza from an all-night delivery service. Lorelei had joined them for the repast and then, with a cheery chortle, had vanished over the edge of the balcony, disappearing into the night with her wedding veil.

The Crystal City Police Department, with a nod to the Guild, was taking full credit for the rescue and the arrests. The assumption made by the police was that the suspects had hoped to get a lot of money out of Rafe Coppersmith by kidnapping his current lover. Rafe and Ella had made no attempt to contradict that conclusion.

There had been no mention in the media of the legendary city of ice and fog.

"I hate to think that the power brokers at the top of Vortex are going to get away with murder," Ella said. "Literally."

"I'm sure the people pulling the strings inside Vortex consider themselves safe, at least for now." Rafe paused. "But if they're smart—and all indications point that way—they may be a little nervous."

"What do you mean?"

"Coppersmith Security and Arcane now have Vortex on their psi-dar. So does the Crystal City Guild and the FBPI. That's bound to make at least a few people inside Vortex a tad uneasy."

"Hmm." Ella swirled the wine gently in her glass. "They'll probably lie low for a while and hope everyone involved forgets about the name *Vortex*."

"Probably." Rafe drank some more beer and lowered the bottle. He studied the glowing ruins. "It was a hell of a shock, you know."

"Realizing that Vortex had grabbed me? Yeah, well, it was a shock getting grabbed so easily, let me tell you. If that kind of thing keeps happening at weddings, my career as a bridesmaid may be in trouble."

Rafe was oblivious to her small attempt at humor. "I should have seen it coming," he said. "Should have realized they might use you to get to me. Should have made sure that you were never alone. If I had been more willing to accept the nature of my new talent, I could have done a better job of protecting you. But I kept fighting the dreams."

"Oh, for pity's sake, your logic is ridiculous." She waved one hand in a grand dismissal of everything he had just said. "I wasn't alone when they slipped that drug into my champagne. I was surrounded by a bunch of bridesmaids and the bride. There was no way to protect me, so stop blaming yourself. What mattered was that you figured out that it was Bob Luttrell who grabbed me and then you found me. That was brilliant."

"You were the brilliant one. You left a message."

"I was feeling very woozy by then. I didn't dare try to write Bob's name even if I could have managed all the letters, which is doubtful, because the room was spinning. He would have noticed and wiped away the lipstick. So I went with the doughnut connection but I wasn't sure if you would understand." She smiled. "But you did. One thing I've been wondering about. How did you come to realize that Special Agent Harding was involved?"

Rafe watched her from the shadows of the lounger. There was a little heat in his eyes. "I used my talent— my new talent."

"No kidding." She was pleased. "You deliberately opened your talent?"

"Figured I had nothing left to lose. You were right. Once I stopped fighting the waking dream and went into it with conscious awareness, I was suddenly in control. A lot of little things that I should have been paying attention to all along suddenly fell into place."

"That is so high-rez, as the kids say." She took another sip of wine. "So, what little things came together for you?"

"Stuff that had been there all along. For example, I went to see him right after I hired you. I'm sure that Bob Luttrell had already sent word that I was in Crystal City, but when I stopped by Harding's office I added the helpful information that I was going to that reception with you. Harding must have scrambled to put that first kidnapping operation together, but he had Vortex resources to draw on. In hindsight it was obvious that he was the only one who could have pulled off the attempt on such short notice."

"Was there anything else about Harding that made you think he couldn't be trusted?"

"A couple of small things," Rafe said. "Those two Alien weapons he confiscated from Vickary's operation disappeared. When I asked him what had happened to them, he told me they were in the FBPI lab. But the FBPI usually calls in Coppersmith when it wants to evaluate Alien tech. I checked with Dad earlier today. Coppersmith never got the call. Also, those two men that Slade escorted to Thursday Harbor and put into FBPI custody have disappeared."

"*What?* When did you find out about that little snafu?"

Rafe winced. "This afternoon, just before the wedding. I didn't want to ruin the mood. I was going to tell you after the reception."

"Hah. How did you discover they went missing?"

"Earlier this afternoon I called Harding to ask him for a status update on the Vortex investigation. I wanted to know what else he had learned from the two men. He said he had sent them to headquarters for further debriefing. But that didn't sound like Harding."

"Of course it didn't," Ella said. "He's a glory-hound. He wouldn't hand off a high-profile case unless he had absolutely no alternative."

"I've worked with him often enough to know that's true. So when he told me that the pair had been transported to FBPI headquarters, it bothered me."

"Your new talent in action, I'll bet."

"Whatever. Anyhow, none of it was proof that Harding was involved, but I decided not to take any chances when I went after you."

"So you brought in your own backup team." Ella hoisted her glass. "Good thinking."

"If Harding had been a good guy there would have been no harm done. But if it turned out he was Vortex, I knew Chief Truett would be thrilled to be able to take him down. But the cops couldn't handle the catacombs alone. They needed a Guild team. I made one more phone call to Marlowe Jones of Jones and Jones. She assured me that Fontana was solid."

"So you put the whole rescue operation into place in less than an hour?"

"That was all the time I had."

"Wow." She smiled. "No wonder your father sent you out to shoot trouble. You're good."

"Thanks. But troubleshooting is not a full-time job, and I'm not going to be able to go back to my old line. My talent for resonating with hot rocks and Alien tech is definitely gone."

"I keep telling you, you've got a new talent. It's just different, that's all."

"A lot of people would call my hallucinations a sign of serious instability brought on by trauma to the para-senses."

"Don't expect any sympathy from me," Ella said. "My talent terrifies people, remember? Bob was sure that I was a Siren. That's why he gave me that powerful suppressor drug. And Harding probably put me on the FBPI watch list."

"I doubt it."

"You're the one who said he was suspicious of me."

"He was. But I think it's very likely that he kept his suspicions to himself," Rafe said.

"Why?"

"For one thing, he was always very secretive about information. He liked to keep secrets close in case he found a way to use them."

"Well, he'll probably blab now. His suspicions will hit the media. I'll lose my clients and have to shut down the Knightsbridge Dream Institute."

"Don't worry." Rafe's mouth twitched at the corner. "First off, very few people will believe anything Harding says now because he's an FBPI agent who went rogue. His credibility is zero. Second, theoretically, your kind of talent doesn't exist. And as for the few who might believe Harding's story—"

"What about them?"

Rafe smiled slowly. "They'll be stuck in the fringe world of conspiracy-ville because it's obvious that you and I are sleeping together and that I'm still alive."

"Oh." She pondered that for a moment. "But maybe they will assume that's a temporary state of affairs."

"Not if we get married."

She felt as if the balcony had given way and she was suspended in midair.

"What?" she whispered.

"You heard me. If we get married everyone will assume that the Coppersmith clan has concluded you're not a threat. You'll have instant credibility."

"Gosh. Thanks. But marriage is a rather extreme way to protect my professional reputation."

"Think about it."

She glared at him. "Are you seriously proposing?"

Rafe drank some beer and lowered the bottle. "Yes, I am. Like I said, think about it."

"Maybe you've had one too many beers."

"Don't think so. Say, how are you feeling?"

"You're changing the subject."

"The other topic didn't seem to be going anywhere."

"I'm feeling peachy-keen," she said through set teeth. "My talent has recovered. And since we're changing the subject, here's a new one for you—the Ghost City."

Rafe sat quietly for a time, contemplating the view.

"You think I should take a team back to the ruins and try to open the portal, don't you?" he said.

"What I think," she said very carefully, "is that if Coppersmith Mining doesn't take charge of the city of ice and fog, other people, including Vortex, are going to keep looking for it and there will be more murders. You know how it is with legends. Sooner or later someone will open that portal."

"You sound like my dad. I saw enough of the Ghost City to know that it is a very dangerous place, Ella. For once, the DND crowd might be right. The city may be one Alien secret that should remain a secret, at least for now."

"Wonderland and the Preserve and the Rainforest are all dangerous places. Heck, the catacombs are dangerous. Since when has danger ever stopped people from investigating secrets? Humans seem to be on an endless quest. Probably something in our DNA."

"I don't have a clue what Coppersmith would be facing

in the city of ice and fog, assuming the company can even find the kind of talent that can access the place. Not everyone can go through that portal and come back out safely."

"That isn't going to stop people from searching for it. Better that Coppersmith takes control than Vortex."

Rafe took another swig of his beer.

"I'll think about it," he said.

"Okay."

"You ready to sleep yet?"

"No. You?"

"No." Rafe set aside his empty beer bottle. "Still pretty rezzed."

"Me, too."

"I can think of one way we could take the edge off."

She rested her head on the back of the lounger and looked at him. "You're talking about us having sex?"

"The thought did occur to me."

"To take the edge off."

"Sex can be very relaxing."

She drank the last of her wine and put down her glass. "You and I have never had relaxing sex."

"I know. We should probably try it sometime. But tonight I'm fine with our regular sex."

She concentrated on the radiant spires of the Dead City. "I think something happens to our auras when we have sex, Rafe. It's kind of weird."

"But in a good way." He paused. "At least as far as I'm concerned. Is this where you tell me that it's not good for you?"

"It's . . . very good. Maybe too good. I'm not sure what

to think. I'm a Siren. We aren't supposed to be able to have the kind of sex that you and I have had."

"Know what I think?"

"What?"

He swung his legs over the side of the lounger, got to his feet, and scooped her up in his arms. "I think you're running scared."

"That's not it."

But it felt good to be held like this, she thought. Better than good—thrilling.

"Sure it is." He carried her through the open slider and headed for the bedroom. "It's kind of funny when you think about it. Here you are, a powerful Siren who can put a man into a coma or kill a dinosaur with her talent, and you're scared to have sex with me."

"That's not how it is."

But he was carrying her down the short hallway into the darkened bedroom and she knew there was no stopping him. She did not want to stop him. This was the one man she could be herself with, and that was a gift she had never expected to receive.

"That's exactly how it is." He stood her on her feet beside the bed, spun her around, and unzipped the back of the bridesmaid gown. "If there's one thing I've learned from you, it's that you have to confront your nightmares."

"That's ridiculous." The dress fell to the rug around her bare feet. She kicked it aside and turned to face him. "Having sex with you isn't a nightmare."

He winced. "Wow. You really know how to make a man feel like a king."

"You're trying to spin my words."

He brushed his mouth against hers. When he raised his head his eyes were hot.

"What I'm trying to do is get you to shut up," he said. "At least until it's time for you to sing."

She looked at him, breathless. Her pulse had kicked up and she was feeling pleasantly buzzed. She decided not to do any more talking for a while.

Rafe reached down and hauled the blanket and sheet to the foot of the bed. He unfastened her dainty bra and slid both palms down her sides.

She shuddered at the power and control in his touch. Excitement sluiced through her, rezzing her talent and—for the moment—pushing aside her concerns about their relationship. He was hers for now, and that was good enough.

His fingers slipped under the scrap of lace around her hips. The panties dropped to the floor. He slid one hand between her legs, cupping her gently, just enough to make her wet.

She sighed and leaned into him.

He lifted her up and dropped her somewhat unceremoniously onto the bed, then sat down beside her and pried off his shoes. His shirt and trousers and briefs followed. He was fully, heavily aroused.

In the next moment he was on top of her, pinning her to the bed with his weight. He caged her with his arms and kissed her with slow, drugging power.

"You're going to sing for me again tonight, Ella," he whispered against her throat. "I want to hear you sing. I need to hear you sing."

She caught his face between her palms.

"Rafe," she whispered.

"Are you going to start talking again?" he asked warily.

"I want you to know that I love singing to you," she said, her throat tight with the intensity of her emotion. "I love you."

He went very still above her.

"Ella," he said finally. "Ella, I love you. I have since the moment I met you."

She smiled. "I doubt that, but it's very nice to hear."

"It's the truth. That's how it is for a Coppersmith man. Like a kick in the gut."

"Okay, that's not exactly the most romantic thing you could have said, but under the circumstances, I'm prepared to run with it."

"It's the truth. You want to know what kind of impression you made on me?"

"Of course." She smiled. "I want to hear every single detail."

"I started dreaming about you right after the explosion in the ruins, when the fever first hit me."

That stopped her. "You dreamed about me?"

"There were times when everyone, including me, was afraid that if the fever didn't kill me I would end up going mad. When things got really bad you would come to me in my dreams and you would sing me back to the surface."

"Oh, Rafe." She blinked the tears out of her eyes. "You survived because you're strong. But I have to say that what you just said is a heck of a lot more romantic than the kick-in-the-gut thing."

"It's all true. You were the one who got me through the nightmares and the cold sweats." He touched the edge of her lips with one finger. "Did you think about me during those three months?"

"I thought about you a lot during those three months, but I can't say my thoughts were romantic. I was mostly pissed off because I was sure that you'd walked away or maybe run away."

"Okay, but you wanted to see me again, right?"

"Sure. If only to tell you that I was pissed off. However, when you said you wanted to hire me instead of date me, I got even more pissed off, and then things got complicated."

"It's been a real roller coaster," he agreed. "But we're good now, right?"

"We may be good, but you owe me a coffee date."

"How about coffee in bed in the morning?" he asked.

"That works."

He held her very still. "Will you marry me?"

She looked into his eyes and saw the certainty of his love. Everything within her responded with the same fierce and abiding certainty.

"I love you," she whispered. "I will marry you."

He rolled onto his back and pulled her down across his chest. "I feel like I've been looking for something all my life and now I've finally found it."

He kissed her.

Energy burned in the bedroom.

Chapter 39

"I WANT TO TALK TO YOU ABOUT THE GHOST CITY PROJ-ect," Rafe said.

Orson tried not to show his astonishment. The Ghost City project had been a forbidden subject within the Coppersmith family ever since it had stolen Rafe's talent and nearly killed him. They had all respected his refusal to discuss the venture in detail primarily because Rafe was as stubborn as everyone else in the clan, and he was the one who had established the unwritten rule.

"All right," Orson said. "I'm listening."

He sat on the business side of his very big desk and studied his second son. Rafe was standing at the floor-to-ceiling windows, silhouetted against the vivid sunset that was painting the Resonance City skyline in fiery shades of orange and red. His legs were braced slightly apart, like a First Generation lawman preparing to face down an outlaw.

But instead of gripping the handle of a gun, his fingers were loosely clasped behind his back.

Cynthia had given him three fine offspring, Orson reflected. He loved them all and he was desperately proud of them. He would have walked into Hell for any of them. But truth be told, Rafe was the one he and Cynthia had worried about the most over the years.

Rafe was the hardest to understand. In a family of highly focused and psychically talented people, Rafe had been the outlier. As Cynthia put it, Rafe had climbed out of his cradle to search for something and he was still looking for it.

His gift for resonating with rock that was infused with energy had made him a valuable point man on Coppersmith exploration teams, but he had preferred chasing bad guys for the FBPI. Orson suspected that Rafe had used the criminal consulting work as a drug to distract himself from his endless quest.

For a while, everyone in the family had begun to wonder if Rafe would join the Bureau as a regular agent. But it soon became apparent that he had no patience for the politics and the rigid hierarchy of organized law enforcement. Orson had figured out early on that there was no point trying to drag Rafe too deep into the family business for the same reasons.

The bottom line was that Rafe was not management material. He was a lone wolf. That type never did well when it came to climbing up a corporate org chart.

Rafe turned away from the scene at the window. "I've been doing a lot of thinking about the Ghost City project, and I've had a few conversations about it with someone I trust."

Now that was interesting.

Orson propped his elbows on the desk and put his fingertips together. "I'm listening."

"You're right, Dad. People—including Vortex—are going to keep looking for the portal to the Ghost City. Sooner or later someone else will find it. I think it would be better for everyone if Coppersmith controls the site. We now know that Vortex is willing to resort to kidnapping and murder to achieve its objectives. The government and the Guilds don't have the technical ability to run a hot-quartz site like the city. Hell, I'm not even sure that we can deal with the power in that place."

"I understand. But better Coppersmith than the other options, is that what you're saying?"

"Yes, that's what I'm saying."

Orson looked at him for a long time. "There's only one way to find it again."

Rafe looked at his gray quartz ring. "I think I can get a team through the firestorm and open the portal. I'm willing to do it. But you're going to have to put someone else in charge of the venture. My old talent is gone, Dad, and it's not coming back."

"You sound like you've made your peace with that."

Rafe smiled. "I had a little help."

Orson's intuition kicked in. "From that young woman you said you wanted to introduce to your mother and me?"

"Ella Morgan. Yes."

The certainty in Rafe's voice told Orson a great deal. "When do we meet her?"

"Today. She's waiting in your reception lobby."

"She's the one, is she?"

"It was like you always said, a kick in the gut."

"Yeah, that's how it is for a Coppersmith man. But take my advice and don't tell your Ella. Think of a more romantic metaphor."

"Too late. I already screwed up with the metaphor thing." Rafe started toward the door. "By the way . . ."

Orson tensed. "What?"

"I've got a new talent."

Stunned, Orson got slowly to his feet. "You're joking."

"No. Turns out that's what the psi-fever was all about. My senses were adapting to the new vibes in my aura. I'm a lucid dreamer now."

"Huh. What the hell can you do with that talent? Please don't tell me that you're going to set up in business as a storefront psychic. Your mother will faint."

"Mom doesn't have to worry. Ella has come up with a new career for me."

"Well? Don't keep me in suspense. What is this new career path you intend to pursue?"

"Why don't you ask Ella?"

Rafe opened the door. Orson knew from the way his son was looking at the whiskey-haired woman sitting in the reception area that he was about to meet his future daughter-in-law.

"Come and meet my dad," Rafe said. "He wants to know about my new career."

Ella put down the glossy magazine she had been read-ing, got to her feet, and walked into the office. She smiled.

"Hello, Mr. Coppersmith," she said.

Orson opened his senses as he crossed the room to greet her. He had always considered himself to be a shrewd judge of character. It was part of his talent. He looked into Ella Morgan's eyes and paid attention to the energy that shivered in the atmosphere around her. Something about the vibe told him that this was the right woman for his always-questing son. He had a feeling that she understood Rafe the way none of the others ever had.

"This is indeed a pleasure, Miss Morgan," Orson said.

"Please, call me Ella."

"Of course—if you will call me Orson. Now, then, what's this I hear about Rafe's new career?"

"It's obvious when you think about it," Ella said. "Rafe likes to hunt for answers. He would have made a great cop or an FBPI agent but he doesn't play well with others. So, I have suggested that he go into business as a private inves-tigator."

Orson let the shock roll over him. When things settled down he got the old, familiar sense of rightness. He looked at Rafe.

"Damn," he said. "Should have thought of that myself."

Chapter 40

IT WAS THE WEDDING OF THE SEASON, A LAVISH, OVER-
the-top affair worthy of an alliance between the powerful Coppersmith family and a legendary music clan.
Invitations to the three-day event at an exclusive resort
on Copper Beach Island were coveted by everyone from
hedge fund investors, Guild bosses, and high-ranking
Coppersmith employees to several members of the reclusive Jones family—that would be the Arcane Joneses
who, according to rumor, had a long-standing friendship
with the Coppersmiths that dated back to the Old World.

The bride's side of the aisle was filled with a glittering
assembly of famous, near-famous, and as-yet-undiscovered
music talents. The bride's mother, the coloratura soprano,
Sophia Morgan, sang a special song written for the occasion by the bride's cousin, a renowned composer. Sophia
hit all the money notes. Someone pointed out that in other

circumstances, tickets to hear her in concert would have gone for astronomical prices.

The bride's brother, Zander Morgan, whose current rez-rock album was at the top of the charts, was scheduled to perform for the crowd later in the evening.

The bride was escorted down the aisle by her father, the conductor of the Resonance City Philharmonic. There was a small but audible gasp of surprise when the cluster of bridal attendants was led by a very small bridesmaid who turned out to be a dust bunny adorned in a somewhat ragged wedding veil.

Upon reaching the altar the dust bunny hopped up onto a pedestal. Having evidently grasped the solemn tone of the occasion, the unusual bridal attendant remained remarkably still until it was announced that the groom could kiss the bride.

When Raphael Coppersmith took his wife in his arms, enthusiastic chortling was heard. A few people surreptitiously checked their cellphones.

SOMETIME LATER RAFE LED ELLA OUT ONTO THE DANCE floor for the opening waltz. A hush fell on the large crowd as everyone turned to watch the couple.

Ella smiled at Rafe, joy sparkling through her. "Mom always told me that Mr. Right would show up sooner or later. And here you are, Mr. Coppersmith. About time."

Rafe tightened his hold on her and whirled her into a long, gliding turn. "There were complications, but I'm here now and I'm going to keep you close for the rest of our lives."

"Works for me."

"You are the most beautiful woman in the world, Mrs. Coppersmith, and I am the luckiest man. I love you. I will always love you."

"I love you, Rafe. You are my forever man."

Together they let the vibrant energy of the music sweep them into a future that glowed with the promise of a love that would last a lifetime.

THE DELIVERYMAN'S NAME WAS TED. HE ARRIVED SHORTLY before midnight on the small, private helicopter that had been sent to the mainland to collect him and his cargo. He had a hard time believing anyone—even folks as wealthy as the Coppersmiths—would have placed the order in the first place, let alone provided such expensive transportation to Copper Beach Island. But he was pretty sure there would be a healthy tip at the end so he didn't complain.

By the time he got to the gate at the resort where the reception was being held, the grounds were awash in hot rez-rock music. He had to raise his voice so that the security guard could hear him.

"Got an order for twelve dozen powdered-sugar doughnuts."

The guard nodded. "Take 'em around to the kitchen. They're expecting you."

Ted wheeled the trolley stacked with boxes of doughnuts to the loading dock behind the resort kitchen. Someone gave him an oversized tip and took possession of the boxes.

"Say, that isn't Zander Morgan and the Resonators, is it?" Ted yelled.

"Live and in person," the kitchen guy yelled back. "Take a listen. Everyone else is enjoying the show. We can arrange to get you back to the mainland later."

"Wow. That is so high-rez. Thanks." Ted paused. "Mind if I ask who ordered the doughnuts? I mean, you guys must have catered this wedding. Why didn't you make 'em?"

"Special request from the bride. We didn't have a dough-nut machine so we ordered in."

The bride's instructions were followed to the letter. The kitchen staff hauled the boxes out into the expansive gar-dens and left them on a picnic table. They collected the empty pizza boxes from the order that had been delivered earlier and returned to the kitchen.

Lorelei, ravishing in her veil, led the visiting-guest dust bunnies back out from under the shrubbery. They were soon joined by the others who emerged from the island's woods and catacombs. The pizza had been a terrific first course but the doughnuts induced pure dust-bunny euphoria.

The twelve dozen doughnuts disappeared rapidly, leav-ing the attendees dusted in powdered sugar. The refresh-ments were followed by a rousing game of hide-and-seek played amid the hedges and the trees.

Humans were born to go looking for answers, and their endless quest inevitably led to trouble. They were com-pelled to take risks and chase dangerous legends. They could not resist the temptation to explore forbidden terri-tory and unlock ancient, potentially deadly secrets.

But they surely did know how to party.